THE DARLING DAHLIAS AND THE POINSETTIA PUZZLE

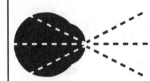

This Large Print Book carries the
Seal of Approval of N.A.V.H.

A DARLING DAHLIAS MYSTERY

THE DARLING DAHLIAS
AND THE
POINSETTIA PUZZLE

SUSAN WITTIG ALBERT

THORNDIKE PRESS
A part of Gale, a Cengage Company

GALE
A Cengage Company

Farmington Hills, Mich • San Francisco • New York • Waterville, Maine
Meriden, Conn • Mason, Ohio • Chicago

$34.99

LIBRARY OF CONGRESS CIP DATA ON FILE.
CATALOGUING IN PUBLICATION FOR THIS BOOK
IS AVAILABLE FROM THE LIBRARY OF CONGRESS

ISBN-13: 978-1-4328-5835-3 (hardcover)

Published in 2018 by arrangement with Levin/Greenberg Literary Agency, Inc.

Printed in Mexico
1 2 3 4 5 6 7 22 21 20 19 18

*For my mother, who could
make a merry Christmas
in the hardest of hard times.*

Remembering.

December 1934
The Darling Dahlias Clubhouse
  and Gardens
302 Camellia Street
Darling, Alabama

Dear Reader,

Christmas in Darling is a special time, so we were glad when Mrs. Albert let us know that she was writing a book about our Darling holiday season. In this modern world, it's easy to get the idea that you need to spend a lot of money on presents, fancy food, and glittering ornaments. Well, take it from us, you don't have to spend money to make merry, and we hope Mrs. Albert makes this plain in her book.

We were also glad because there was a bushel of Darling holiday doings this year. The big event was the Holiday Jigsaw Puzzle Tournament, and the

Dahlias sponsored a team! Another big thing: Earlynne Biddle and Mildred Kilgore decided to scrape their pennies together and open a bakery. This did not go as smoothly as hoped, and they need a little more practice with their bread, but we can recommend Earlynne's croissants without a quibble. The first-ever Merchants' Association Holiday Window Contest was a smashing success, too, although the competition got a little heated at times.

But Christmas was not all candy canes and carols. Myra May and Violet are still shuddering over the threat to their little family. (We won't tell you what it was because that might spoil Mrs. Albert's story.) The sheriff and Mr. Moseley had to figure out what was going on at the Jericho State Prison Farm and put a stop to it. And Liz Lacy (our Dahlias' president and everybody's friend) is faced with what looks like a pretty big decision.

In case this is the first time you've read one of Mrs. Albert's books about us, you might be interested to know that our garden club is named for Mrs. Dahlia Blackstone, who had one of the greenest thumbs God ever gave His children. If you live north of the Mason-Dixon Line, we hope you won't be too mad at us if we tell you that winter is a glorious time in our Southern gardens: pansies, snapdragons, honeysuckle, and sweet peas are blooming, along with camellias (our state flower) and winter jasmine. But if you don't have a winter garden to make you happy, don't despair. Just get out there and sow some smiles and compliments. As Aunt Hetty Little says, "One kind word will bloom all winter long."

Well, that's enough for now. We'll let you go so you can turn the page and start reading. Or if you're in the mood to bake, Mrs. Albert says you have her permission to skip to the end of the book for some good old-fashioned Southern holiday desserts — always a sweet way to end any party!

Happy holidays to you!
The Darling Dahlias

P.S. Mrs. Albert also wants us to tell you that she's included some notes at the bottom of certain pages to remind you of the other stories she's written about us, in case you want to read (or reread) these, too.

THE DARLING DAHLIAS CLUB ROSTER

WINTER, 1934

Club Officers

Elizabeth Lacy, president. Garden columnist for the Darling *Dispatch* and part-time secretary to Mr. Benton Moseley, attorney-at-law.

Ophelia Snow, vice president and secretary. Until quite recently, a reporter, Linotype operator, and advertising manager at the Darling *Dispatch.* Now works full time at the CCC camp. Wife of Darling's mayor, Jed Snow, who also owns Snow's Farm Supply.

Verna Tidwell, treasurer. Cypress County treasurer and probate clerk, organizer of the Darling Girl Scout troop. A widow, Verna lives with her beloved Scottie, Clyde. She is in an on-again-off-again relationship with Alvin Duffy, the president of the Darling Savings and Trust.

Myra May Mosswell, communications secre-

11

tary. Co-owner of the Darling Telephone Exchange and the Darling Diner. Lives with Violet Sims and their little girl, Cupcake (Violet's niece), in the flat over the Diner.

Club Members

Earlynne Biddle, a rose fancier and hobby baker. Married to Henry Biddle, the manager at the Coca-Cola bottling plant. Earlynne and Mildred Kilgore are about to open a new bakery in downtown Darling.

Bessie Bloodworth, owner of Magnolia Manor, a boardinghouse for genteel elderly ladies. Bessie is Darling's local historian and grows vegetables and herbs in the Manor's back yard.

Fannie Champaign, noted milliner and proprietor of Champaign's Darling Chapeaux. Recently married to Charlie Dickens, publisher and editor of the Darling *Dispatch.*

Mildred Kilgore owns Kilgore Motors with her husband Roger. They live in a big house near the ninth green of the Cypress Country Club, where Mildred grows camellias. She and Earlynne Biddle are about to open a bakery on the courthouse square.

Aunt Hetty Little, gladiola lover, senior member of the club, and town matriarch. A "regular Miss Marple" who knows far too many Darling secrets.

Lucy Murphy grows vegetables and fruit on a small market farm on the Jericho Road. Married to Ralph Murphy, who works on the railroad and is never home.

Raylene Riggs, Myra May Mosswell's mother. Cooks at the Darling Diner, manages the garden behind the Diner, and lives at the Marigold Motor Court.

Dorothy Rogers, Darling's librarian. Knows the Latin name of every plant and insists that everyone else does, too. Resident of Magnolia Manor.

Beulah Trivette, owner of Beulah's Beauty Bower, where all the Dahlias go to get beautiful. Artistically talented, Beulah loves cabbage roses and other exuberant flowers.

Alice Ann Walker, secretary to Mr. Duffy at the Darling Savings and Trust. Alice Ann grows iris and daylilies. Her disabled husband, Arnold, tends the family vegetable garden.

CHAPTER ONE:
"NOTHING UNUSUAL EVER HAPPENS IN DARLING"

Friday, December 14, 1934

"I don't think I heard that right," Elizabeth Lacy said as she began setting up the card table in the front room of the Darling Dahlias' white-frame clubhouse (the parlor, when club founder Dahlia Blackstone had lived in the old house). "Earlynne and Mildred are opening a *bakery*?"

"It's true," Aunt Hetty Little replied energetically. "I heard it from Beulah at the Beauty Bower yesterday morning. Beulah said she heard it from Alice Ann, who got the word straight from Mildred herself, when she came into the bank to open the bakery's checking account."

Past eighty and the oldest member of the club, white-haired Aunt Hetty sometimes complained of arthritis in her knees and often walked with a cane, fancifully carved by her nephew, Billy Ray. But she was full of pep and vinegar and could be found out

15

in her garden at the crack of dawn on a sunny day, planting, pruning, and picking.

"Earlynne started baking when she could stand on a stool to reach the top of the table," Bessie Bloodworth said. She added doubtfully, "But baking for a hobby is not the same thing as baking for a business. And Mildred isn't much of a cook. She admits that herself."

Aunt Hetty chuckled. "Well, you know Earlynne. She's got enough confidence for the two of them. Not to mention that hoard of recipes. That woman has more recipes than Carter has little liver pills."

"Confidence is one thing, stick-to-it is something else," Verna Tidwell said skeptically. "Earlynne never met a new project she didn't love — for a week or two. Not to be critical," she added. "Just stating a fact."

"Well, we'll just have to wait and see, won't we?" Aunt Hetty said. "Verna, did you bring your magnifying glass?"

"Here it is," Verna said, putting it on the table. Slender and olive-skinned, Verna kept her dark hair short in an easy-care style. She was the first woman in the entire state of Alabama to be elected to the important job of Cypress County probate clerk and county treasurer. She was not one to waste time putting on makeup — a quick dash of vivid red lipstick was usually enough for her, and sometimes she didn't even bother with that. "I'm not sure the rules allow us to use a magnifying glass, though," she added.

"Well, I don't know whyever not," Aunt Hetty replied tartly. "Some puzzle pieces are so itsy-bitsy that they're impossible to see. We're allowed to wear our eyeglasses, aren't we? What's the difference between wearing eyeglasses and using a magnifying glass?"

"A magnifying glass ought to be okay," Elizabeth Lacy said. "But I'll ask Miss Rogers. She's the one who's making the rules."

"Dorothy Rogers makes too many rules, if you ask me," Aunt Hetty muttered.

Liz (as her friends called her) tried not to smile, but it was true. Miss Rogers had read about the jigsaw puzzle tournaments that were all the rage across the nation and decided that a competition would be a good wintertime community activity for their little town. And since she was the town's librarian and the puzzle contest was *her* bright idea, she had decided to set it up as a fundraiser for the library, which was perennially short of money for new books.

As the organizer of the tournament, Miss Rogers had made all the rules: sixteen of them, to be exact, because she always liked to have things spelled out. There was a three-dollar non-refundable entry fee for each four-person team, and so far, six teams had entered. The first team to finish its puzzle in the two-hour contest period would win. If no teams were completely finished at the end of two hours, the team that had assembled the most pieces would win. The prize was a big box of items donated by local merchants, to be shared by the winning team.

"Probably won't amount to a hill of beans," Aunt Hetty had grumbled. "They won't want to give away anything they think they might sell." But Liz had reminded her that the contest was a fundraiser, and that the prize wasn't the most important thing.

When the Dahlias learned about the competition, they voted to sponsor a team. Bessie, Liz, Ophelia Snow, and Aunt Hetty (all avid puzzlers) volunteered, and Liz was chosen as the team leader. Then Ophelia — who worked three days a week at the Darling *Dispatch* and two days at the new CCC camp, outside of town — got an offer of a full-time job from the camp's commandant.

"I hate to drop out," she told Liz, "but I don't think I should take on anything else right now." Luckily, Verna was as passionate about puzzles as Ophelia and agreed to take her place.

The Dahlias' team tried out a long list of possible names and finally agreed on Verna's suggestion: the Darling Dahlias Puzzle Divas. Tonight was their second practice session, with a five-hundred-piece puzzle they had rented from Lima's Drugstore for five cents a day. (If you want a three-hundred-piece puzzle, Mr. Lima will rent it to you for just three cents a day. If you're looking for a thousand-piece puzzle, expect to pay a dime.)

A few years before, game manufacturers had begun marketing cheap, mass-produced cardboard jigsaw puzzles, replacing the expensive, hand-cut wooden ones. The new low price created a puzzle mania that swept the country, with sales peaking at an incredible ten million a week. The most popular of these new cardboard puzzles was the Picture Puzzle Weekly — a different puzzle was released each week — which was sold as the "perfect family entertainment." Depending on the size, the Puzzle Weeklies sold for ten to twenty-five cents, and people rushed to buy them. Adding to the interest, retail stores had begun offering free advertising puzzles with the purchase of a toothbrush, a flashlight, a can of Dauntless cherries, or a box of Cremo five-cent cigars. What better (if more devious) way to help customers remember your brand name than to put them to work assembling a picture of your product?

Some suggested that puzzles were popular because they gave millions of unemployed people a cheap, absorbing way to fill the empty hours. But Lizzy thought it was more than that. You might be out of a job, but you could tell yourself that you were "at work" on the puzzle. Finishing a puzzle could give you a sense of accomplishment that was hard to come by when you weren't bringing a paycheck home every week. You might even begin to feel that you were in control of something, at a time when most people felt that they were at the mercy of outside forces.

"Who's got a wristwatch?" Liz asked, as she began setting the four folding chairs around the card table. The last time they did a five-hundred-piece puzzle, it had taken them over two hours to finish it. To be competitive, they would have to work much faster. But this was only their second practice, and the tournament was over a week away.

"I'll time us, Liz," Verna volunteered, taking her wristwatch off and putting it on the table. "How many pieces are there in this puzzle?"

Bessie — comfortably round, with graying curls, a little fringe of gray bangs, and a ready smile — leaned across the table and picked up the box. "This one has straight border edges, not like that crazy round one we practiced with last week. Miss Rogers says the one we'll be doing for the tournament will have straight edges."

"And all the teams will get the same puzzle, I hope." Aunt Hetty adjusted her eyeglasses. "Since we're racing against one another, it wouldn't be fair if some of us got an easy one and some got a hard one."

"Yes," Liz replied. "Everybody gets the same puzzle, although poor Miss Rogers is going a little crazy." She pulled out a chair and sat down. "There are seven teams, so she's trying to round up seven copies of the same five-hundred-piece puzzle — with *no* missing pieces." That was the frustrating problem with "used" puzzles. They were inevitably missing a piece or two.

Bessie sat down in the chair to Liz's right. Changing the subject, she said, "Does anybody know the name of Earlynne and Mildred's new bakery?"

"Mildred and Earlynne's Folly?" Verna suggested drily.

"Now, you be charitable, Verna." Aunt Hetty hung her wooden cane on the back of a chair and sat down. "Last I heard, they were still debating what to call it, Bessie. But they've rented a place to put it."

"Earlynne Biddle and Mildred Kilgore, in business together. Now *that* will be something to see." Bessie put her elbows on the table. Those two bicker, bicker, bicker, all the livelong day."

"You say they've rented a place, Aunt Hetty?" Verna sat across from Bessie. "Where?"

"That old frame building next to Fannie Champaign's hat shop," Aunt Hetty said.

Verna settled herself. "Oh, that's where AdaJean LeRoy used to have her cake shop. Remember that place? The front part is about the size of a bathtub. Put three or four customers in there at once, and you'll have a crowd. But as I remember, there's a nice big oven in the kitchen, and a sink and an icebox."

"They've got their work cut out for them, then." Bessie shook her head. "Nobody's been in that building since poor AdaJean broke her hip and went to live with her nephew up in Montgomery. And that was . . . oh, three years ago, at least."

"More than that," Aunt Hetty said. "I

know, because I got a Christmas card from her last year. She mentioned that she'd missed five Darling Christmases and wished she could be here for the holiday." She sighed reminiscently. "I told her we missed her, too. She made the best gingerbread. Maybe I'll write tonight and ask her for her recipe. Earlynne and Mildred might want to add it to their list."

"I wonder if they've got my recipe for Red Velvet Cake," Verna mused.

Liz cleared her throat, feeling that if she didn't take charge, they would never get around to working on the puzzle. "Shall we get started?" She held up the puzzle box so everybody could see the picture on the cover. "This one is Milton Bradley's *Dutch Bargain.* Two little Dutch girls are trading dolls — and it looks like the bigger girl is taking advantage of the smaller one."

"So *that's* what 'dutch bargain' means," Bessie mused thoughtfully. "Somebody taking advantage of somebody else. Seems like life is full of dutch bargains."

"It looks pretty easy," Liz said. She dumped the pieces in the middle of the table, then propped up the lid where everybody could see the picture.

"Let's turn all the pieces right-side up first," Verna said, always the organizer. "And we don't have to stay in our chairs. We can walk around the table for a better view."

"I'll stay where I am and work on the border," Aunt Hetty said. "Once I get the corners, the rest will go faster."

"I'll sort the sky and the grass," Bessie said. "Looks like those are mostly greens and blues."

"I'll work on the windmill." Verna pointed to the picture on the box cover. "Orange, brown, black, and a little yellow."

"I'll look for the girls' pieces," Liz said, and made a note of the time on Verna's watch. "On your mark, ready, set, *go.*"

You're probably curious about the Dahlias' clubhouse and gardens, so while the Darling Divas are working on their puzzle, we'll have a quick look around.

The Puzzle Divas are meeting in the little four-room frame house that Mrs. Dahlia Blackstone bequeathed to Darling's garden club. Last year, the club members — who call themselves the Dahlias, in honor of their founder — tore down the wall between the two front rooms to make a bigger space for their meetings and other get-togethers. They stacked up several brick-and-board shelves in the back room for their gardening library and seed collection. And they installed new linoleum in the kitchen, where they make jams and jellies and can home-grown vegetables. The Depression has been hard on everybody, so they donate their canned goods to the Darling Blessing Box, to help folks who can't garden and need a little help putting a meal on the table.

Behind the house, a wide lawn — brown now, after the early-winter frosts — sweeps down toward a clump of woods, a large magnolia tree, and a clear spring smothered in ferns, bog iris, and pitcher plants. There are curving perennial borders on both sides of the lawn, and several "island" gardens of lilies and roses. The garden had once been so beautiful that it was featured regularly in magazines and newspapers across the South. But as Mrs. Blackstone grew older and infirm, the more self-assertive plants had taken advantage, crowding out their smaller, meeker neighbors and (as you might expect) turning the garden into a jungle.

When the Dahlias inherited the garden, they launched a salvage operation. They pulled the weeds (mostly dog fennel, henbit, ground ivy, and Johnson grass) out of the perennial borders, permitting the scruffy phlox, larkspur, iris, asters, and Shasta daisies to shake themselves, take a deep

25

breath, and begin their new lives. They disciplined the roses — the climbers, the teas, the ramblers, the shrubs, and a charmingly frowsy yellow Lady Banks — and more. They dug and replanted the unkempt Easter lilies and the orange ditch lilies, which had leapfrogged over the spider lilies and landed in the oxblood lilies' bed. They restrained the rowdy cardinal climber and cross vine and mandevilla on the fence and repaired the trellis so the confused Confederate jasmine could stretch up and out. Gardens are always a labor of love, and every time a Dahlia set foot on the place, she saw something new to love. As Aunt Hetty likes to say, when its sleeves are rolled up, love can always find something else to do.

And that's what happened. Once they got the garden beds cleaned up, the Dahlias hired Mr. Norris to bring his old horse Racer and plow up the large empty lot on the corner. In the early spring, they planted peas, carrots, green onions, and lettuce. A month later, it was time to plant green beans, eggplant, okra, sweet corn, watermelons, squash, pumpkins, and sweet potatoes. As the summer wore on, people from all over town came to work in the garden, watering, hoeing, and pulling weeds in return for all the vegetables they could pick. Mrs. Blackstone, the Dahlias thought, would be pleased — and there was always more than enough okra to go around.

In the house, the Divas were still at work, each one paying attention to her own sections of puzzle but occasionally putting a piece or two in elsewhere. They were so engrossed that they didn't speak much, except to say things like "Here's another windmill piece for you, Verna," or "Liz, I think this must be part of the little girl's apron."

They even forgot to check the time until finally, Bessie plugged in the last piece of green grass. "Jigsaw!" she exclaimed — which, according to Miss Rogers' rules, was what you were supposed to say when your team put in the very last piece. "How long did it take us, Verna?"

Verna consulted her wristwatch. "One hour and thirty-two minutes."

"That's quite an improvement over last time, girls," Liz said encouragingly. "We're getting faster."

Aunt Hetty frowned. "But we still need to shave off — how much?"

"At least a half hour," Liz replied. "How about if I return this puzzle and rent another

27

from Mr. Lima. Tomorrow's Saturday. Would you be able to practice again then?"

"If we do it in the afternoon." Aunt Hetty began to take the puzzle apart. "I have choir in the morning — we're practicing carols for the Christmas Eve service."

"I promised to help Mrs. Bechtel with her recitation for the Ladies Club," Bessie said, "but I can squeeze in a couple of hours in the afternoon." Bessie owned and managed the Magnolia Manor, next door to the Dahlias' clubhouse. Mrs. Bechtel was one of the four elderly ladies who rented rooms from her.

"Works for me," Verna said cheerfully, scooping up the puzzle pieces and putting them back in the box. "Al and I are going to the movies, but that's later." Alvin Duffy, the president of Darling Savings and Trust, was Verna's more-or-less-steady boyfriend. Verna's friends sometimes wondered why they didn't get married, but when they asked her, she just smiled.

"What do I want with a husband?" she would say with that faintly ironic smile of hers. "My job pays the bills, I have plenty of books and time for reading, and Clyde snuggles up next to me in bed. What more could I want?" Clyde was Verna's bossy black Scottie. He and Al got along about as well as two bulls in the same pasture, which might be one reason for Verna's hesitation.

Bessie folded her chair and leaned it against the wall. "What I want to know is when Earlynne and Mildred are going to open their new bakery. Has anybody heard?"

"Before Christmas, Mildred said." Aunt Hetty reached for her cane.

"They'd better hope for a Christmas miracle, then," Verna remarked, folding up Aunt Hetty's chair. "The last time I looked through the front window, AdaJean's old shop was a mess. Must be wall-to-wall spiders and mice, not to mention cockroaches."

"Well, you know Mildred," Aunt Hetty said, winding her scarf around her throat. "If anybody can whomp up a miracle, she's the one. I never did see such a fine organizer."

Bessie reached for her coat. "You don't think it'll *snow*, do you?" She paused, looking doubtfully out the front window. "It's awfully dark. And downright chilly." It rarely got very cold in southern Alabama, but the last week had seen nighttime temperatures near freezing.

"Snow?" Verna pulled a bright red knit cap over her dark hair. "The last time it snowed in Darling was the year Calvin Coolidge got elected. Nineteen twenty-four."

"That was the second time women could vote for president," Bessie said. She liked to keep up with politics.

"Such a pretty snow that year," Aunt Hetty said reminiscently. "That was the winter my little granddaughter Rosie was born."

Liz raised her voice to get people's attention. "Puzzle practice here tomorrow at one?"

"Yes, ma'am," Verna said, taking her mittens out of her pocket.

"I'll be here," Bessie replied, "unless something happens."

"It won't," Aunt Hetty said, starting for the door. "Nothing *ever* happens in Darling."

CHAPTER TWO:
"WHAT WE NEED
IS A MIRACLE"

Monday, December 17
Mildred Kilgore wrung out her mop into the bucket and straightened up slowly against the kink in her back. "I don't care what you say, Earlynne. I can see the handwriting on the wall. We are *not* going to open this bakery next week. Or the week after that. Or maybe even by Christmas." She pushed her dark hair out of her face and propped her mop against a wall. "What we need is a miracle."

"Oh ye of little faith," Earlynne Biddle said airily. Moving easily in her blue denim coveralls, she climbed down from the ladder, a paintbrush in her hand. "Anyway, I just painted over that handwriting on the wall, so you can stop worrying about it." She stepped back and gazed at her handiwork. "White paint really brightens this old room. Don't you think?"

Mildred took another look. The painted

walls helped, and now that the linoleum floor was scrubbed and waxed, Ada-Jean's old shop didn't look half bad. But in her opinion, its best feature was the big glass front window where they could arrange an attractive holiday display. She could already see how charming it would look, with tiered plates of Christmas cookies and little ginger-bread houses surrounded by green pine boughs crusted with artificial snow (Ivory soap flakes whipped up with starch and hot water) and decorated with Christmas tree ornaments. Charming enough to take first place in the Merchants' Association Holiday Window Contest.

But Mildred never liked to agree too readily with Earlynne. "White walls are so stark, Earlynne," she said. "I still prefer green."

"Green would make you look like a corpse," Earlynne retorted briskly. She put down her paintbrush and tucked her brown hair back into its bun. "White makes people cheerful. Cheerful people spend more money."

Mildred couldn't come up with a clever rebuttal (although she knew she *would,* within the next five minutes). Anyway, there was no point arguing for green walls when she had already given in and told Earlynne to paint them white, if that's what it took to make her happy. But she didn't want to be seen as yielding too easily.

So she said, "Well, people can't buy *anything* until we get a display case of some kind in here. The best thing would be something with glass shelves and a glass front and glass top, with sliding doors at the back." She pointed. "It needs to go right *there*. Along the back wall. With enough space behind it for us to work."

Earlynne fished in the pocket of her coveralls, took out a compact, and peered into the mirror to see if she had paint on her face. "I've already thought of the display case," she said in a superior tone, and closed her compact. "Henry is having it built for us, out at the plant. It'll be delivered tomorrow." Henry was Earlynne's husband. He managed the Coca-Cola bottling plant outside of town.

"But it doesn't go on the back wall," Earlynne added. She pointed. "It goes *there*. Along that side wall. With the sales counter and the cash register at the end nearest the door." She pointed again. "Right there."

"No, that's all *wrong*, Earlynne," Mildred said flatly. "The counter has to go in front of the back wall, because that's where the door to the kitchen is. We have to be able to carry trays of pastries in and out without getting in people's way."

"The counter ought to be where people can see it the minute they walk in," Earlynne declared. "We'll have shelves on the back wall."

"No, the shelves go *there*," Mildred said firmly, pointing to the side wall.

What followed was a snappy back-and-forth argument about where they should put the display case, the cash register counter, and the shelves, with each of them arguing for *her* idea, until finally Earlynne heaved a dramatic sigh and gave in.

"Oh, for *pity's sake*," she said, drawing it out. "Have it your way if you must, Mildred. We'll put it against the back wall, if that will satisfy you."

Now, if you didn't know Mildred and Earlynne, you might think that a business belonging to two women who argued about every single little thing was doomed to failure before it began. But this pair had been disagreeing vigorously since second grade. Earlynne had a barbed wit and Mildred had a sharp tongue. Each was as stubborn as an Alabama mule, and they rarely saw eye to eye. But they had managed to remain close friends in spite of their differences, which must be some sort of testimony to the fundamental perversity of the human spirit.

Still, there were signs that their partnership was not going to be a piece of cake. For instance, while Earlynne and Mildred had more or less agreed that they wanted to start a bakery (as opposed to, say, a tea shop or a florist shop) they had disagreed about when to launch it.

Mildred had argued that Darling was still suffering the lingering effects of the Depression and that it was a bad time to go into business. "Just look around the courthouse square," she said. "Most of the merchants are still having a tough time. How are we going to make it with a new bakery when they're having so much trouble?"

But Earlynne had dreamed of owning a bakery since she was big enough to climb on a kitchen chair and roll out a crust for a pecan pie. Since she could now glimpse forty just over the horizon, she was convinced that this was the right time.

But just as importantly, she felt that the Darling economy was due for a turnaround, what with the Vanity Fair plant opening up after the first of the year over at nearby Monroeville. The new plant meant that Darling people who had been without jobs for a while would be working again. Especially women, since Vanity Fair was a lingerie company and they would be hiring anybody who could run up silk panties on a sewing machine. When women had paying jobs away from home, they needed somebody to do the baking, didn't they? They couldn't let their families go without bread.

Mildred had been willing to listen to Earlynne's proposal because she had a little extra money of her own to spend. Her uncle (who managed her deceased father's substantial estate) had been more generous than usual this year. But she had been in the habit of saying *no* to Earlynne's ideas, so she put off saying *yes* for quite a while — until her husband Roger told her that he had heard a lot of stupid business ideas in his time, but opening a Darling bakery took the cake. It was (he said) the most ridiculously idiotic idea anybody had ever dreamed up.

Well. When Roger said that, Mildred naturally had to stand up for herself. Setting aside for the moment that the bakery was really Earlynne's idea, she told him loftily and in no uncertain terms that it was *her* money and *her* time and she couldn't think of a better way to put both to work than to invest them in a business that was *hers*. Well, half hers, anyway. She and Earlynne would contribute equally to the bakery's success and split the profits down the middle. If there were any. Profits, that is.

The partnership responsibilities were fairly clearly divided. Earlynne could contribute the baking expertise but no money, and while Mildred was no baker, she could contribute some money. She agreed to pay six months' rent on AdaJean LeRoy's old cake shop and buy what they needed to get started — the electric refrigerator they absolutely had to have and the newfangled electric Sunbeam Mixmaster that Earlynne craved. Then there were the basic baking supplies: flour, sugar, shortening, yeast, and so on.

Mildred had some experience in management, so she would handle the purchasing, the shop sales, and the advertising as well as keeping the books. Earlynne would do the actual baking. Mildred didn't argue about that. Earlynne had turned out gorgeous baked goods — pastries, pies, rolls, fancy cakes — ever since she was a girl, and her sticky buns were absolutely beyond compare. She promised Mildred she would get to work and whip her recipes into shape for commercial baking just as soon as they banished the mice and spiders and cockroaches, made sure the oven was working properly, got the new refrigerator installed, and fixed the leak under the sink.

But above all, they needed a name, and they were still arguing about that. Earlynne had narrowed her list to Darling DeLites, The Cakewalk, and The Upper Crust. (Her husband Henry liked The South Is Risin' Again, but Earlynne viewed that as a joke.) Mildred's list was topped with two names: The Doughnut Depot and Pie in the Sky. Her husband Roger threw in Two Tarts, but that was a joke, too. And not a very funny one.

They couldn't agree, of course. Earlynne objected that Mildred's favorite names wouldn't work since they were going to sell much more than just doughnuts and pies. Mildred, on the other hand, argued that DeLites was misspelled, cakes weren't the only things they were selling, and The Upper Crust made it sound like they were catering to rich people, of whom there were precious few in Darling.

After an extended and rather acrimonious debate, Mildred threw up her hands and said, "Why don't we just call it The Flour Shop? That way, everybody knows what it is. And we can sell anything we like."

"The Flower Shop?" Earlynne snorted. "You're saying we should give up the bakery and turn ourselves into *florists*?" Another snort. "I imagine the Dahlias might like that, but *I* wouldn't."

Mildred had to find a piece of paper and a pencil and write it down, but finally, Earlynne got it. "Good grief. *Flour* Shop." She gave an exasperated sigh and rolled her eyes, although Mildred could tell that she thought it was a pretty good idea. She pretended to mull it over, and said, with pretended reluctance, "Well, I guess it'll do until we think of something better."

But they hadn't. So The Flour Shop it was, and The Flour Shop it stayed. Mildred hired Pinkie Parsons, Darling's resident sign-painter, to paint it on the front window, in big black letters in a classy script that Mildred loved and Earlynne said made her feel cross-eyed:

The Flour Shop

At which point people began to stop in front of the window, cup their hands to the glass, and peer inside, hoping to find out what was going on. And both Mildred and Earlynne began taking their project a little more seriously. Now that it finally had a name, it began to seem that The Flour Shop was really going to happen. Maybe.

But first they had to decide what they

were going to sell. Earlynne felt that she was the expert on this subject. "I have recipes for the most wonderful French pastries — beignets, croissants, eclairs, petit fours. That's what I've baked all my life. People will *love* our pastries. And cakes." She clasped her hands and added dreamily, "Wedding cakes, birthday cakes, anniversary cakes, special-occasion cakes. Chocolate cake, sponge cake, cheesecake, angel food cake —"

"Bread," Mildred interrupted firmly. "Nobody can have their baloney sandwiches or toast and jelly without it. And right now, all they can buy is Wonder Bread or Butternut, which by the time it gets to Mrs. Hancock's grocery shelf is already three or four days old. What they buy from us, on the other hand, will be *fresh.*" She wrote down *just-baked bread* at the top of her list. "What else? But not all that fancy French stuff, please. Let's give people something familiar to start with."

Earlynne chewed on her lip. "Well, then, scones. Tarts. And cinnamon buns and orange nut bread. Cookies are easy to make." She brightened. "We could have a glass bowl of Christmas cookies on the counter and give one to every customer, free. That'll get everybody into the Christmas spirit, don't you think? Oh, and we need a Christmas tree, too, Mildred. Right over there." She pointed to the front corner opposite the window. "Let's get the tree up as soon as we can. People will *love* it!"

"The tree, yes," Mildred said. "But it should go in the other corner." *Cookies,* she wrote impatiently, then *tarts.* "What kinds of tarts?"

"Apple, I suppose. And peach." Earlynne squared her shoulders. "And don't rush me about the list. We can decide all that later. I'll sit down and go through my recipes and —"

"For heaven's sake, Earlynne," Mildred said testily. "*Everybody* has apples, and even I can bake a peach pie. And Raylene and Euphoria, over at the Diner, make the best pies in the world. If people are going to fork over good money, they want something they can't make for themselves. And can't get at the Diner."

Earlynne, who had forgotten all about Raylene and Euphoria, looked uncomfortable. "I said don't *rush* me, Mildred." She pressed her lips together. "Give me a little time, and I'll make a list."

"Well, okay," Mildred said. "But get me the list tomorrow. Put bread at the top, please. And put down what you think we ought to charge. How much for the bread, for the scones, etcetera." Half under her breath, she added, "And the tree goes in the *other* corner."

Ah, the prices. Mildred thought that since people were paying nine cents for a loaf of Wonder Bread at Hancock's Grocery, they should sell their bread for less. Otherwise, people would keep on buying cheap three- or four-day-old bread at Hancock's.

"We should sell for seven cents a loaf," she had declared. "That makes our bread affordable as well as fresh."

Which seemed like a good idea — until she began figuring out how much it would cost to produce a loaf. She calculated that a pound of flour would make one loaf of bread. Mrs. Hancock was selling forty-eight pounds of King's flour for $2.25, which came out to almost five cents a loaf — just for the flour!

And flour was only the beginning. She also needed to figure in the cost of the rent on Mrs. LeRoy's building. At twenty dollars a month, it sounded cheap enough, until you realized that twenty dollars a month came out to sixty-seven cents a day — and that you would have to sell ten loaves of seven-cent bread just to pay a single day's rent! There was also the cost of the electric lights and the gas to run the oven and a once-a-week ad in the *Dispatch* and a telephone and the cash register to ring up the sales and paper bags to put the bread in.

There was more. If Earlynne was going to bake tarts and cheesecakes and cookies, they would need sugar (twenty-five pounds for $1.25 at Hancock's), brown sugar (fifteen cents for two pounds), shortening (forty-five cents for a three-pound can of Snowdrift), cream cheese (seventeen cents a pound), and eggs, fifteen cents a dozen. And they weren't in the bakery business just for the fun of it. They wanted to make a profit, didn't they?

By the time Mildred finished adding up all the numbers, she had a rip-roaring headache. She could also see that they could *not* afford to buy their supplies retail. They had to find a wholesale source of flour and sugar, which meant driving to Mobile: eighty miles in each direction at twenty miles to a ten-cent gallon of gas, plus a day of her time. A whole darn day, just to buy flour!

Mildred flung down her pencil and whooshed out a deep, despairing sigh. She had been *stupid* to invest her good money in Earlynne's foolish dream without taking the time to figure out the real costs and the possibility of profit.

No doubt about it, Roger was right. As the world's most idiotic idea, their bakery really did take the cake.

If they were to make a dime, it would take a miracle.

CHAPTER THREE:
"WHAT DO YOU MEAN, IT DOESN'T MATCH?"

Tuesday, December 18

Just up the street from The Flour Shop, past Fannie Champaign's Darling Chapeaux and the Darling Savings and Trust, across Ben Franklin Street and behind Snow's Farm Supply, sits a four-room frame house. There are bushes in front and a battle-scarred tomcat, black as the ace of spades, guarding the sagging front porch. Miss Josephine Crumpler lived in this house for fifty-two years, until the Savings and Trust foreclosed and she went to live with her niece in Nashville.

Now, Miss Crumpler's house belongs to Cypress County and is the office of Sheriff Buddy Norris, Deputy Wayne Springer, and the cat. The jail is conveniently located next door, on the second floor of Snow's Farm Supply, making it handy for the sheriff and his deputy to keep an eye on prisoners. There's not much crime in Darling, but the jail's twin cells are often occupied on weekends, when one or two of the town drunks are locked up to sleep off their overindulgence in Bodeen Pyle's white lightning.

In the room that served as his office (Miss Crumpler's front bedroom, which still had her pink and green honeysuckle wall-paper), Sheriff Buddy Norris was sitting with his boots propped on his desk, trying to puzzle something out. At his elbow was a mug of black coffee, strong enough to stop a cougar in its tracks; that's how Wayne made the coffee so that's how Buddy drank it. He was reviewing the report of the late-October death of a prominent Darling businessman, Whitney Whitworth. A member of Darling's acclaimed barbershop quartet, the Lucky Four Clovers, Mr. Whitworth was tragically killed when his Pierce-Arrow somersaulted off the Jericho Road and down an embankment at the bottom of Spook Hill, landing upside down on top of the unfortunate driver. The wreck had taken place on a quiet Sunday night, at an hour when most Darling folk were paying rapt attention to Wayne King's Orchestra on their parlor radios, humming along with "Dream a Little Dream of Me" and "Goodnight, Sweetheart."

At first, it was thought that this was just an unlucky accident. But when Deputy Springer looked carefully at the wrecked automobile, he suspected that the crash had involved another car. There appeared to be no eyewitnesses, however, and both Buddy and Wayne judged that the chances for figuring out just how it had happened were slim to none.*

And then they had some good old-fashioned luck. Miss Lacy — Liz Lacy, who worked in Mr. Moseley's law office — had been contacted by somebody who knew somebody who had seen the crash and said it was no accident. Another car had *deliberately* struck the Pierce-Arrow in the rear. What's more, this eyewitness was able to identify both the car *and* the driver. His tip took Buddy and Wayne to the Jericho State Prison Farm, where they intended to interrogate Jimmie Bragg, the assistant to Warden Burford.

But they were too late. Not an hour before they got to the prison farm, Bragg had shot himself, leaving behind a typewritten note apologizing to Mr. Whitworth's widow for

* You can read about that accident, the investigation, and its aftermath in *The Darling Dahlias and the Unlucky Clover.*

accidentally running into her husband's auto. While there was certainly a discrepancy between Bragg's confession and the word of the eyewitness, the sheriff had to admit that the man's suicide seemed to wrap up the case very tidily.

Darling thought so, too. Lionel Noonan, of Noonan's Funeral Parlor, outdid himself with Mr. Whitworth's funeral. Every pew in the Presbyterian church was filled, and the polished bronze casket was almost buried under an avalanche of flowers. The Lucky Four Clovers (with Deputy Springer stepping in at bass for the unlucky Mr. Whitworth) provided appropriate music — "Life's Railway to Heaven" and "When They Ring Those Golden Bells" — for the deceased's journey to the afterworld. Mr. Whitworth was interred in the Darling Cemetery, with full military honors provided by the Sons of Confederate Veterans. (Mr. Whitworth's daddy had worn the gray in the famous Alabama Brigade.)

Mr. Bragg was shipped back to his mother in a plain pine box — the less said about him the better.

The Darling *Dispatch* also seemed to think the confession wrapped up the case. Editor and publisher Charlie Dickens ran a front-page story on the tragic crash in the *Dis-*

patch, under the headline Prominent Darling Man Killed in Accident. The story
appeared with a human-interest sidebar by
Ophelia Snow reporting that Mr. Whitworth's widow, "fragile but lovely in her
grief," had generously agreed to honor her
husband's business commitments to the
Darling Telephone Exchange for a badly
needed new switchboard system. Frustrated
Darling telephone subscribers enthusiastically welcomed this news. It had been a terrible nuisance to have every other call
dropped, some calls not go through at all,
and some go through but to the wrong
person, which you might not realize until
you'd said half of what you intended to say
and then had to apologize, hang up, and
feel like a fool for the rest of the day.

On page three of the same issue of the
Dispatch, under an advertisement for Ex-
Lax ("Children *love* this delicious chocolate
laxative!"), there was a brief paragraph
about Mr. Bragg's suicide.

But it was the suicide — or rather, the *ap-
parent* suicide — that was perplexing Sheriff
Norris at the moment. To the Whitworth
file, Deputy Springer had added another
report that had just arrived. It had to do
with the weapon that had been found with
Bragg's body. The old Colt single-action six-

shooter had Bragg's fingerprints on it, which for the ordinary person might have clinched the matter, especially when he read Bragg's suicide note. But not for Deputy Springer, whose experience as a lawman had lent him a certain skepticism.

A few words about the recent history of the Cypress County Sheriff's Office may be helpful here. Earlier in the year, Darling's beloved Sheriff Roy Burns had met his maker in the form of a bad-tempered rattlesnake down at the bottom of Horsetail Gorge, where the sheriff was spending a pleasant Sunday morning in the company of his trout rod. (Leona Ruth Adcock was heard to remark that the rattler wouldn't have bit the sheriff if he'd been in church, but small-minded people always like to criticize.)

Buddy Norris had been Roy Burns' deputy for over two years and seemed to be his logical successor. But Buddy ran into a couple of problems when he was campaigning. He was in his late twenties but was a dead ringer for the boyish aviator Lucky Lindy, which is to say that he looked like he was about fifteen-and-a-half, so some folks said he was too young. Other folks said he was too cocky, especially after he arrested the visiting revival preacher for driving his

1926 Studebaker under the influence of something more intoxicating (and illegal) than communion wine. They felt he should have had the sense to show more deference to a man of God.

But it all came out in the wash, as Buddy's mother liked to say. His only opponent in the special sheriff's election was Jake Pritchard, who owned the Standard Oil station on the Monroeville Highway. Jake had recently raised the price of gas from ten to fifteen cents a gallon, and some folks felt that making Jake sheriff was giving him too much of a monopoly. So they voted for Buddy instead.

Once elected, the new sheriff hired himself a new deputy. Wayne Springer was pushing thirty-five, a tall, dark-haired man, stringbean lean but muscular, with the high cheekbones and bronzed skin that usually came with some Cherokee blood. He had five years of law enforcement experience over in Jefferson County and a reputation for being willing (if not eager) to use his .38 Special. What's more, because he had come from a large sheriff's department (Birmingham was the biggest city in Alabama), Wayne had been trained in modern police methods.

It paid off. After they got Bragg in his coffin and on his way home to his mama, Wayne had looked carefully at the Colt six-shooter, the one with Bragg's fingerprints. There was a .45-caliber round left in the gun. He had test-fired it, then examined the bullet under his microscope (*his* microscope; the sheriff's office didn't have one), comparing it to the slug Doc Roberts had dug out of Bragg's body during the autopsy Buddy ordered.

It didn't match.

Buddy scowled when Wayne gave him the news. "What do you mean, it doesn't match?"

"It's not the same caliber." Wayne put both bullets on his worktable, side by side. "The one left in the Colt is a .45." He pointed to the bullet on the left. "The slug that killed Bragg is a .44."

Buddy wished he knew more about guns. "Could that Colt have fired a .44?"

"It could have," Wayne said. "But there's something else, Buddy. When you fire a six-shooter, the spent cartridges stay in the gun. So when Bragg shot himself and dropped the gun, there should have been a spent cartridge in the chamber."

"Yeah." Buddy knew that much, anyway. "So what's your point?"

"My point is that there *was* no cartridge

in the chamber."

"Hmm." Buddy let out a long breath, seeing the implications. "So we've got ourselves a problem. Right?"

"Right," Wayne said briskly. "What we need is a *real* expert. A ballistics expert." He picked up the bullets, juggled them for a moment, and put them down again. "Remember Goddard?"

"Goddard?" Buddy asked uncertainly.

"Yeah. Calvin Goddard. Remember that article in *Popular Science* I showed you not long ago? The one on ballistics? Calvin Goddard wrote it."

"Oh, that one," Buddy said. "Yeah, I remember." Apologetically, he added, "Not in detail, though. Remind me."

"Goddard says that every gun leaves a fingerprint on every bullet it fires. Not a real fingerprint — that's just a manner of speaking. He's talking about the impression left on the bullet by the grooves inside the gun barrel. Some guns have five grooves, others have six. Some grooves give the bullet a right-hand spin; others, a left-hand spin. That's called rifling, and it's specific to a given maker and model. But bottom line, every gun is unique." He glanced at Buddy with a raised eyebrow.

Buddy nodded, although he hoped there

wasn't going to be a quiz.

Wayne pointed to the two bullets on his work table. "Judging from the rifling on the two bullets, I'm pretty sure — maybe about eighty percent sure — that they weren't fired from the same gun. So even though Bragg's prints are on that Colt and it had been recently fired, it isn't the weapon that killed him."

"Ah," Buddy said. He wasn't surprised. From the beginning, something had told him that Bragg had not died by his own hand. But he *was* surprised that two bullets could tell a story like that. And that Wayne could figure it out just by looking through that microscope. When *he* looked through it, all he saw were his eyelashes.

"But I'm no expert," Wayne went on, "You'd never want me to testify on ballistics in front of a jury. These slugs ought to be examined — and photographed — under Goddard's fancy new comparison micro-scope. He runs a crime lab for the police department in Chicago. I'll bet he'd be glad to do the testing for us. He might not even charge us for it."

A crime lab. Buddy wasn't sure what that was, but it sounded like what they were looking for. He glanced down at the two bullets, thought of the consequences, and

54

nodded slowly.

"I reckon we ought to do that. Ask Goddard if he'll write up something that we can include in the report when we get those bullets back. It sounds like we've got more work to do."

Wayne had nodded. "Yeah. If Bragg wasn't killed by that Colt, there's another gun out there somewhere — the one that *did* kill him." He paused. "And the killer."

That conversation had taken place a day or two after Bragg was buried. Now, some seven or eight weeks later, Goddard had returned the bullets, along with magnified photographs, a description of his testing procedures, and his findings, all impressively typed up on the letterhead of the Chicago Police Department's crime lab. Goddard's final two sentences endorsed Wayne's earlier observation.

The rifling patterns evident on the two bullets are distinct and substantially different. The examiner could find no points of comparison. It can be said with near 100% certainty that the .44 caliber test bullet fired from the Colt revolver and the .45 caliber bullet removed from the victim's body were fired from two different guns.

Buddy tossed the file on his desk, picked up his coffee, and leaned back in his chair. Two bullets, fired from two different guns. The Colt was locked in the safe on the other side of the room. Where was the gun that killed Bragg?

Who had fired it? Why? Was this killing just a random act — maybe even an accident, covered up to look like a suicide?

Or was it part of something bigger?

And how in the hell was he supposed to come up with answers to these questions?

He put his feet on the desk, took a swig of coffee, and began to think.

CHAPTER FOUR:
"SHE'S CUTER THAN SHIRLEY TEMPLE!"

Wednesday, December 19

Over at the Darling Diner, Myra May Mosswell and Violet Sims are finally getting the hang of the new Kellogg switchboard that had been recently installed in the Darling Telephone Exchange, in the Diner's back room. The money for the switchboard was generously contributed by the widow of their former partner, Whitney Whitworth, who had opposed the new equipment. Mrs. Whitworth had not only given them enough to purchase the new switchboard, she actually *gave* them her share in the business, which she inherited from her deceased husband.

Myra May (who has a square jaw, a strong mouth, heavy brows, and a cynical gaze) had trouble believing that this was actually happening until the week before Thanksgiving, when the Kellogg Switchboard Company sent a man from their Chicago plant to install the new equipment. Violet (brown-haired, petite, pretty, and cheerfully optimistic) and her team of switchboard operators got busy learning to manage it. In the very same week, the paperwork on the transfer of Mrs. Whitworth's share of the business was completed. Incredibly, the Exchange now belonged entirely to them! At Thanksgiving, they had a great deal to be thankful for.

Both Myra May and Violet had been astonished by Mrs. Whitworth's unexpected generosity. Raylene Riggs, however, wasn't at all surprised. She had seen it coming.

Raylene — a tall, striking woman with auburn hair streaked with gray — was Myra May's mother. A gifted cook and manager, she ran the Diner's kitchen with the help of Euphoria Hoyt (recently returned from a stint at the Red Dog Saloon, across the tracks in Maysville, the colored section of Darling). But Raylene had another gift, in addition to her extraordinary skills in the kitchen. She often (but not always) knew when something was going to happen. Sometimes she even knew why, and what would happen as a consequence.

Raylene didn't advertise her gift, but she didn't make any secret of it, either. Folks who knew usually didn't think anything of it one way or another. It was just a nice sort of thing to have, like curly hair or the ability to play "Dixie" on a kazoo.

Resourceful and even-tempered, Raylene was a rock when things went wrong in the kitchen. But lately, she had seemed . . . well, disturbed. Her concern seemed to center on four-year-old Cupcake, Violet and Myra May's little girl and the apple of Darling's eye.

Cupcake had a bouncy mop of strawberry blond curls, the bluest of blue eyes, and a sweet smile. She loved to help out in the kitchen when Gramma Ray was cooking, pulling the pots and pans out of the cupboard and pretending to make biscuits or bake a cake. But even more, she loved to sing, and Violet loved to teach her songs from the radio.

"Tiptoe Through the Tulips" was one of Cupcake's favorites. Violet bought her Nick Lucas' recording of it and showed her how to play it on their Victrola, so she could listen whenever she wanted. Then, when Raylene found a pair of taps and applied them to a pair of Cupcake's shoes, the little girl quickly invented a tap dance to go with the music. Soon, she was tapping as easily as she walked.

This surprising ability amused Myra May

and Raylene, but it delighted Violet, who had once wanted to be a dancer herself. She began to encourage Cupcake to dance for the customers in the Diner. They loved it, and pretty soon people were asking if Cupcake would sing and dance for them while they ate.

"She's cuter than Shirley Temple!" they exclaimed admiringly. "And every bit as good a dancer. She could have a career in the movies!" Which thrilled Violet, who loved it when people admired her little girl.

Given Cupcake's natural talent, it wasn't long before Violet decided to enroll her in Nona Jean Hopworth's kiddy tap dance lessons in nearby Monroeville. Nona Jean was a former Ziegfeld showgirl who had danced professionally as Lorelei LaMotte. After leaving Ziegfeld (and starring in a less-than-stellar role as gangster Al Capone's girl-friend) Nona Jean had come to Darling to live with her aunt, old Miss Hamer.* After her aunt died, she married Howie Hopworth, the owner of a chiropractic clinic in Monroeville.

Nona Jean was so impressed by Cupcake's

* You can read about Nona Jean and her partner, Lily Lake, in *The Darling Dahlias and the Naked Ladies*.

native abilities that she immediately included her in a dance recital with her older students, just before Thanksgiving. With one of the older girls, Cupcake sang and tapped "Baby Take a Bow," Shirley Temple's show-stopping routine from the movie *Stand Up and Cheer,* which had been released that summer. To Violet's great delight, Cupcake earned a standing ovation and did her "Tiptoe" dance as an encore.

After the recital, Nona Jean was so enthusiastic about her new pupil that she offered to teach Cupcake for free. But Myra May hated to be beholden and said no to that offer. So Violet was paying Nona Jean fifty cents every week for an hour's lesson with the older kiddies. And she got Beulah (at the Beauty Bower) to show her how to wrap the little girl's hair in rags to create sausage curls — not the fifty-six curls that Mrs. Temple was rumored to wrap for Shirley every night, but enough curls to make Cupcake extra-pretty. Beulah even gave Violet a bottle of her homemade quince-seed setting lotion, which helped to hold the curls in Cupcake's baby-fine strawberry blond hair.

Raylene, however, didn't seem quite so enthusiastic about Cupcake's great success. For some reason, the recital seemed to trouble her, and for the past several weeks, she'd been watching little Cupcake with a hawk-like intensity. Whatever her suspicions, she was keeping them to herself. But she warned Myra May and Violet (both of whom were mystified) to lock all the doors at night and keep a close eye on their little girl.

Cupcake wasn't just *theirs*, however. She seemed to belong to all of Darling, just as little Shirley Temple — now one of the brightest stars in the entire Hollywood galaxy — belonged to all of America. President Roosevelt, Shirley's most important fan, was deeply impressed by her heart-warming smiles and merry optimism. "As long as our country has Shirley, we will be all right," he said. Darling folk felt the same way about Cupcake. As long their town had Cupcake to cheer them up, they could survive just about anything.

Which did not bring any special comfort to Cupcake's Gramma Ray. She often seemed to be looking off into a future that nobody else was seeing, and it was clear that something was worrying her. Puzzled, Myra May and Violet both realized that she wasn't her usual quietly contented self, and each of them, privately, asked what was on her mind.

But she always shrugged off their questions with a dismissive, "Oh, it's nothing, really." She would smile and go on with her daily work, keeping the Diner's kitchen humming and turning out those delicious pies that made Earlynne think twice.

Nevertheless, Raylene paused every now and then to give Cupcake a special hug. And as Christmas got closer and closer, she kept a wary eye out for strangers.

CHAPTER FIVE:
"YOU CAN'T POSSIBLY GET BY ON FIFTEEN DOLLARS A WEEK!"

Thursday, December 20

The frame building next door to the Darling Diner boasts two stories. On the first floor is the editorial office, production plant, and print shop of the Darling *Dispatch,* which is owned and published by Charlie Dickens. On the second floor is the office of Moseley and Moseley, Attorneys at Law, which is reached by a steep flight of open stairs that angle up the west side of the building.

For the past few years, there has been only one Mr. Moseley: Benton Moseley, who inherited the firm from his father, grandfather, and various uncles who practiced law at the same location for the past seventy-some years. Mr. Moseley (who once served a term in the state legislature and is still deeply involved in the state's Democratic politics) also has an office in Montgomery. He's in the habit of spending three or four days a week in the state capital.

But Liz Lacy, Mr. Moseley's longtime secretary, is always at her desk: attractive, smiling, and ready to help, no matter what sort of legal hot water you've gotten yourself into. Mr. Moseley often says that Liz is indispensable, and that she knows so much about the law that she would doubtless pass the state's bar exam with flying colors. But Lizzy understands that he's joking — at least about the bar. There are no female lawyers in Alabama.

Recently, however, there'd been a change of schedule. Miss Lacy could be found at her desk from eight to twelve in the mornings *only,* and the office was closed most afternoons. It was a matter of economics. In October, the country had observed the fifth anniversary of Black Tuesday: the day the Wall Street stock bubble had burst, destroying the get-rich-quick dreams of millions of Americans. The New Deal was helping many families keep body and soul together, but the Depression still had a stranglehold on the nation's overall economy.

Like many lawyers across the country, Mr. Moseley was having a hard time keeping his Darling practice afloat. While his clients in Montgomery mostly paid their legal bills on time and in cash, the citizens of Darling were more likely to pay late and in kind. Three laying hens, for instance, or even a fat pig. A bushel of sweet corn in July. A half-cord of firewood in December. Recently, Mr. Moseley had told Liz that he could afford to pay her for only twenty hours a week.

"I can't tell you how sorry I am to do this, Liz," he'd said gravely. "The minute things start looking up again, I'll want you back at your desk full time."

There's more to this story, for Liz and Benton Moseley were not just coworkers but friends. Years earlier, when she'd first come to work for him, Lizzy had labored under the weight of an enormous, soul-shaping crush so powerful that it threatened to consume her. She was conscious of it every moment, and had to work hard — oh, so hard — to pretend to be what he thought she was: a secretary who did her work professionally and dispassionately.

Over time, Lizzy's romantic fantasies had given way to practical reality, and now the two of them occasionally shared dinner and a movie, just for fun. In fact, Mr. Moseley (who had been married and divorced) had a socialite lady friend in Montgomery and often visited her when he was in the state capital.

Liz understood the situation and no longer yearned to be anything more than Mr. Moseley's "Girl Friday," as he sometimes called her. Still, she couldn't help feeling that it wasn't quite fair of him to assume that she would be available to come back to work full time as soon as he beckoned. Maybe he didn't mean to take advantage of her, but that's how she saw it. It made her feel uncomfortable and just a little resentful.

Naturally, she didn't tell her boss any of this. What she said was "I understand, Mr. Moseley. We'll just have to do the best we can."

Twenty hours of paid work amounted to just fifteen dollars a week, half her normal salary. But that was fifteen dollars more than some people were earning, and while things would be awfully tight, Lizzy felt she could manage. Her house was paid for and she didn't need any new clothes. She walked or rode her bike around town; she didn't own a car. If worst came to worst, she could give up her telephone. And she could economize on food: she had a large garden that provided all the vegetables she could eat and chickens for her breakfast eggs and even an occasional Sunday chicken-and-noodles dinner.

Her mother had recently married the owner of Dunlap's Five and Dime. When Lizzy told her what had happened, the new Mrs. Dunlap said, "Don't you worry about a thing, dear. Mr. Dunlap and I would *love* it if you would work for us at the Five and Dime. Why, you can start this afternoon! We'll be glad to pay you twenty-five cents an hour."

Lizzy shook her head firmly. "That's a lovely offer and I thank you, Mama, but no. I have other things I want to do."

"But *what*?" her mother cried. "And how will you *live*, Elizabeth? You can't possibly get by on fifteen dollars a week!"

"Just watch me," Liz muttered testily, under her breath. Aloud, she said, "Oh, I have a little cash saved up. I'm sure I'll be all right."

Some people might have been at loose ends without a job to go to every afternoon. But Lizzy knew exactly how to spend those hours: on the novel she was writing, her second. Her first, a historical novel about the War Between the States, would be published the next April by Scribner, one of the three or four top publishing houses in the country — an unbelievable bit of luck, she thought, pinching herself for the umpteenth time to make sure she wasn't dreaming. The book, called *Inherit the Flames,* told the story of Sabrina, a young Alabama woman whose family plantation was plundered by Yankee soldiers. Sabrina had to choose between marrying a wealthy older neighbor and struggling to manage on her own.

Lizzy's editor, Maxwell Perkins (the same editor who had made F. Scott Fitzgerald and Ernest Hemingway famous) had written a gracious note saying that she was a talented writer with a great career ahead of her. Her agent, Nadine Fleming, had said that *Inherit the Flames* was a "wonderful" debut novel but warned that the Depression had already killed off a great many potential bestsellers. Writers were forced to find whatever work they could: giving advice to the lovelorn, doing screenplays, ghostwriting. Liz shouldn't get her hopes up.

"The best thing you can do is keep on writing," Miss Fleming had said. "I want you to be ready with plenty to offer when this horrible Depression ends and books start selling again."

So Lizzy was determined to put her now-free afternoons to good use. She was satisfied (no writer is ever entirely happy) with the progress she was making with her second book. She felt as if she understood the story she was telling about the War Between the States, and she admired her characters, a pair of orphaned sisters who had to look out for each other.

Her evenings, however, were another matter.

The difficulty was Grady Alexander, who lived just down the street. He and Lizzy had once been what Darling folk called a "number." Lizzy herself had planned to marry Grady — when she felt ready to make a lifetime commitment. What had kept her from it was her longtime dream of being a writer. Being a housewife and a mother and a writer . . . well, it was a little hard to imagine finding time in the day to be all *three*.

That's what she had told herself, anyway. But lurking in a dark corner of her heart was another, more veiled reason. She had worried that — while she certainly had a deep affection for Grady (who was an all-around nice guy and would make a more than acceptable husband), she didn't love him quite enough to sign a lifetime contract. Maybe, if she waited just a little longer, she would love him more.

So she had held back when Grady pressed her to go all the way. It wasn't that she was "saving herself for marriage," as the magazines coyly put it. Rather, she felt that if she gave Grady what he wanted, he would take it as her pledge that she would marry him. And she just wasn't ready for that.

Lizzy's dilemma had ended abruptly when Grady got a young woman in trouble and had to marry her. His new wife, Sandra, gave birth to a healthy Grady Junior, but she hadn't lived to enjoy her son and husband. She was buried under a pink granite headstone in a quiet corner of Darling Cemetery. She left behind a shocked and grief-stricken family and a few pious individuals who remarked that her death was plain proof that you couldn't transgress God's law and get away with it.*

After his wife's death, Grady had a predictably difficult time managing child care. He had a good, full-time job as the agricutural extension agent for Cypress County. During the week, he left his son with Sandra's mother. On weekends, he brought him home — to a house that was just up the street from Lizzy's.

And therein lay the problem for Lizzy.

* You'll find the story of Grady's marriage in two previous books: *The Darling Dahlias and the Silver Dollar Bush* and *The Darling Dahlias and the Eleven O'Clock Lady.*

71

Grady wanted to pick up their relationship where they had dropped it when he and Sandra had impulsively done the deed that resulted in Grady Junior.

"We can start over again," he'd told Lizzy. "It will be better this time, because we know what's important. We can have a family of our own — give little Grady a sister and a brother." His tone was imploring. "Please, Liz, I *need* you."

Lizzy's first response had been a quick no. "We can't turn back the clock," she'd said. "What's done is done. We're different people now."

Which in spite of being terribly clichéd was also terribly true. Grady was now a widower and a father. Lizzy was about to be a published author, with a second book in her typewriter. She was also Mr. Moseley's indispensable assistant, and she intended to keep that job. She had more than enough on her plate.

But Grady had meant it when he said, "You're not getting off so easily, Liz. I won't allow it."

He didn't. He called her at work, sent her notes and little gifts, and never let more than a few evenings pass without dropping in to see if she needed any chores done.

And after she'd given him her answer,

Lizzy had been bombarded by second thoughts. She understood how truly terrible the past months had been for him — losing his wife, whom he surely must have loved, and being left with the care of a motherless baby. A part of her still loved him, she supposed. And still another part was pure and simple Darling: a woman was meant to marry and take care of her husband and children. Any woman who didn't do that wasn't living up to her God-given role as a woman.

Even if some big, important editor in New York said she had a great career ahead of her as a writer.

Mr. Moseley wouldn't be back from Montgomery until the next day, so the office was still dark and quiet when Lizzy came in at eight on that Thursday morning. She turned on the lights, plugged in the coffeepot, and glanced around, appreciating the look of Christmas. The wreath of pine boughs hanging on Mr. Moseley's office door was fresh and green, with a red velvet ribbon, silvery bells, and a bright holiday scent. A small Christmas tree sat on a table in a corner of the reception area, with Lizzy's funny little gifts for Mr. Moseley — a Betty Boop necktie, a box of big gold-colored paperclips, a pen in the shape of a feather quill — prettily wrapped and nicely arranged under it. There was a bright red poinsettia on the coffee table in the waiting area, and another on Lizzy's desk.

And hanging in Mr. Moseley's closet, wreathed in the seasonal scent of camphor, was the fur-trimmed, red flannel costume he always wore when he played Santa Claus at the annual children's Christmas party at the courthouse across the street. It was a tradition Lizzy remembered with delight from her own Darling childhood, when Mr. Moseley's father and uncles had given candy and treats to the children of the town — wearing that very same suit. She was glad that Mr. Moseley was keeping up the Christmas tradition.

The office was full of things that suggested traditions, and Lizzy loved them all. The polished floors were made of sturdy oak planks from Briar Swamp, installed when the building was built by Mr. Moseley's grandfather, before the War Between the States. The Oriental rug had been brought from Turkey by Mr. Moseley's father in 1914, the year the Great War began. The gilt-framed diplomas and certificates of three generations of Moseley attorneys hung on the walls. And the front window looked out across the street to the Cypress County courthouse, where the American flag and the Alabama flag fluttered against the gray December sky.

When Lizzy first came to work for Mr. Moseley as a young high school graduate, it had seemed to her that Darling's solid, sturdy courthouse symbolized justice, while the law books on the shelf in Mr. Moseley's office spelled out all the rules in black and white. Between the law books and the courthouse, there could never be any mistake in distinguishing what was right and what was wrong — or so she had thought,

But over the years, she had learned that justice was far more slippery than she had imagined. "The law is full of tricks and bluffs and compromises," Mr. Moseley said. "It doesn't always go by the book."

At first, Lizzy had felt this to be both confusing and dissatisfying. If the law played tricks on people, where was the justice? But after she thought about it — and watched Mr. Moseley confront, compromise, negotiate, and settle — she began to understand. The law might look solid enough, but in reality there were holes in it, like a good Swiss cheese. On the page, the rules seemed black and white, but in practice, they were various shades of gray. It was the very elasticity of justice and the deft skills of its practitioners that made it work. This wasn't a comforting idea, but it fit the facts.

The coffee was ready now, so Lizzy poured herself a cup and settled down at her desk to type a brief in a civil suit over a client's broken leg, scheduled for a preliminary hearing the next day. The client was suing Mr. Hokum, the owner of the cotton gin where he worked, because a rotten wooden floor had collapsed under him. She was a good typist and didn't make many mistakes — thankfully. The brief had to be done in triplicate, so even a little error meant that she had to get out the eraser shield and correct the original and both carbon copies. She had been working at this tedious task for about fifteen minutes when the phone rang.

"Good morning, law office," Lizzy said. She flexed the fingers of her right hand, glad for the interruption.

"Mr. Moseley, please." The caller, a man, was obviously not a Southerner.

"He's not in the office today," Lizzy said. "Perhaps I can help you?"

"I would be grateful if you could give him a message," the man said. "My name is Peter Price. I'm an attorney in Los Angeles, California. I represent Mr. Neil Hudson, also of Los Angeles. Mr. Hudson is looking for his daughter, Dorothy, whom he thinks may be living in your town. I hope Mr. Moseley can help."

Calls often came in from other lawyers, and Mr. Moseley always responded, as a matter of professional courtesy. "I'll be glad to tell him," Lizzy said. She picked up a pencil and made a note of the time and Mr. Price's name in her telephone log.

She added, "This is a small town and I know most of the residents. I don't remember ever hearing of a Hudson family, though."

"That's not the name," Mr. Price said. "Mr. Hudson says that his daughter, who is four years old now, is living with her aunt."

"I see," Lizzy said, making another note. "And the aunt's name?"

"Violet Sims. *Miss* Violet Sims." The lawyer's voice sounded disapproving. "The lady is unmarried. We understand that she works in a café."

Violet Sims. Lizzy felt a chill across her shoulders. For a moment, she couldn't think how to respond. Then she heard herself saying, with remarkable evenness, "Thank you, Mr. Price. Your telephone number?" She wrote it down in the log. "I'll give Mr. Moseley your message. If he has any information, he'll be sure to call you."

"Thank you. I would appreciate that very much," Mr. Price said. He paused. "I should add that at this point, Mr. Hudson views this as a simple family disagreement. He hopes to resolve it amicably, without pressing criminal charges against his former sister-in-law. But you might tell Mr. Moseley that Dorothy's aunt took the child without her father's permission, after the death of her mother. We don't want to involve the police — unless that becomes necessary, of course."

"I see," Lizzy said. That last bit sounded like a threat.

Smoothly, the lawyer went on. "We're hoping that Mr. Moseley will be willing to go to the aunt and explain the situation. If she will return the child, all will be forgiven and forgotten. Mr. Hudson will be glad to pay for Mr. Moseley's services and the railroad fare for sending the child to Los Angeles." He paused, then added, as an afterthought. "If the aunt is reluctant, perhaps Mr. Moseley could sound her out on the amount she would accept."

"Amount?" Lizzy asked.

"Well, we're hopeful that Miss Sims will simply yield Dorothy to her father," the lawyer said. "But she could reasonably request a reimbursement of her expenses for the support of the child for the past four years. We would be willing to go as high as, oh, say, a hundred dollars a year — although a lesser amount would naturally be preferable."

"Naturally," Lizzy murmured drily.

"We feel that, depending on her circumstances, she might respond better to that suggestion than to the threat of a kidnapping charge." The lawyer's voice took on an edge. "But we will involve the police if we have to." This time, there was no mistaking the threat.

Lizzy took a deep breath. It was all becoming quite clear — and ugly. "Thank you," she said. "I'll pass this along to Mr. Moseley."

"Thank you. Do you know when he'll be back?"

Lizzy knew that Mr. Moseley had to be in court the next day, but she found herself saying, "Early next week, I believe."

"Good. If I don't hear by the middle of next week, I'll assume he's not able to help and will get in touch with another attorney in Darling. I have a couple of other names to try."

Lizzy said goodbye and replaced the receiver on the hook, feeling as though she had just been tossed off the back of an L&N caboose.

Violet Sims was her friend and fellow Dahlia, the co-owner (with Myra May Mosswell) of the Darling Diner and the Telephone Exchange. And while the name — Dorothy — puzzled her, she knew the child Mr. Price was looking for.

She was Darling's adored little Cupcake.

CHAPTER SIX:
"WHATEVER IT TAKES"

Darling is no different from many small towns in the South. Its major historic event was the War Between the States, which took a generation of Darling boys into the Confederate Army and didn't give them back. The War also taught Darling women that they could manage the work on the home front better than anybody might have predicted — a lesson that most were quick to forget when their men came home.

The second big thing was the telegraph and the Louisville & Nashville railroad spur, both of which arrived at the same time, for better or worse connecting Darling to the rest of the world. (The L&N also delivered the final, fatal blow to boat traffic on the Alabama River. Trains and railroad tracks were faster, more reliable and cheaper to operate than the old-fashioned paddle-wheelers, which had a tendency to catch fire, blow up, and sink.) The third was the telephone, which came to town around the time Woodrow Wilson was elected president and pretty much dealt a death blow to the telegraph. And after that came the Great War, which took another generation of Darling boys and didn't give them back, either. War, it seems, is like that.

Like many other towns across the country, Darling has commemorated its war dead by building a granite monument to them on the courthouse lawn. The courthouse, the most important structure in town, is an imposing two-story red brick building with a bell tower and a white-painted dome with a clock that strikes the hour so loudly that it can be heard all over town. In the summer, the courthouse is surrounded by lush green grass and bordered with marigolds, zinnias, nasturtiums, and cosmos — planted, watered, and weeded by the Dahlias — for the enjoyment of all Darlingians.

By autumn, the summer flowers have given way to yellow and orange chrysanthemums, blue asters, and pansies with curious, upturned faces. The courthouse steps are lined by jack-o'-lanterns carved by Darling schoolchildren, and their drawings of Pilgrims, Indians, and turkeys decorate the courthouse windows.

Then, as the year drifts to a close, the

jack-o'-lanterns are replaced by pots of bright red artificial poinsettias, and the courthouse lawn sprouts a collection of painted Christmas figures made by Hiram Hill the year McKinley was shot and Teddy Roosevelt moved into the White House. Hiram's life-size plywood figures — six shepherds, three wise men, two angels, eight reindeer, one sleigh, one Santa, and a cadre of elves — are stored in the courthouse basement and set up every year by volunteers from the Benevolent and Protective Order of Elks.

Then, the weekend before Christmas, men from the Loyal Order of Moose put up a tall, beautifully proportioned Christmas tree hung with tiny lights and dozens of painted cardboard stars made by Darling's first and second graders, with each child's name on his or her star. The lights are turned on in a festive display, and all the children in town are invited for carols and candy, handed out by Santa Claus himself, played with a jolly flourish of ho-ho-hos by Benton Moseley in a red suit that always smells a bit like camphor.

The courthouse Christmas party is organized by the County Clerk's office, which means that Verna Tidwell — who is both probate clerk and county treasurer — is in charge. It's fair to say that Verna loves being in charge of things: when she's in charge, she can be sure that things are done right.

The County Clerk's office is upstairs on the second floor of the courthouse. It's a busy place, because that's where people pay their property taxes, get their marriage licenses, file birth certificates and adoption papers and death notices, and register liens and property sales. It's also where votes are tallied. Verna regards election management as one of her most important jobs, especially now that *women* can vote.

The office is open from eight to twelve and from one to five, which gives Darling folk plenty of time to do their business there. They are waited on by Verna's assistant, Madge Shoemaker, who answers questions and gives directions, manages the part-time lady who files and sorts the mail, and cleans the canary cage. Madge inherited the canary (named Bing Crosby) from her sister. But Bing sang so loud and so often that Madge's husband wouldn't let her keep him at home. So Bing now lives in the office, where he freely and fervently bestows his song on everybody who comes through the door.

Verna and Liz have worked across the street from one another for years and are in the habit of eating their lunches together a couple of times a week. In the summer, they picnic on the lawn. In the winter, they eat indoors, at Verna's office or Liz's.

On this particular Thursday, Verna picked up the phone in mid-morning and found Liz on the other end of the line. "Something's come up, Verna, and I need your advice. How about lunch today?"

From the tone of Liz's voice, Verna suspected that Liz had something pretty serious on her mind — something personal, probably. She had already confided her rock-and-a-hard-place predicament with Grady Alexander, and Verna had offered her opinion. Grady had had his chance and had blown it. He had no business telling Liz they should reignite their romance. In Verna's considered opinion, Grady was an opportunist who was taking advantage of Liz's compassionate heart. She ought to tell him to find somebody else to be a mother to his little boy and get on with her life.

But as it turned out, Liz had an entirely different subject in mind, although she didn't get to it until they had finished eating. Verna poured mugs of coffee and they opened their lunch bags by the window in her office, where they could look out at the Moose men putting up the last of the plywood reindeer while they ate and chatted about Darling doings.

When they were finished, Liz folded her arms on the table and said, "I got a very strange phone call this morning, Verna. It's worrying me."

"A phone call?" Verna rolled her eyes. "From Grady, I suppose. With another proposal. Really, Liz. When are you going to —"

Liz shook her head. "No, it was from an attorney named Price, in Los Angeles. He has a client who is looking for his four-year-old daughter, Dorothy. The client's wife is dead and the baby was taken from him shortly after her birth by his sister-in-law — his wife's half-sister. At least, that's what the lawyer — Mr. Price — says. He thinks the sister-in-law and the little girl are living in Darling, and he wants Mr. Moseley to find her." She paused. "Mr. Price says he'll pay for Mr. Moseley's trouble. He'll even pay the aunt to give up the child. If she doesn't, he intends to press criminal charges. Kidnapping, I suppose."

"Criminal charges?" Verna scowled. "Sounds like a threat. And the payment sounds like a bribe."

"That's what I thought, too," Liz said. "He said he'd pay as much as a hundred a year for the four years she's had the child — unless she'll take less."

Verna pursed her lips. "It also sounds *sleazy,* if you ask me. I don't think I know of any four-year-old Dorothys in Darling. What's the aunt's name?"

"Violet." Liz knotted her fingers together. "Violet Sims."

"Violet?" Shocked out of her usual equanimity, Verna stared at her. "*Violet?* Oh, my God, Liz! Then Dorothy must be —"

"Yes," Liz said bleakly. "She must be Cupcake. That's why I wanted to talk to you, Verna. I don't know what to do."

Verna sipped her coffee, thinking. "I'm trying to remember the details, but I don't think I ever knew what happened, exactly. All I can recall is that Violet was out of town for a while, then appeared one day with the child. Cupcake was just a baby at the time, wasn't she?"

"I remember the day she came back," Liz said. "It was in September, about four years ago. Bessie Bloodworth and I were visiting the cemetery. Our car quit on us, so we started to walk back home. Just then Violet came along, in Mr. Clinton's taxi. She had gotten off the train in Monroeville, but there wasn't a train to Darling until late that evening, so she paid Mr. Clinton to take

87

her home. When she saw us walking, she asked him to stop and pick us up."

"And the baby?"

"Violet was holding her. She was just a tiny thing, no more than a few weeks old, all wrapped up in a pink flannel blanket with nothing showing but her face and a little curled-up fist. I remember Violet telling us that her sister — the baby's mother — had died in Memphis. I think she said that the baby's father couldn't keep her, or didn't want her, something like that. He was going to send the child to an orphanage. Violet was the only family the little girl had, so she decided to raise her."

Verna pushed her lips in and out, thinking. "Did she have any papers to prove that she had a right to the child?" Violet was a sweet, compassionate person. Anybody who knew her would understand that whatever she did, she did with the best of intentions. But if you were the little girl's father and you wanted her back, it might not be too hard to convince people that she had *kidnapped* that baby.

"If she did, I didn't see them," Liz said. She pulled in a ragged breath and blew it out again, looking distressed. "Mr. Price said they would prefer to treat it as a simple family disagreement. But he made it clear that they'd go to the police if they don't get Dorothy back right away."

Verna turned her coffee mug in her fingers. After a moment, she said, "When you talked to Violet in the taxi, did she seem at all frightened?" Maybe her brother-in-law had threatened her, or the baby. If that's what had happened — if she had taken the baby because she was afraid the father couldn't take care of her, or might even harm her — it could change the whole situation. "Did she look as if she'd been slapped around? Violet, I mean. Or like she was running away from something?"

"Not that I remember," Liz said slowly. "To me, she just seemed happy to be getting home. The only thing that was worrying her was Myra May." She smiled a little. "She was afraid that Myra May might not want the baby. If that happened, she wasn't sure where she would go."

"Wouldn't want the baby?" Verna gave a wry chuckle. "That child has Myra May wrapped around her finger. And her grandmother Raylene, too. Their lives seem to center completely around Cupcake. If they lose her, they will be devastated."

And Cupcake would be, too. Violet and Myra May and Raylene were her family. They were her whole world, from the very beginning of her life. Darling was the only home she had ever known. Everyone in town was her friend.

Liz gave Verna a direct look. "I told the lawyer I would give his message to Mr. Moseley. But now I'm thinking that's not a good idea, at least until we know a little more about this situation. It also occurred to me that we might have nothing to worry about. You have all the county adoption records here, don't you? Perhaps Violet and Myra May have already —"

But Verna had understood where this was going. She pushed back her chair and got up from the table. A few quick steps took her to a tall wooden filing cabinet in a corner of the office, where she pulled out the third drawer. In it were a dozen manila folders, alphabetically arranged — not many, because adoptions in Cypress County were usually informal agreements among friends or family members. Going to court cost money, and if they didn't expect a challenge, people didn't bother. She was sure she would have remembered Violet's application, but she ran her fingers across the tabs anyway, checking the labels.

"No, sorry," she said, straightening up. "Violet has never filed for adoption here." She went to her desk and got her cigarette

90

case. "And even if she had, it might not matter. In the cases I've seen, the judge asks for a signed release from one or both of the parents, if they're still living. It sounds as if Cupcake's father never gave her that." She took out a cigarette. "But we don't know what really happened, do we? All we know is what that lawyer *said* his client told him. And lawyers are as likely to lie as the next person, when they think it's to their advantage."

"What do you think I should do?" Liz asked worriedly. "If I tell Mr. Moseley, I'm afraid he might . . ." She bit her lip.

Verna flicked her lighter to her cigarette. She knew what Liz had been going to say. As a member of the Alabama bar, Mr. Moseley had an obligation to the law. In this case, the law could be on the father's side. They needed to know more about the situation before they involved Liz's boss.

"Did Price say what he was going to do — and when he was going to do it?" she asked.

"If he doesn't hear from Mr. Moseley by the middle of next week, he plans to call somebody else — another attorney, I suppose. He said he had a couple of names."

"Gerald Cankron and Homer Box." Verna blew out a stream of smoke. "Either of them will be glad to cooperate with him, I'm sure, especially if there's a little money involved."

"That means we have to do something pretty quick," Liz said.

"Right." Verna pulled an ashtray toward her and tapped her cigarette ash into it. "You need to talk to Violet and Myra May this afternoon. Tell them about the phone call. Find out what really happened in Memphis, when Violet took the baby. Maybe she was afraid for Cupcake's well-being. Maybe she knows something about the father that would cast doubt on his claim to the child." She pulled on her cigarette. "After all, she and Myra May have had her for four years. Where has the man been? Why hasn't he stepped forward before now?"

"I was going to work on my newspaper column this afternoon," Liz said. "But it's not due until next Wednesday. And I see your point. Those are good ideas — and questions that have to be answered." She gave Verna a grateful look. "Thank you. I feel better already."

"I'll keep trying to think of something else," Verna said practically. "But I'm afraid there aren't a whole lot of options." She cocked her head. "How about if I go with you to talk to Violet and Myra May? I can lend a little moral support. And maybe they'll tell us something that will give us some more ideas — *before* you say anything to Mr. Moseley."

"I would love it if you would come, Verna," Liz said emphatically. She glanced up at the clock over Verna's desk. "Myra May and Raylene are busy with the lunch crowd right now, and Violet is probably giving them a hand. Maybe we should wait until the middle of the afternoon?"

"I'll meet you there at three," Verna said. "I had to work late a couple of times last week, so I'm due to take a little time off. And the planning for the Christmas party is just about finished." She paused, quickly scanning her to-do list in her mind. "Does Mr. Moseley's Santa Claus suit need to go to the drycleaners? If so, you can leave it with Mrs. Hart. They'll send it over to Monroeville." The Harts ran Hart's Peerless Laundry, cattycornered from the courthouse.

"No, it's fine." Liz smiled. "Smells a bit like camphor, though. I took it out of the box and hung it in the closet to air out." Her smile faded. "I'm afraid it won't feel much like Christmas if Cupcake is gone. We have to do *something.*"

"You're right on that score," Verna said

fervently. "Whatever it takes, we have to keep that from happening."

Liz pushed her chair back and stood up. "Yes," she said, with determination. "Whatever it takes."

CHAPTER SEVEN:
"NOW, ABOUT THAT PROPOSITION"

In the newspaper office across the street from the courthouse, Charlie Dickens pulled off his wire-rimmed glasses and rubbed his nose. It was nearly two o'clock. It would take him another half hour to finish making up page five, and Thursday was already sliding past at breakneck speed.

Every Thursday night Charlie revved up the Babcock flatbed cylinder press — the cantankerous Black Beast, already old when his father bought her thirty years ago — and printed the week's *Dispatch*. On Friday morning, he would feed the subscribers' copies through the mailing machine to label them with names and addresses. Then he would haul the copies to the post office, so Tom Wheeler could deliver them to his RFD route on Saturday. (If Tom's ancient Model T didn't break down, that is. If that happened, Tom would hitch Old Fred to his buggy, and it might be late Saturday night before all the newspapers were delivered.) On Sunday afternoon, after church and a fried chicken dinner, the men would pull their rocking chairs up close to the stove and read the paper out loud while their wives (or mothers and sisters) did the dishes, then sat down to darn socks and sew on a few buttons. Unless they were Hardshell Baptists, that is, in which case the men read the Bible and the sewing got put off until Monday.

The *Dispatch* was an eight-page weekly. Charlie bought the four pages of ready print (world and national news off the wire services, commentary, comics, the market report, and the women's page) from a syndicate called the Western Newspaper Union. The weekly ready-print sections (pages two, three, six, and seven, with the other pages left blank) were produced by a shop in Mobile and shipped to Darling on the Greyhound bus. They usually arrived at ten on Thursday morning. If they didn't (which happened more often than not, given the fact that the bus was about as old as the Babcock and the tires weren't young, either), the paper didn't go out until Monday. Or Tuesday.

But the ready-print pages had arrived that morning, so Charlie knew he'd be working late that night. He would warm up the Babcock and print the four home-print pages (one, four, five, and eight) on the blank pages of the ready print. Page one was local news, four was local news and an editorial, and five and eight were ads and whatever local news was needed to fill the columns.

The home-print pages were all compiled right here in the shop. Charlie and Ophelia Snow, his roving reporter, collected the news and wrote the stories. Ophelia sold ads and operated the Linotype machine. Charlie did the final edits, made up the pages from Ophelia's Linotype slugs, and ran the press. The end result was a quite respectable small-town newspaper, if Charlie did say so himself, with something in it for every reader in the county.

At least, that's how the newspaper had been operating. Charlie showed up every day and spent Thursday nights running the Black Beast, praying it wouldn't break down. Ophelia came in on Mondays, Wednesdays, and Thursdays, and worked Tuesdays and Fridays in the commandant's office at Camp Briarwood, the Civilian Conservation Corps camp a few miles outside of town.

97

Recently, however, Ophelia had hit Charlie with some very bad news. Captain Campbell, the Briarwood commandant, had offered her a full-time job — at double the money Charlie was paying her. She had given him two weeks' notice.

Charlie felt like he'd just been sucker punched. With Ophelia in the office, things had been running more smoothly than ever before, especially with advertising and subscription sales. She was a halfway decent reporter, too, at least where the small-town doings were concerned. And she wrestled that cranky old Linotype like a pro. He got a lump in his throat at the thought of losing her — and he flinched at the thought of finding somebody to replace her. He knew just about everybody in town, in the whole county, for that matter. Nobody had Ophelia's skills.

As for Ophelia, she was obviously torn. "I've loved working here, Charlie," she said sadly. "And I feel just terrible about leaving you in the lurch. But with two kids in high school, Jed and I really need the extra money."

Charlie knew that she might have added "And with my husband's business going down the drain," but she didn't. Snow's Farm Supply was in deep trouble, because the farmers who depended on Jed Snow for their livestock feed couldn't pay him and pay their grocery bills, too. Charlie knew that Jed hadn't wanted his wife to take even one job, and that he cringed every time he thought that she was keeping the family afloat. But Jed had had to face facts: if it weren't for Ophelia's two jobs, the Snows would be dead broke — and in debt to boot.

Charlie had to face facts, too. So he dredged up a grin from somewhere and said, "Well, Opie, you gotta do what you gotta do. Don't worry about me. I can handle things here."

"Are you *sure*?" she said doubtfully.

"No," Charlie had said, and grinned. "Hell, no, I'm not sure. You know how I hate that damn Linotype. And I'm not worth a plugged nickel when it comes to selling ads. But that's life. We do what we gotta do and get on with it. You tell Campbell I told you to take that job. And tell him if he fires you, I'll kill the sonuvabitch."

"Thank you," Ophelia said, misty-eyed. Then, to his surprise, she leaned forward and kissed him on the cheek. He sighed, turned, and busied himself with the papers on his desk, hating the thought of managing the *Dispatch* on his own.

A longtime newsman with investigative

reporting experience in such premier newspapers as the *Cleveland Plain Dealer* and the *Baltimore Sun,* Charlie had reluctantly assumed his father's place as editor and publisher of the *Dispatch* after the old man died a few years before. In fact, he had intended to sell the paper and the in-house job printing business and go back to the big city, where there were crimes to report and fires and train wrecks and political corruption to write about. The city was where headlines happened. Charlie had grown up in Darling, and he knew that *nothing* happened there. Ever.

But then the Crash happened on Wall Street and the Depression happened everywhere. The *Dispatch* subscribers' list was reduced by more than half, and the job printing business was nearly wiped out. At that point, Charlie couldn't *give* the damned newspaper away, much less sell it. He was stuck in Darling and stuck with the *Dispatch.* He had the sour, empty feeling that his life was over.

And then something else happened, something quite miraculous. Her name was Fannie Champaign, and Charlie fell for her, hard. He was a crusty old newspaperman without a smidgeon of romance to soften his cynical soul. But somehow, beneath all of his pessimism and distrust, Fannie found his heart and touched it — and changed his life. It was still the case that important headlines didn't happen in Darling, but Charlie was reconciled to that discouraging fact as long as he could go home to Fannie every day.

What's more, he had even found a renewed interest in the *Dispatch,* especially in the past year, for he had begun to realize that the little newspaper was the emotional glue of Cypress County. In good times, good news gave people something to celebrate. In bad times, bad news made them feel connected to their neighbors. Even though they might have differences of opinion, they felt as if they were all in the same boat, everybody trying to make it through rough waters. Some pessimists said that radios and Movietone newsreels would make newspapers obsolete in a few years, but Charlie didn't believe that. People would be reading newspapers until kingdom come, because that's where they found the news. And good or bad, the news gave them something to hold on to.

There had been a whale of a lot of news lately, coming from all corners of the globe. In Canada, all five of the amazing Dionne quints were reported to be "safe and snug for the winter." In Great Britain, Winston Churchill, always the worrywart, was sounding yet another alarm about Adolf Hitler's Nazi party. "Germany is arming," he announced in stentorian tones, "secretly, illegally, and rapidly." And Japan, he warned, had military ambitions. But nobody liked Churchill after he got so many boys killed at Gallipoli. And nobody was listening, anyway. They were too busy watching Windsor Lad win the Derby, the *Queen Mary* take to the seas, and the Edinburgh-to-London Flying Scotsman become the first steam locomotive to reach a hundred miles an hour. Britain, Britons thought, was on top of the world.

But a few of them may have acknowledged that Churchill was right. In Berlin, Adolf Hitler had declared himself Führer and required members of the Wehrmacht — the German armed forces — to swear the oath of loyalty to him instead of the German constitution. And in faraway Japan, the Imperial Navy (already the third largest in the world, after Great Britain and the United States) had just launched the fifth of five cruisers and destroyers to be built that year.

There was news from the United States, too. In Washington, DC, the government reported that the economy was improving. Unemployment had fallen to 22 percent (from a high of 25 percent the year before), while the gross national product had risen by 8 percent. But even as the New Dealers put down their pencils and congratulated each other on the brightening economic situation, they looked up in the sky and saw dark clouds of tumbling topsoil, blown all the way from the Dust Bowl to the Atlantic. And in Virginia, clouds of a different sort had gathered. A federal grand jury had recently indicted nineteen moonshiners and nine corrupt local officials, including the county sheriff, in what newspapers all over the country were billing as the "Franklin County moonshine conspiracy."

Distractions helped. In New York, Babe Ruth hit his seven hundredth home run. On Broadway, the new Cole Porter musical, *Anything Goes,* starred Ethel Merman, whose voice was every bit as powerful as the Babe's bat — and maybe more. In Chicago, the final head count at the Century of Progress Exposition was reported to be nearly thirty-nine million visitors, a record turnout for any World's Fair. In Hollywood, Will Rogers, Clark Gable, and Janet Gaynor were stealing the box office, but little Shirley Temple was stealing everyone's heart. The six-year-old was already a goldmine for Fox Studios, which was about to release her latest movie. It was called *Bright Eyes* and would be playing at Darling's Palace Theater early next year. Word was already spreading that Fox planned to sponsor Shirley lookalike contests across the United States and that (in addition to the cash prizes) the studio had the option of sending the winner to Hollywood as a movie double for Shirley. Mothers everywhere were rolling sausage curls and teaching their daughters to tap.

The Cypress County news wasn't nearly so exciting, and Charlie knew that there wouldn't be any big local headlines between now and the end of the year. Oh, there was lots going on — it just wasn't *news*, that's all. Miss Rogers, at the library, was organizing a jigsaw puzzle tournament. The merchants were holding a window-decorating contest, with a prize for the most attractive holiday-themed window. The annual children's Christmas party would take place as usual on the courthouse lawn, with Benton Moseley playing Santa. A couple of women with more energy than sense — Earlynne Biddle and Mildred Kilgore — were opening a bakery on the north side of the square, next door to Fannie's hat shop.

Ah, Fannie. Charlie's wife, and both the

source of his joy and — these days — the source of his perplexity. When he married Fannie, the first thing he'd had to get used to was her independence. The next was her astonishing ability to make money. You'd think that a newspaperman would be open-minded and even progressive about women's rights, wouldn't you? Well, Charlie was certainly no old fogey with his head buried in the sand. But he was still trying to come to terms with the fact that his pretty wife was now able to vote when he discovered that her ladies' hat business was bringing in some $2,400 a year.

Twenty-four hundred dollars! By any measure, this was a small fortune. It was fifty percent more than the average American male earned in a year. It was twice as much as Charlie was making from the newspaper and his job printing business put together. And she made it by making *ladies' hats*!

Fannie had always been reticent about her accomplishments. When they got married, Charlie had no idea that her hats (which he viewed with a patronizing masculine amusement) had already been made famous by Lilly Daché, a renowned French milliner, or that leading lady Joan Crawford had worn one of her millinery creations in the movie

Grand Hotel. The *Hollywood Reporter* quoted Miss Crawford as saying that she "simply adored Miss Fannie's clever little hat" and caused quite a hullabaloo when she stole it from the studio wardrobe department to wear to one of Hedda Hopper's Hollywood parties. After that, Fannie's fame went up like a Fourth of July rocket. She had to hire three girls from the Academy to help in the shop after school, but she still couldn't begin to make enough hats to fill the demand.

But Fannie's earnings weren't the only surprise in Charlie's life. Back in October, he had discovered that she was shelling out the astonishing sum of fifty dollars a month to someone who went by the initials J. C. He had learned this on the sly, so to speak, when he was surreptitiously going through Fannie's account books. This secret monthly payment perplexed him no end. But what bothered him even more than the fact of this payment was the *mystery* of it.

Damn it all, why was she keeping it from him? Didn't she trust him? Or was she afraid to tell him because it involved some terrible secret from her past? Was she paying *blackmail*? This was an appalling thought, but it got lodged in his brain and he couldn't shake it loose.

And because he had made this discovery when he was poking his nose where it didn't belong, he couldn't just come straight out and ask his wife who the devil was getting six hundred dollars a year from her, and why. It was a *lot* of money, really, especially in these challenging days. And it rankled. Oh, it rankled.

But just yesterday, and quite by accident, Charlie had made some unexpected progress in his research into this frustrating domestic puzzle. He had happened on a cancelled check that Fannie had dropped on the floor beside her desk in the little cubby she called an office, behind her hat shop salesroom. It was made out in the amount of fifty dollars, payable to the Georgia Warm Springs Foundation. In the memo line at the bottom of the check, she had written the name J. C. Carpenter.

Charlie had stared at the check with a bemused astonishment. He knew very well what the Georgia Warm Springs Foundation was — he had done a story about it some years ago, when he was a reporter with the *Cleveland Plain Dealer*. Franklin Roosevelt had been partially paralyzed by polio in 1921 and was determined to restore himself to health. In 1924, he visited Warm Springs, a complex of thermal springs in the foothills of Pine Mountain in west Georgia. The springs were long reputed to have healing properties, and an inn and a collection of rickety resort cottages had been built around them.

After a few days in the pools, FDR felt that his paralyzed legs had greatly improved, and he began to make extended visits to the remote springs. Then an article appeared in the *Atlanta Journal,* saying that FDR was "swimming his way to health." Polio was a much-feared scourge, Roosevelt was already famous, and the article got national attention. Other "polios" began to flock to Warm Springs. A couple of years later, Roosevelt bought the place, created the Georgia Warm Springs Foundation, and built a house for himself on a hillside near the pools. Now known as the Little White House, it was a personal retreat where the president could go for working vacations. The foundation constructed a school, a chapel, an infirmary, and a cafeteria and administrative building, and physicians and physiotherapists worked with the polios to improve their chances of recovery.

Charlie felt that this was all very interesting, but what could it have to do with Fannie? Why was she donating so much money every month to Warm Springs?

So this morning, Charlie had taken what he hoped was a definitive step toward finally solving the puzzle. He had telephoned the foundation office at Warm Springs and asked to speak to J. C. Carpenter. The girl on the switchboard seemed to be new, though. She said she didn't know who that was and everybody was off for the day at the annual Christmas party. Someone would call him back. He was still waiting.

With a sigh, Charlie put his glasses back on and went back to his work. He was setting page five, which contained Liz Lacy's Garden Gate column, news from the women's clubs, and ads. He was already finished with the Mercantile's Christmas toy sale ad brought in that morning by Archie Mann's wife, Twyla Sue. (Puzzles and games, 9–19 cents; fire-engine red scooter with roller bearings, $1.19; Shirley Temple doll, $2.99.) The Mercantile ad was on the same page as the announcement for the new bakery, The Flour Shop, which was having its grand opening on Saturday, featuring "delicious fresh-baked" bread at 11 cents a loaf. He pulled the copy Mrs. Hancock had brought in for her grocery ad and scanned it. Wonder Bread was only 9 cents a loaf — two cents *cheaper* than the new bakery. He was just getting started on it when he was interrupted by a voice.

"Yo, Charlie — got some time to talk?" It was Buddy Norris, the sheriff. He was leaning against the counter that divided the front part of the Dispatch office from the working area and pressroom.

Charlie was about to ask him if the conversation could wait until tomorrow, but he changed his mind. He'd been at the makeup table for a couple of hours. It was time for a cigarette break. He took off his ink-stained denim apron and went toward the editor's desk.

"Come sit for a spell, Buddy," he said. "Let's have a smoke."

Buddy came around the counter and took a chair. Charlie sat down behind his desk, put his feet up, and pulled a crumpled pack of Camels out of his shirt pocket.

"Don't mean to interrupt," Buddy said.

"No problem," Charlie said, lighting his cigarette. "I'm ready to take a load off." He had never hit it off with the former sheriff, Roy Burns, who (as Burns himself had vividly put it) didn't "have no truck with them goldurn newspapermen. They ain't nothin' but a bunch of muckrakers." Charlie had cheerfully acknowledged himself as Darling's chief muckraker and a thorn in the sheriff's side.

But he and Roy Burns' successor shared the common pragmatic view that, under the right circumstances, law enforcement and the press could work together for the advantage of both. Charlie reserved the right to keep his sources confidential, and Buddy reserved the right to conceal important details of an investigation — although Charlie's sources were hardly private and Buddy admitted that "investigation" was a pretty fancy word to describe what he usually did.

Now, Buddy dropped his knitted wool hat on the floor, unbuttoned his jacket, and tilted his chair against the wall, hooking his heels on the rungs. Unlike Roy Burns, he didn't favor uniforms or even a sidearm. "Darling ain't the wild West," he'd say. "It's the civilized South." (Which was not entirely true. Bootleggers created their own kind of lawlessness.) But he did go so far as to pin a badge on his khaki shirt, and his blue jeans were pressed.

"Chilly out there?" Charlie asked, glancing out the front window. It had been cold and gray all week, with an occasional drizzle, and he'd built a fire in the woodstove at the back of the workroom.

"Yeah. Heard on the radio that it's snowing up in Montgomery. Probably not here, though. Just cold enough to make you think it's gonna. Windy, too." Buddy fished in his coat pocket and took out a pack of Lucky Strikes and a matchbook. "Got something for you, Charlie. A tip, you might call it." He struck a match with his thumbnail and put it to his cigarette. "But you got to promise to keep it under your hat until I say you can print it."

"I can do that, I reckon," Charlie said, but added cautiously, "What do I have to trade for it?" The sheriff was usually fair, but cagey. He wouldn't give you anything unless you gave him something in return.

Buddy hesitated. "What I'm looking for is kinda out of the ordinary. Maybe even a little . . . well, dangerous. If you don't feel up to it, I'll understand. You can keep the tip regardless."

Dangerous? Which meant that Charlie was immediately ready to do it, whatever it was. But all he said was, "Let's hear what you got."

Buddy tipped his chair back down and leaned his elbows on his knees. "What I've got is a report from a crime lab run by the Chicago Police Department. Goddard — the guy who directs the lab — is an expert on firearms, and specifically on bullets. He's got this idea that every bullet has a kind of a fingerprint on it, from the gun that fired it." He gestured with his cigarette. "Well, not a fingerprint, exactly. See, guns are made with little grooves inside the barrel, to put some spin on the bullet. When a round is fired, it gets marked by the grooves. Every gun is different, so somebody who knows what he's doing can tell whether a particular bullet has come out of a particular gun."

"I've read about Goddard," Charlie said. "Invented a microscope that lets him look at two bullets side by side and tell whether they came from the same gun."

Buddy looked disappointed, as if he'd just lost his punchline. "Yeah. That's the guy. Goddard."

Charlie blew out a stream of smoke. "So what's this report you've got? Something new you're working on?"

If it was, Charlie had no idea what it might be. Darling had been characteristically quiet over the Thanksgiving holiday. Witness the fact that a new bakery and a puzzle tournament were big news.

Buddy pulled on his Lucky Strike. "You remember Jimmie Bragg?"

"Sure," Charlie said. Back in October, he'd been a headline in the *Dispatch,* following on the heels of the story that had reported Whitney Whitworth's fatal wreck on the Jericho Road. "Bragg was the warden's fair-haired boy, out at the prison farm. He ran Mr. Whitworth off the road, felt guilty about what he'd done, wrote a suicide note, and shot himself. Used an old Colt six-shooter, if I remember right. His fingerprints were on the gun."

Charlie had written the story himself, and details like that six-shooter stuck in his mind. It was odd, though. He had encountered Bragg at the scene the morning after the accident happened, and the man had acted like it was all news to him. What's more, he had shown no remorse at all, at least not then.

"That's Bragg," Buddy agreed. "And yes, his prints were on that Colt. But before Noonan sent him off to Monroeville for burial, I had Doc Roberts dig out the slug. Then Wayne went out in the back yard and fired a test round from the Colt. We sent both bullets to Goddard. That's the report I just got." He looked around for an ashtray and Charlie shoved an empty Bush's hominy can toward him. "Turns out that only one of the bullets was fired from the Colt."

Charlie blinked. "Want to run that by me again?"

Buddy tapped his cigarette ash into the can, dragging out the suspense. "Goddard says that the only bullet that came from the Colt was the one *Wayne* fired. The test round. The bullet that killed Jimmie Bragg came from a different gun."

"Ahhh," Charlie said, beginning to understand.

"What's more, when we got the Colt, there was one round left in the gun. But no spent cartridge." He pulled on his cigarette. "It's a revolver, Charlie. The spent cartridge stays in the chamber until it's ejected."

"Which Bragg couldn't do because he was dead," Charlie said quietly. He could feel the goosebumps rising on the back of his neck — familiar goosebumps. They had always been a reliable indicator that he had just run right smack into a real story and it was time to saddle up and do something about it.

"Yes," Buddy said. He had the grace to add, "Wayne is the one who knew about Goddard and came up with the idea of comparing bullets." He gave a rueful grin. "He keeps up with this stuff better than I do."

"Springer is a good man," Charlie said. And experienced in ways Buddy wasn't, which made him a smart hire. He thought for a minute.

"So now you've got a dead man, but not

the gun that killed him. Which means that you're looking for the murder weapon — and the fella who pulled the trigger." He shook his head. "That's a tall order. All the action, as I understand it, took place at the prison farm."

The Jericho State Prison Farm was several miles south of town. Its nearly fifteen hundred acres of open pastures and farm fields spread out far beyond the fenced and guarded central compound. It ran by its own rules, under the by-the-book management of Warden Grover Burford, who knew everything that went on in *his* prison. Charlie seriously doubted that Burford would be hospitable to inquiries about Bragg's death by lawmen from the outside — especially because whatever had happened out there had happened under Burford's watch. Likely, with his consent.

Which led to the puzzler: What did Buddy want from *him*?

"A tall order is *right*," Buddy said with a lopsided grin. "And like I say, it could maybe be a bit dangerous. But there's a story in it. A big story, potentially. Which is why I've got a proposition for you."

Charlie was about to find out what the sheriff had in mind. But not right away. The door opened, and Mildred Kilgore came in, a wool cap pulled down over her ears, her coat belted tightly around her.

"Hey, Charlie," she said. "I've got a job printing order for you — the new flyer for our new bakery." She saw Buddy Norris and added pleasantly, "Oh, hello, Sheriff. How are you today?" Without waiting for an answer, she turned back to Charlie. "I need two hundred copies this afternoon, please. For The Flour Shop."

Charlie got up from his desk and went to the counter. "Earliest, Saturday morning, nine o'clock. I can't get to it until I get the *Dispatch* out of here."

Mildred pulled down the corners of her mouth. "That long? But we need it *tomorrow,* Charlie! We're having our grand opening on Saturday and we planned to distribute the flyers to the merchants around the square on Friday."

"That long," Charlie said firmly, resisting the urge to say *take it or leave it.* He hated the job printing part of the business. People always put off getting their printing done until five minutes before they had to have it, then pitched a hissy fit if he couldn't produce it on the spot. "If you want something on Friday, you need to bring it in on Tuesday. I have a newspaper to publish, you know."

Mildred heaved a dramatic sigh. "Well, if that's the best you can do, I guess we'll just have to live with it." She pushed a sheet of paper, handwritten, across the counter. "Here's what we want. The name of our bakery on the front in big letters. The list of items we're selling and the prices are all on the inside."

Charlie scanned the page, then went back to the top, reading it aloud to make sure it was correct. "Bread, eleven cents a loaf. Scones, seven cents. Gingerbread, five cents. Cinnamon buns, two for nine cents. Cupcakes, two for fifteen cents. Assorted Christmas cookies, fifteen cents a dozen." He looked up. "Sounds good — but the bread seems a bit pricey. Mrs. Hancock sells it for . . . what? Eight cents a loaf?"

"Nine," Mildred said, puffing out her cheeks. "And it's already two or three days old by the time she puts it on the shelf. Our bread is freshly baked every day. Except on Sundays," she added. "We have to have one day off."

Charlie scanned the list again. "Is this all you're going to sell? What about Danish? Apple Danish would be good in the morning."

"And shoofly pie," Buddy put in helpfully. "I'll bet you could sell a *lot* of shoofly pie at breakfast time. But not doughnuts. Folks get their doughnuts at the Diner." He smacked his lips. "Raylene Riggs makes the *best* doughnuts. Jelly doughnuts, too."

"We'll be adding items as we go along," Mildred said stiffly. "This is just for our opening week. And we wouldn't *think* of competing with Raylene." She gave a brief smile. "We want buttercup yellow paper, please, Charlie. And we'd like the flyer folded in thirds."

Charlie bent down to look under the counter at the paper supply. Straightening up with a sheet of paper, he said, "All I've got is this pale green. And far as folding is concerned, I'm afraid you're out of luck. The folding machine stopped working a couple of days ago. I've ordered the part," he added, "but it has to come from Chicago, and it isn't here yet."

"Oh, *drat.*" Mildred narrowed her eyes at him. "Really, Charlie. *Green?*"

"You could take it over to Pitter Pat's Print Shop, in Monroeville," Charlie suggested helpfully. He pushed Mildred's handwritten sheet back toward her. "Pat might have yellow. And he'd be glad to fold it for you."

"I am *not* driving to Monroeville," Mildred muttered, pushing the sheet back to

Charlie. "We'll take the green paper. And we'll fold it ourselves."

Five minutes later, she had left and Charlie returned to the chair behind his desk. "Now, about that proposition," he said, picking up where he and the sheriff had left off. "Let's hear it, shall we?"

Buddy lit another cigarette. "Okay, here it is."

With increasing apprehension, Charlie listened to what the sheriff had to say. Yes, that was dangerous! Worse than dangerous, it was an easy way to get himself dead.

But Charlie had been an investigative reporter for decades. He had an unerring nose for news, and he knew a story when it popped up in front of him. This one could be big. Big enough to keep his mind off the sad job of replacing Ophelia. Big enough to make the wire services. Big enough to put the *Dispatch* on the map, maybe. Not big enough for a Pulitzer — but you never knew about that, did you?

Yes, it could be a big story, he thought. If he lived to write it.

CHAPTER EIGHT:
"WHAT ABOUT BREAD?"

"Not until *Saturday*?" Earlynne cried, pushing the hair out of her eyes with a floury hand, leaving a wide white streak across her forehead. Her white apron was streaked with chocolate and what looked like peach juice. "But we're opening on Saturday morning! Didn't you tell Mr. Dickens that?"

"Yes, I told him." Mildred took off her coat and wool cap and hung them on the hook beside the back door. The oven had been on all morning, and the kitchen felt pleasantly warm after her chilly walk across the square. It smelled good, too — a rich, yeasty fragrance, warmed by scents of orange and cinnamon. And fresh-brewed coffee. The electric percolator on the shelf beside the gas stove was bubbling merrily.

"But Saturday was the best he could do," she added. "And the flyer is going to be green, not yellow, because that's all the paper he has right now. If we want another color, we have to order it, and it won't come in on time. What's more, his folding machine is broken, so we'll have to fold it ourselves." She scowled. "You know, if you'd given me your list when I asked for it, we'd have the flyer today."

"Oh, stop lecturing, Mildred," Earlynne said irritably. She broke an egg into her mixing bowl. "I couldn't give you the list until you told me how much money each item is going to cost to make."

"And I couldn't tell you how much each item would cost until I knew what items we were talking about, could I?" Mildred demanded in a reasonable tone. "And then I had to calculate all the prices, which was not an easy job. Don't forget, Earlynne, we are not in this for fun. It would be nice if I could get some of my money back, which can only happen if we make a profit."

She glanced at the new floor-to-ceiling shelves they had installed along one of the kitchen walls, now stocked with several trays of baked goods. On the warming shelf over the gas range, two bowls of yeasty dough were rising under damp dishtowels. There were new lights hanging from the ceiling, fresh shelf paper lining the shelves in the pantry, and the linoleum was clean as a whistle. They had put several long days into

122

getting the kitchen spruced up and functioning again — which had also meant getting Scooter Dooley, Darling's handyman, to fix the drippy faucets in the old porcelain sink and make sure the large gas oven was working right.

Mildred nodded toward the shelves. "Cinnamon buns and scones. Looks like you've been busy."

"I came in early to practice," Earlynne said, breaking another egg into the bowl and giving the batter an energetic stir. "I have to get used to the equipment and to working in this kitchen. I've been practicing at home, too, but every oven is different. And I need to get a routine worked out, so we can have a nice variety of baked goods in the display case all day long." She added, "The stuff on the shelves is just practice, but you can take some home for you and Roger, if you like. I've arranged to donate the rest to the orphanage out on Schoolhouse Road. I thought the children would enjoy them."

"The orphanage is a nice idea," Mildred conceded, filching a scone. "But if you had donated to the Ladies Guild, you might have created some customers." Sampling it, she added, with genuine enthusiasm, "Earlynne, this is delicious! So flaky, too."

Earlynne smiled. "Scones are easy. Just

123

flour, baking powder, salt, and sugar in a big bowl. Chop cold butter into little pieces and rub it into the flour with your fingers until it feels like cornmeal." She put her mixing bowl under the new Sunbeam electric Mixmaster and turned it on. "Add the wet stuff, eggs and milk," she said, over the noise of the mixer. "Roll it out and cut it into wedges. *Voilà!*"

"That certainly looks easy," Mildred said. She watched as the twin beaters whirred busily, whipping every lump out of the batter. Electric mixers for the home kitchen had been around for fifteen years, but the Mixmaster was the first to be reasonably priced — if you had a job and could afford eighteen dollars (more than half a week's average paycheck). "And just think of the work it saves."

"And the wear and tear on your arm muscles," Earlynne said. "It has ten speeds." She demonstrated by turning a button, and the beaters speeded up. "You can even take the mixer off the stand, if you want to use it that way. You'll have to get used to using it, Mildred."

Mildred wasn't sure about this, for the same reason she didn't like her cousin's electric sewing machine, which whizzed along so fast you couldn't see where the

124

fabric was going. It made her shiver to think what would happen if she accidentally got her fingers under the needle, or in the beaters. She peered into the mixing bowl. "What are you making now?"

"A batch of Christmas cookies," Earlynne said. "These have just five ingredients, so they're easy. And cheap," she added, switching off the mixer. "And since they're cookies, they'll keep for our grand opening. When you've got them decorated, you can put some of them in the display in the front window and the rest into our new glass pastry case. I'm going to make some sweet potato cookies. They don't cost much, either. And some simple gingerbread houses. They're easy, and when you've decorated them, they'll look swell."

"Cheap is definitely good," Mildred said, remembering how much money she had spent on her shopping trip to Mobile the day before. The car had been so loaded with bags of flour and sugar, tins of shortening, and all the other supplies that it had nearly dragged its bottom along the road. She gave Earlynne an inquiring look. "*I'm* decorating cookies? And gingerbread houses?"

"I thought you'd want them for your holiday window," Earlynne said primly, plumping the cookie dough onto a floured board and starting to roll it out. "When I get through with these, I'm going to bake some pecan cupcakes. They're nice because they keep so well." She smiled blissfully. "Baking all day is pure *heaven.*"

Mildred made an impatient noise. "If you want to take a day off from paradise, you can go shopping with me in Mobile. But I can decorate the cookies — although you might have told me earlier."

She paused, then added cautiously, "I know you like to do pastries and sweet things more than anything else, Earlynne. And the scones are certainly delicious. But it seems to me that we're going overboard on all that stuff. How many different items are you going to make?"

"As many as I feel like making." Earlynne tossed her head. "A batch of this, a batch of that. We need a lot of *different* things in that display case, Mildred. Things that look as good as they taste. We want to tempt people to spend a little extra on impulse, you know."

Mildred gave an impatient huff. "Haven't you ever heard the phrase 'too much of a good thing'? In my opinion, we're going to have way more of those sweet and savory items than we need." She lifted her chin. "What about bread?"

"What about bread? What about it?" Wielding her rolling pin, Earlynne scowled down at her cookie dough. "Really, Mildred, I wish you would stop harping on bread."

"Harping on it?" Mildred asked sharply. "Pastries are fine, Earlynne, but *bread* will be our most important item. Plain white sandwich bread, like Wonder Bread, but fresher and better-tasting. We'll sell more bread than anything else, and it'll keep customers coming back."

Earlynne whacked the cookie dough with her rolling pin but said nothing.

Mildred went on. "I'm figuring we'll sell maybe fifteen loaves a day the first week or so. That's mostly to our friends. If they like it and tell *their* friends about it, we'll sell twenty a day the next week. Or maybe more — especially after the Vanity Fair plant opens and people have a little more money."

"*Twenty loaves?*" Earlynne stood stock still. Her eyes widened and she gave a little gasp. "That many — every day?"

"That many," Mildred replied emphatically. "So you have to decide on one basic recipe and be sure you've got it right. Then you can branch out and bake whatever different breads people want — rye, pumpernickel, sourdough, whatever you like. But for now, let's focus on plain, ordinary white

127

bread and be sure we've got it right. Okay?"

Earlynne squared her shoulders and took a deep breath. "Well, you'll be glad to know that I've baked three different test loaves, just for you," she said stiffly. "They're over there on the bottom shelf. You've been making such a fuss about the bread — I thought you could give them a taste test and tell me which of the three you like best. In your expert opinion," she added, with a clear hint of sarcasm.

"Well, *fine,*" Mildred said, with her own hint of sarcasm. She couldn't pretend to be an expert baker, like Earlynne. In fact, she had never baked a successful loaf of bread in her life — it was just too much trouble. But she had been eating bread several times a day ever since she was old enough to say "peanut butter and jelly." She knew what bread was supposed to look like — and how it was supposed to taste. "I'll check them out right now, before I start on the cookies."

She took a bread knife out of the drawer and put the three loaves on the pine-topped worktable. Studying them critically, the first thing she noticed was that they were not the same shape or size, and that none of the crusts were evenly browned. They were not at all pretty, she thought, trying to picture how they would look in the display case. Obviously, Earlynne was going to have to work on producing *uniform* loaves.

The crust of the first loaf was fairly soft and easy to slice, but the bread was dense and heavy at the bottom — soggy, almost. The crust on the second loaf was rock hard, and the inside was distinctly doughy. The top of the third loaf was flat and slightly sunken in the middle, while the inside was pocked with irregular holes and — worse! — laced with ribbons of unincorporated flour.

"Well?" Earlynne put down her rolling pin. "How do they taste?" she asked hopefully. "Which loaf do you like best?"

"We've got a problem, Earlynne." Mildred gestured at the loaves. "Actually, *three* problems — and I haven't even tasted them yet."

Earlynne came over to look, and for once in their long friendship, she didn't get all defensive and tell Mildred to go fly a kite. She stared at the loaves for a few moments. Her shoulders slumped. And then, to Mildred's enormous surprise, she dissolved into tears.

Mildred stared at her. She had known Earlynne since they were girls, and she had never seen her cry — not even when Laurabelle Rombauer was named Homecoming Queen and Earlynne had to be content with second runner-up. Her instinctive response was to snap, "Stop crying and pull yourself together, Earlynne Biddle. Nobody cries over *bread.*"

But instead, she found herself putting her arms around her friend and holding her, patting her back awkwardly. "It's okay, Earlynne. Really — I'm sure you can figure out what went wrong. Maybe the yeast didn't work. Maybe you ought to knead it a little less — or more, maybe? Or let it rise longer, or bake it at a lower temperature, or . . ."

She ran out of possibilities and stopped. "But what do I know?" she said with a sympathetic laugh, smoothing Earlynne's brown hair out of her eyes. "*You're* the expert baker."

But at that, Earlynne gave a despairing wail and burst into tears all over again. Mildred led her to a chair at the worktable, then went to the stove and poured two cups of coffee. She put Earlynne's cup down in front of her and handed her a tissue.

"Wipe your eyes and blow your nose," she commanded, "and tell me what's wrong."

Earlynne wiped her eyes, blew her nose, then blew her nose again. Then she crumpled the tissue in her hand and just sat there, staring despondently down at it.

At last, in a very small voice, she said, "I am a fraud, Mildred. A complete fraud."

Mildred was taken aback. Earlynne was always supremely self-confident, especially about her baking. "A fraud?" she asked in astonishment. "What in the world is *that* supposed to mean?"

Earlynne sighed. "I was hoping I could . . . That is, I thought I could get by without anybody finding out —" She broke off, shaking her head miserably. "But I guess it's time to come clean."

"Come clean?" By now, Mildred was feeling very impatient. "Come clean about *what*?"

"Those loaves —" Earlynne took a deep breath. "They're the *best* ones."

"The . . . *best* ones?" Mildred asked, aghast.

Earlynne bit her lip. "The other six are in a bag in the pantry. I thought I would give them to Liz to feed to her chickens. I didn't want you to see them."

Mildred began to feel desperation welling up inside. "But Earlynne," she began, "surely, if you had a little more practice —"

"The truth is that if you judge my baking by my bread, I'm a failure," Earlynne said dramatically. "I have never in my whole life managed to bake a halfway decent loaf. Not one!"

"You can't . . ." Bewildered, Mildred felt for a chair and sat down, hard. "You can't bake *bread*?"

Earlynne shook her head. "I can make all kinds of wonderful things — rolls and tarts and sticky buns. I bake the most marvelous angel food cake, and my eclairs are out of this world. Really, Mildred, you won't *believe* my eclairs! When I told you I wanted to open a bakery, that's what I was thinking about. It didn't even occur to me that we would have to sell *bread*. Especially not when Mrs. Hancock has shelves and shelves of Wonder Bread, with every loaf looking perfect — exactly the same as every other loaf. I couldn't make bread like that in a million years!"

"But I don't understand," Mildred said. "Bakers always get their start baking bread, don't they? If you have never baked a loaf of bread, how can you call yourself a baker?" Her voice was rising. "How could you possibly imagine —" She fought down the urge to cry, thinking of all the money she had invested in this ridiculous project — and what Roger would say when he found out. "How could you even *imagine* opening a bakery, if you can't bake *bread*?"

Earlynne sniffled into the tissue. "To tell the truth, I didn't even think about bread until you started bringing it up. All I thought of was making pastries." She leaned forward eagerly. "The thing is, Mildred, I'm so good at that, and I love it. Macaroons and beignets and Napoleons — oh, I make the most *wonderful* Napoleons. They're even better than my eclairs." She closed her eyes and clasped her hands. "Layer upon layer of the thinnest, flakiest, most delicate puff pastry and the most delectable pastry cream, topped with —"

"Stop!" Mildred commanded. "I am not disputing your ability to make Napoleons. But you can't solve our problem by waving your hand and saying, 'Let them eat pastries.' You have to get up from that chair and start making *bread.*" She pounded her fist on the table, punctuating her words. "Right now — do you hear? I don't care what recipe you use. Just choose one and do it. Plain white bread can't be that hard, can it? All you need is practice. Over and over. Until you get it right."

Earlynne's shoulders slumped. She was the picture of dejection. "It's no use, Mildred. Believe me. I have tried to make bread for years and *years,* and that —" She pointed to the three failed loaves. "That is the very best I can do. There is absolutely no sense in going through the exercise again."

"Well, *hell,* damn it," Mildred said, between gritted teeth. "We are opening on Saturday. We've advertised our bread in the *Dispatch,* and it's in our flyer, for eleven cents a loaf. What are we going to do?"

Earlynne gave her a long, searching look. Then she said, "Have *you* ever tried baking bread?"

CHAPTER NINE:
"NOTHING SAYS CHRISTMAS LIKE A POINSETTIA"

It was not quite one o'clock that afternoon when Liz left Verna's office in the courthouse. She had a couple of hours to kill before she and Verna planned to meet at the Diner, to let Violet and Myra May know about Mr. Price's telephone call. She was headed home, but she needed a couple of things at Dunlap's Five and Dime, so she went there first.

Darling was too small for a Woolworth's, but nobody cared because their Five and Dime was just as good. Like other dime stores across the country, Dunlap's sold just about anything your heart desired, as long as it was under a dollar. Because Darling shoppers could get five or six or even more items for every dollar (some of which they might have needed), the bargain-basement prices made them feel rich. So even though the shadow of the Depression continued to darken the prospects of many businesses,

Darling's Five and Dime was holding its own.

Nowadays, Lizzy had a personal reason to care about the Five and Dime, for her mother — long a widow — had recently married its owner, Reginald Dunlap. The marriage had been as much of a surprise as Grady's marriage to Sandra Mann, but a pleasant surprise, even a delightful one, and for good reason. Lizzy's mother had always believed that she wasn't doing her maternal duty if she wasn't instructing her only daughter in the management of her life: not only what to wear and how to fix her hair, but what goals to set and how to reach them.

As a girl, Lizzy had found it hard enough to handle this matriarchal tyranny. But as she grew older, Mrs. Lacy's meddling became almost intolerable — especially when she began pushing Liz to marry Grady Alexander.

"It's *time*, Elizabeth," she would say, in a doomsday voice. "You're not getting any younger. I'm telling you this for your own good, you know. You should say yes to that fine young man *now*."

And when Grady got Sandra pregnant, Mrs. Lacy actually told Liz it was all *her* fault — which Lizzy took to mean that if she'd given Grady what he wanted when he wanted it, he wouldn't have gone to Sandra. (Unfortunately, this was near enough to the truth to make Lizzy feel uncomfortable, although she refused to go so far as to blame herself for what Grady did.) When she heard the astonishing news that her mother was getting married, Lizzy was jubilant. From here on out, the new Mrs. Dunlap would be Mr. Dunlap's problem.

But Mr. Dunlap probably thought he had gotten a gem, for his wife (who had been dying for something significant in her life) rolled up her sleeves and took command of the Five and Dime. She cleaned the place top to bottom, reorganized the inventory, and rebuilt all the displays. This afternoon, when Lizzy got to the store, she saw that her mother had also redone the big front window. She had created a clever snow scene, with a miniature Christmas tree, Santa's sleigh, a toy train, and elves, surrounded by pine boughs twisted with colored lights and dusted with glittery fake snow. It was really quite charming.

Her mother opened the shop door. "Well, how do you like it, Elizabeth?"

The former Mrs. Lacy was a large, heavy-bosomed woman with a shrill voice — so large and formidable, in fact, that Lizzy had never quite figured out how Mr. Dunlap (a small, mild-mannered man with gray hair and thick spectacles) had summoned the courage to propose. But appearances had to be deceiving. Her mother had confided to her that, when they were alone together, Mr. Dunlap was a "tiger."

"I think it's lovely, Mama," Lizzy said, quite honestly.

"It's for the Merchants' Association window-decorating contest," her mother said. "Just between the two of us, I'm sure it will win. I stopped at Mann's Mercantile this morning and looked at Twyla Sue's window. It's not at all creative, just a few boots and shoes stuffed with pine branches and lots of fancy ribbon. And the window at Hancock's Grocery — well! A pyramid of canned Heinz soups, decorated with a string of popcorn and dried cranberries? Mine looks *so* much better, if I do say so myself." She paused, giving Liz a critical look. "Speaking of looking better, isn't it time you got your hair cut, Elizabeth? You're looking awf'lly shaggy."

"I have an appointment at the Beauty Bower next week, Mama," Lizzy said, although she was letting it grow out and only intended to get it washed and set.

Her mother seemed satisfied. "Good.

Now, let me show you this eggbeater we just got in. I know you'll want it."

Fifteen minutes later, Lizzy was on her way home through the chilly afternoon, bending into the blowing wind and wishing she'd thought to wear her mittens and a muffler. Her paper sack contained the fingernail polish (ten cents), bobby pins (seven cents), and elastic garter belt (fifty-three cents) that had been on her list, plus the "new, improved" rotary eggbeater (thirty cents) her mother had insisted she buy. Lizzy had learned long ago that it was easier to get along with her mother if she gave in on the small things (like the eggbeater) and saved her energy for significant battles. Her house had been one of those battles.

Lizzy and her cat, Daffodil, lived in a beautiful yellow house about the size of a dollhouse, across the street from her mother's house, where Lizzy had grown up. She had secretly purchased the rundown old place and had it remodeled without telling her mother. When it was done, she announced that she was moving and moved — the very next day. This had provoked a series of hysterical eruptions that continued for weeks. But Lizzy was doing what she knew she *had* to do: move out of her mother's house, even if it was only just across the street.*

And as far as Lizzy was concerned, her tiny house was perfect. There was a postage-stamp parlor, a miniature kitchen, and two small upstairs rooms with slanted ceilings, one for her bedroom, the other for her writing studio. Upstairs and down, her house was only about six hundred square feet. But it *felt* bigger, because there was a front porch just wide enough to accommodate a white-painted porch swing, and a screened-in back porch where she often ate.

And the back yard — oh, my! It was many times bigger than the house, and incredibly lovely. In the summer, the grass was lush and green and there were sunflowers and pink roses and a graceful weeping willow. Even now, there were sweet peas, honey-suckle, and sweet-scented winter jasmine. And summer and winter, there were fresh vegetables in the kitchen garden.

To Lizzy, her dollhouse seemed simply perfect. It was even more perfect because it was hers, and she could (and did!) lock the door against her mother — politely, of course. And because it was hers *alone,* a

* The story of Lizzy's house is told in *The Darling Dahlias and the Cucumber Tree.*

truth she found difficult to explain, even to her friends.

And especially difficult to explain to Grady, who just couldn't get it into his head *why* she loved her house so much and why she wanted to live there alone — especially now that he was a widower and they could begin their relationship again. He agreed that her house was too small for a family, but he couldn't see any reason why she wouldn't marry him and move into *his* house, which was just down the street.

"We could rent your house," he suggested in a practical tone. "It would bring in enough money so you could quit your job."

But the idea of somebody else living in her beautiful little house made her shudder. And what if they didn't take care of it?

She thought of this again, when she walked up the porch steps on this gloomy December day and saw a beautiful red poinsettia sitting beside her front door. It was brilliantly, splendidly red, the pot wrapped with silvery paper and tied with a red velvet ribbon. A small white envelope was tucked into the foliage.

With a sigh, Lizzy scooped up the plant. It was truly lovely, yes — and timely, to boot. She was writing next week's Garden Gate column about this very plant. This could be the inspiration she needed to get started.

But the poinsettia could only be from Grady, who was in the habit of dropping off small gifts and flowers — for example, the pot of bronze chrysanthemums he'd left beside her front door on the day before Thanksgiving. He would phone that evening to ask how she liked it and suggest that they go to a movie — which she didn't want to do. Going out with Grady encouraged him to think they could be a couple again.

Lizzy sighed. The poinsettia obligated her, and she was a woman who took her obligations seriously. She viewed this as a serious character flaw, and perhaps a particularly female one. Men never seemed to feel obliged to meet other people's expectations. Or maybe it was Southern, or a product of her vexed relationship with her mother, whose expectations she had for years forced herself to meet, no matter how much she resented them.

Daffodil had heard her key in the lock and was meowing an enthusiastic welcome on the other side of the door. She pushed it open and went in, with the poinsettia in her arms. "Hey, Daffy," she said happily, as her orange tabby wound around her ankles, turning up the volume on his purr. She put

142

the plant on the hall table and picked him up, rubbing her cheek in his luxuriant fur and wishing that her other relationships were as simple and straightforward as her relationship with Daffy — unconditional, uncomplaining, unreserved affection on both their parts.

After a moment, Daffy asked to be put down and she set him on the floor. She took off her coat and red woolen cap and hung both up on the hallway rack. Then she turned to Grady's poinsettia.

"It's lovely, isn't it, Daffy?" she said, touching the bright red leaves. "Nothing says Christmas like a poinsettia. I just wish . . ." Her voice trailed off. It was too bad that she couldn't accept it in the same spirit in which Grady sent it.

The envelope was about half the size of a penny postcard. Her name — Miss Elizabeth Lacy — was written in black ink in a strong, masculine hand on the outside. Not Grady's hand, she thought, in some surprise. There was no florist in Darling, so perhaps he'd had the plant delivered from the flower shop in Monroeville. Extravagant of him, she thought.

She opened the envelope and pulled out the card, expecting it to say something like "From Grady, with love. Looking forward to spending Christmas with you."

But it didn't. The note was in the same strong hand that had addressed the envelope. It said:

I've been thinking about our October conversation and will be getting in touch again soon. In the meantime, please accept this poinsettia and my best wishes for a happy holiday season.

Yours,
Ryan Nichols

Lizzy stared for a moment at the hand-drawn sketch of the four-leaf clover, remembering Ryan Nichols' surprising visit and feeling an odd little flutter around her heart. And then she smiled.

And smiled again.

CHAPTER TEN:
"IMAGINE! OUR LITTLE GIRL IN THE MOVIES!"

Over at the Darling Diner, it was the middle of the afternoon. Myra May was finishing the lunch cleanup and getting ready to start supper prep. The last lunch customer was gone, and she no longer had to listen to the men's conversations about the piss-poor cotton yields, the CCC camp's tree-clearing project in Briar Swamp (which most people thought was a waste of good labor), and the gruesome end of Baby Face Nelson, Public Enemy Number One, who was dead after a wild shootout with federal agents.

It was Myra May's first quiet hour in a busy day, and she was enjoying the interlude. Lenore Looper was handling the switchboard — the *new* switchboard, so well-designed that one operator could do the work of two with half the effort. Violet was upstairs in their flat, putting Cupcake down for her afternoon nap. Raylene had gone home after lunch and would be back

145

soon to make the meatloaf and apple pie on the Thursday night menu.

Meanwhile, the Philco radio on the shelf behind the counter was tuned to Mobile's station WALA (which supposedly stood for "We Are Loyal Alabamians"). Jack Hylton's Orchestra was playing "You're the Cream in My Coffee." Myra May, dressed in neatly pressed khaki slacks, plaid blouse, and apron, was happily singing along as she stacked the clean coffee mugs. "You're the cream in my coffee, you're the salt in my stew, you will always be my necessity, I'd be lost without you."

This was one of the songs that Violet was teaching to Cupcake, who had already made up a cute little tap dance to go with the tune. The customers loved it, and always dropped a penny in Cupcake's fancy china pig, which sat on a shelf at the end of the lunch counter.

But Myra May often wondered about the wisdom of letting Cupcake show off her talent. Was it a good idea for a little girl to get so much attention? Would the applause turn her head? Would the attention spoil her? Would she grow up believing that all she had to do to succeed in the world was sing and dance and smile prettily? That might work for an adorable four-year-old, or even five or six. But what would happen when Cupcake lost her baby prettiness and became a gawky teen?

Myra May was still considering these questions when the door opened and Liz Lacy and Verna Tidwell came in. They brought with them a puff of chilly air that cleared out some of the cigarette smoke left behind by the lunch crowd.

Myra May turned from her work. "Well, hi, girls," she said with a warm smile. "Haven't seen the pair of you for a while." She reached for mugs. "Got time for coffee? A piece of pie?"

But Liz's unsmiling response — "We need to talk to you and Violet" — told Myra May that her friends weren't just taking a mid-afternoon coffee break. And when Verna added, "Someplace where we won't be interrupted," she knew that something was up. Something serious.

"Let's go upstairs," she said, and hung the Closed sign on the front door.

A few moments later, they were sitting around the kitchen table in the large, comfortable flat that Myra May and Violet shared. The parlor looked out over the courthouse square, while the kitchen at the back looked out across the large garden that supplied the Diner's kitchen with beans, peas, corn, carrots, and lettuce. And although the December sky was bleak and the air was chill, Violet's red geraniums at the window, the fragrant coffeepot perking on the stove, and the red-and-white checked oilcloth on the table made the kitchen seem warm and cheerful.

"So what's this all about?" Myra May asked, after Violet had joined them. She was wearing a sunny yellow cotton housedress and a blue-checked wraparound apron. She smiled when she saw their company but quickly sobered at the expressions on their faces.

She sat down at the table and echoed Myra May's question. "Something's up, isn't it? What?"

"I got a phone call from a Los Angeles lawyer this morning," Liz said. "He wants Mr. Moseley to help him locate a missing child — a four-year-old girl named Dorothy — and her aunt, Violet."

Myra May's heart seemed to skip a beat and she gasped. Violet gave a little cry and reached out to Myra May. The two of them held hands while they listened to Liz, who reported the phone call from start to finish.

"I talked to Verna about it," she concluded, "because I wasn't sure what I should do. Tell Mr. Moseley right away and ask him what we should do? Or talk to you first, and figure out where to go from there."

"We decided it would be better to talk to you," Verna said. She opened her purse, took out a cigarette, and lit it. Her voice was somber when she added, "We know this is awf'lly hard, girls. We want to help in any way we can."

By now, Violet was crying, her head down, her shoulders shaking with hard sobs, and Myra May got up to stand behind her and gently stroke the back of her neck. She always felt utterly helpless in the face of Violet's tears, but this was worse. It was as if a hurricane wind was suddenly blowing their tranquil world apart. She thought of herself as the strong one, the one who was responsible for protecting Violet and their daughter. But there was nothing she could do against this threat. She was nearly overwhelmed by a wave of helpless impotence.

Still, for Violet's sake, she had to say something. She bent over and gave her a hug, then took a deep breath and forced herself to sound resolute. "Chin up, sweetie. We'll fight this, and we're going to win. Nobody is taking our Cupcake away from us. Not her father, not some big-shot Los Angeles lawyer. *Nobody.*"

But as she took her seat again, she had to admit she was not surprised that this had happened. Ever since the day Violet had walked through the door with the blanket-wrapped baby in her arms, Myra May had been afraid that Cupcake's father would show up and stake his claim. As time went on, the fear — as fears usually do — had faded into the sunlit background of their busy daytime lives. But it still returned as a nightmare terror that left her shaken and breathless in the long, dark hours of the night. And now that fear loomed over her like a menacing storm cloud, poised to sweep over the horizon and obliterate them.

Liz folded her arms on the table. "It would help us to hear the whole story, Violet — about you and Cupcake. I know it's painful, but if we understood everything that's happened, maybe we could figure out how to deal with this. Can you tell us?"

They all waited. Violet looked to Myra May, asking what she thought. Myra May forced herself to smile. "Go ahead, dear," she heard herself say in a comforting voice. "They're here to help. Tell them." The words seemed to come from somewhere very far away, and she knew the comfort in her voice was false.

Violet took a handkerchief out of her

apron pocket and blew her nose. "Cupcake's real name is Dorothy," she said. "She's my niece. My half-sister, Pansy, was living in Memphis. She asked me to come up and help her when she had the baby — her first." Her voice grew bitter. "She knew she couldn't count on help from Neil. Neil Hudson. He was the man she was living with. The baby's daddy."

"So they weren't married?" Liz asked, and Violet shook her head.

"Did he have a job?" Verna asked.

Violet leaned forward. "He had a regular song-and-dance act at the Orpheum, which is one of the biggest vaudeville theaters in Memphis. Before the Depression, that's where all the important entertainers appeared — Eddie Cantor, Louis Armstrong, Duke Ellington. Pansy met Neil there when she auditioned as a dancer. Right away, she became part of his act, and then they moved in together. Within a few months, she got pregnant. He was upset when she told him, because it meant she couldn't dance — and her salary was helping to pay the rent. He pressured her to get an abortion, but she stood up to him. She *wanted* the baby."

"Good for her," Liz murmured. Myra May, who had heard this story before, felt a wrenching sadness. She also knew that

Violet had once considered a dance career for herself and had decided against it, for which Myra May was eternally grateful.

Violet picked up her coffee cup and took a sip. "The birth was hard, and when Pansy came home from the hospital, the doctor said she had to stay in bed. I took care of her and the baby and cooked for Neil and did his laundry and the baby's diapers." Her voice took on a sharper edge. "He was always out until the small hours of the morning. Part of it was the work, but there was also a lot of drinking. He was jealous of the baby, because she took so much of Pansy's attention. Wasn't it bad enough that she was sick, without him acting like a spoiled little boy?"

Myra May felt her insides twist, but she made a small encouraging sound. They didn't talk about this often, because each of them was so afraid — afraid that Cupcake's father would show up one day and take her away from them. And now that awful possibility was looming in front of them, like an evil genie escaped from its bottle.

Violet's hands were trembling and she put the cup down. "Pansy died three weeks after Dorothy was born, and things went from bad to terrible." She glanced at Myra May. "I loved the baby dearly, but my life was here in Darling, and I told Neil I couldn't stay indefinitely. He was acting like a jerk, but I tried to see it from his point of view. He had just buried Patsy, and he was faced with the task of taking care of a baby all day. On top of that, he had to work all night. How in the world would he manage? And to make matters worse, the Orpheum's owner had just put the theater up for sale. He wasn't even sure he'd have a job the next week."

Verna wrinkled her forehead. "Was Neil any good? As a performer, I mean."

"Pretty good, yes. He also helped to manage the theater," Violet said. "When the Orpheum began to fail, I think he just gave up. Without saying a word to me about what he was planning, he went to an adoption agency and signed some papers. Then he came back to the flat and told me that the baby was going to an orphanage until somebody came along and adopted her. He said I had to get her ready to go with the social worker."

"But how *could* he do that?" Liz asked, baffled. "How could he give his baby away?"

"Sounds like he didn't have a lot of choice," Verna said in a practical tone. "I'm surprised that he didn't ask you to marry him, Violet. From his perspective, that

153

would have been ideal."

Violet bit her lip. "Actually, he did, which made things even worse. I told him it was out of the question. He . . . didn't want to take no for an answer."

Myra May, who knew something of the ugly episode that Violet was leaving out, reached for her hand again, feeling a deep concern. Violet wasn't as strong as she looked. It had taken a long time for her to get over what had happened in Memphis that night. The man had been drunk, which was a convenient excuse. But his apologies hadn't changed anything. The pain of the violation was still there and this was bringing it up all over again. She could feel Violet's hand trembling in hers.

There was a moment's silence. Then Liz said, "Did you *offer* to take the baby, Violet?"

Violet started to say something, then bit her lip again and looked down. Mutely, she shook her head.

There was a hard lump in Myra May's throat. She tried to clear it but couldn't. She spoke around it. "That was *my* fault, Liz. Violet was thinking of me. She was afraid I wouldn't want the complications of a baby, with all we have to do here — the Diner and the Exchange. That year was

154

really tough. She knew I wasn't crazy about kids and she didn't want to impose a baby on me."

"It was *not* your fault, Myra May!" Violet retorted hotly, retrieving her hand. "It was *my* fault. I should have telephoned you. If we had discussed it, you would have told me to ask Neil if we could take Dorothy. He would have said yes, and then we wouldn't be in this fix."

"But there was no phone in Neil's flat," Myra May reminded her. "The nearest phone booth was blocks away, and you couldn't leave the baby."

"And even if he had given you permission to take her," Verna said, "there was no guarantee that he'd let you *keep* her. She is his child. He could come and get her any time he felt like it."

Violet gave a muted whimper. She turned her head as if she had been slapped. Her hand went to her throat and her face was white. Without a word, Myra May got up, found the bottle of rum on the shelf beside the sink, and splashed a hefty slug into Violet's half-empty coffee cup.

"Drink," she commanded, and put her hand on Violet's shoulder. She frowned angrily at Verna. "Really, Verna. Did you have to say that?"

Still, she knew that it was the truth — the brutal truth that she and Violet had been evading, all these years. They couldn't evade it any longer. They had to face it.

Obediently, Violet drank, coughed, then drank again. After a moment, the pink came back to her cheeks. She took a deep breath and said, "I know you're right, Verna. But still, if I'd had any idea what Neil was planning, I would have begged him to give Dorothy to me and taken my chances with Myra May." She took another sip of the rum-laced coffee. "Anyway, it all came apart when Neil told me to get her ready to go to the orphanage. I just couldn't do that."

"You didn't consider meeting the social worker and telling her you wanted to adopt the baby?" Liz asked.

Violet nodded. "I thought of it, yes. But I'm not married, and I was afraid she would tell me I couldn't provide a real family for the baby. I didn't sleep a wink that night, thinking about it. So after Neil was safely asleep, I packed her diapers and the little things I'd bought for her and the two of us left the apartment. I walked to the station with Dorothy in one arm and our suitcase in the other and caught the earliest train heading south. I didn't even leave a note."

"So what happened after that?" Verna

stubbed out her cigarette in the glass ashtray in the middle of the table. "He had to know that *you* had taken her, Violet. Did he get in touch with you? Did he come looking for her? Did the social worker contact you?"

"We never heard anything from him," Myra May said emphatically. "Not from the social worker, either. Cupcake has been with us for almost four years, and not one word."

Violet pressed her lips together. "To be honest, Verna, I didn't make it easy for him to get in touch with me. I took my letters — the letters I'd written to Pansy — as well as her address book. She was my half-sister, you see, and we had different last names. I doubt that he ever knew mine. Our parents are dead, and Pansy and I were the only ones left. There wasn't any way he could reach me — or so I thought." She knotted her fingers together. "And at the time, the Depression was hitting hard. People were on the move everywhere. Neil was in the entertainment business, so after we were gone, I thought he'd go to California, or maybe New York."

"Sounds like he chose California," Liz said, "since the lawyer called from Los Angeles."

"But he *was* here," Raylene said gravely. "Cupcake's father, I mean."

Startled, they all turned to see Myra May's mother standing in the doorway. She was wearing her usual working outfit — a plain white short-sleeved blouse, dark poplin skirt, and a bibbed gingham apron. Her gray-streaked auburn hair was twisted into a knot at the back of her head.

Violet half-rose from her chair. "Neil was *here?*" Her voice was shrill. "Here in *Darling?*" She sank back down again, helplessly. "How do you know, Raylene?"

"Not here, exactly," Raylene amended. "He was in Monroeville. I know because I saw him." She joined them at the table.

Myra May got up again, went to the stove, and poured a cup of coffee. "When did this happen?" She put the cup in front of her mother.

"And how do you know it was him?" Violet's hands were knotted into fists and her voice was frantic. "You don't know what he looks like, Raylene! I never even told you his name."

Her mind racing, Myra May sat down again. She was remembering that her mother had recently begun to keep a close eye on Cupcake. Something had seemed to be worrying her. But when she asked, Raylene just shook her head and said, "Don't worry, dear." Myra May hadn't questioned her further.

Myra May was a direct and practical person and not especially intuitive or sensitive to others' moods — with the exception of Violet's, of course. She and her mother had been reunited just a couple of years before, and she still hadn't fully accommodated herself to Raylene's "gift."*

Which was pretty darn creepy, when you stopped to think about it. Who wanted another person peering into your private thoughts, knowing how you felt about things? On the other hand, predicting what a customer was going to order for lunch seemed like a silly parlor trick, something somebody might do to amuse people and keep them coming back. Sometimes, Myra May had to confess, she thought the whole thing was a bunch of foolishness. Her mother was making it up — and people were going along with her, just for the heck of it.

Myra May narrowed her eyes at her mother. "Answer the question," she said bluntly. "If you've never seen Neil Hudson and didn't know his name, how did you

* Myra May hadn't even known that her mother was alive. Their reunion is related in *The Darling Dahlias and the Texas Star.*

159

know who he was?"

"I just *knew,* my dear," Raylene said softly. She looked at Violet. "He was in the audience at Cupcake's dance recital. He was sitting in the back."

"I didn't see him," Violet said. "Are you sure —"

"He saw *you,* Violet," Raylene went on. "He knew right away who you were. And after the recital, when he saw you with Cupcake, he guessed immediately that she was his daughter. She's the right age. And he thought she looked a lot like her mother, with all those strawberry blond curls."

"Oh, no," Violet whispered. "And yes, she does look like Pansy." She dropped her face into her hands.

Raylene went on, still softly. "I drove over with my friend Pauline that evening, remember? After you and Cupcake left, I hung back. I heard him talking to the man who was with him. It was a complete surprise to him — discovering his daughter, I mean. Seeing how talented she is. At first he was simply floored. He had all but forgotten about her, and he could hardly take it in. But he's a quick thinker." Her voice hardened. "By the time he and his friend left, he was already beginning to come up with a plan."

Violet's head jerked up. "A *plan*?" Her words were barely audible.

"What kind of a plan?" Myra May demanded.

"He's going to promote her," Raylene said. "When she did her dance number, he got very excited. He thinks she has an extraordinary potential. I heard him tell his friend that he intends to make her part of his act. He's going to turn her into another Shirley Temple."

"Oh, *no*!" Violet wailed.

Verna's eyebrows shot up. "His act? You mean, he's still in vaudeville?"

"Yes, he's still in vaudeville," Raylene replied. "But he has bigger ideas. He thinks he can get Dorothy into the movies. With *him*. As a father-daughter duo. A song-and-dance act."

"Oh!" Violet cried, and put her hands over her ears. "Oh, no, no, no!"

"Yes." Raylene was resolute. "He was planning to find out where you lived, Violet, so he could come and take Cupcake away. But he has a friend who's a West Coast lawyer. He decided he'd try the legal route first."

"That must be the lawyer Liz talked to this morning," Verna said.

"Mama," Myra May demanded fiercely,

"If you knew all this, why in the world didn't you *tell* us? Maybe we could have done something!"

Raylene's smile was sad. "Would you have believed me, dear? And what could you do? At least, until he showed his hand."

In the silence, Myra May knew her mother was right.

Raylene straightened her shoulders and went on more briskly. "What's more, thinking is one thing and doing is another. I had no idea whether this man would actually *act* on his idea. After all, Neil Hudson didn't come to Monroeville looking for his daughter, or for you, either, Violet. The discovery was a complete surprise to him. When he left, he was still quite stunned, and the idea of a father-daughter duo had just popped into his head. I was hoping he would think about her welfare and decide to leave well enough alone."

Liz leaned forward. "Why *was* he here? In Monroeville, I mean."

"It was accidental," Raylene said. "After the recital, I asked around and learned that he was with a touring vaudeville troupe that had performed at the Lyric Theater over in Birmingham. They were on their way to New Orleans by auto. Someone who knew Nona Jean from her Ziegfeld days told Neil that she had a student who was a phenomenal look-alike for Shirley Temple. Out of curiosity, he decided to drop in on the recital. It wasn't until he saw Violet and Cupcake together that he realized who she was."

"Well, now that he has a lawyer," Verna said, "we can assume that he's determined to act on his intention. And if he's looking at Shirley Temple and thinking that he can duplicate her success, he's thinking *big* money. I read the other day that Shirley is under contract to Fox for a hundred and fifty dollars a week, with another twenty-five dollars for her mother."

Myra May gave a little gasp. "You've got to be joking!" Violet exclaimed.

"No, she's not," Liz put in. "I read that, too."

"But the Temples are asking for even more," Verna went on. "They want a thousand a week for Shirley and two hundred and fifty for her mother, with a fifteen-thousand-dollar bonus for every movie the little girl completes. They're likely to get it, too."

There was a stunned silence around the table. Finally, Myra May shook her head. Numbly, she said, "A thousand a week! Why, it would take us four or five *months* to make a thousand dollars!"

"And fifteen thousand for a movie?" Violet's eyes were large and round in her pale face. "That's *incredible,* Myra May! Just think what that kind of money would mean for Cupcake's future. College and new clothes and a car and . . . and *everything!*" She gulped a shaky breath. "Imagine! Our little girl in the movies! Why, she would be *famous!*"

For an instant, it seemed to Myra May that her heart stopped beating. "Violet, I can't believe that you would even consider . . ."

But her voice trailed away and her unfinished sentence hung in the silent air between them. Surely Violet wasn't imagining their daughter following in Shirley Temple's footsteps! That would mean that she and Cupcake would go to Hollywood — and they might never come back! Just the thought of it made her feel cold and empty, as if winter had suddenly frozen her in its icy grasp.

Verna was the first to break the silence. "Well," she said in a practical tone, "before I let the child go anywhere, I'd have to be *very* confident that Mr. Hudson had the connections to get himself and Cupcake into the movies. I've read that every week, hundreds of mothers line up outside the Hollywood studios, hoping against hope that their children will be discovered. Almost all of them go home disappointed."

Liz cleared her throat. "But even if he could," she said gently, "would you *want* him to? Is the Hollywood life something you'd want for Cupcake?"

Myra May knew the answer to that. "No!" she cried, and smacked the table with the flat of her hand, hard. "No, of course not! It's out of the question. Tell them, Violet. Tell them!"

But Violet was silent.

CHAPTER ELEVEN:
"I MAY HAVE BAKED
A LOAF OR TWO"

Friday, December 21

When Earlynne asked, "Have you ever tried baking bread?" Mildred had said no. Then, forcing herself to be more or less honest, she had reluctantly corrected herself. "Well, yes. I may have baked a loaf or two."

Because she had. But that had been quite a few years ago, and if you'd asked her, she couldn't have told you what went wrong. But something had gone *very* wrong, and the result was a misshapen mound of gummy, indigestible dough encased in a crust so hard you couldn't crack it with a jackhammer. She guessed that she had somehow failed to follow the recipe, and had buried the disaster in the bottom of the garbage pail before Roger could find it and make fun of her.

And that was the end of Mildred's bread-baking career. In her opinion, life was far too short to bother doing anything that required a great deal of regular practice, like perfecting her golf swing or learning to play the piano — or baking bread. In fact, baking bread fell into the category of things it might be nice to do someday, but were definitely not necessary to her everyday happiness. Her experiment had taken place before the Crash, when Roger was making gobs of money selling new cars, and at the time, she'd had a cook who baked the family's bread.

Then, just when Mildred had had to let her cook go because the economy had foundered and people had stopped buying cars, Wonder Bread had come along. It might be a little doughy and bland, but every loaf was perfectly uniform and evenly sliced, just right for sandwiches — even if the loaves were several days old by the time they got from the big Continental Baking Company's bakery in Atlanta to Mrs. Hancock's grocery shelf and then to the Kilgore breadbox. Wonder Bread was a miracle. Mildred couldn't think of a single reason to give bread-baking another try.

But she held the firm belief that a bakery that didn't sell bread didn't deserve to be called a bakery. So, faced with Earlynne's shocking admission of bread-baking ineptitude, she decided that she would simply have to learn. Women had been baking bread for their families since the beginning of time, hadn't they? If they could do it, so could she. Her previous disaster, she was sure, had been caused by her failure to follow the recipe.

This time, she would be more careful.

So Mildred asked Earlynne to write down her recipe. She took it and a bag of flour and some baker's yeast home to her own kitchen, where she could practice in private, with no one to get in her way. Since Roger was out of town, she didn't have to worry that he would walk in on her. Undisturbed, she could bake for hours. Until she got so tired, she couldn't stand up.

Or until she produced the perfect loaf, whichever came first.

She didn't stop to ask herself what would happen after that. Would she have to make a career of baking the daily bread for The Flour Shop shelves? If she had thought about *this* daunting prospect, she might not have embarked on the experiment. She was thinking only as far ahead as Saturday.

So she got up very early Friday morning and began. But things didn't go quite the way she expected. The recipe said that the yeast would get bubbly when she added warm water to "prove" it. But she couldn't

168

see a single bubble in the yeast for her first batch. She couldn't decide what was wrong. Was the water too hot? Too cold? Was the yeast *dead*? She threw it out and started over.

The yeast for the second batch bubbled up nicely, but the dough stuck to her hands when she was kneading it. So she added more flour — so much that the dough got all stiff and sulky and refused to rise. And she hadn't been very careful when she was tossing the flour around, so there were drifts of the powdery white stuff all over the kitchen floor, which had to be mopped before she could try again.

The third batch was a different story. She must have let the dough rise too long, because while it looked beautifully light and puffy before it went into the oven, it collapsed with a despairing sigh the minute it felt the heat. She baked it anyway, but when she sliced it, it had the texture of a mud brick and the taste of a crepe paper sandwich. Maybe she had forgotten the salt.

And the fourth batch? Well, the less said about that the better, since the neighbor's cat climbed into the warm bowl while the bread was rising and got sticky dough all over its fur and whiskers. It howled like a banshee while she tried to clean it up.

By this time, Mildred had spent hours in the kitchen. It was early afternoon. The grand opening was tomorrow, and she had to face the bitter truth. She had followed Earlynne's recipe precisely (or thought she had), and she had failed. She could not bake even one perfect loaf, let alone produce enough loaves to justify calling The Flour Shop a *bakery*. They would have to tell their customers to continue to buy stale bread from Mrs. Hancock. All they had to offer were sweet treats.

And now that she understood something of the work that went into a perfect loaf of bread — a loaf that she and Earlynne would be proud to put on the shelf at their bakery — she couldn't even think of anybody who *could* do it! When Wonder Bread came to town, the art of baking bread had pretty much gone the way of all the other old-fashioned crafts that sheltered and clothed and fed people. Like building your own log cabin or weaving your own cotton cloth or making your own sauerkraut. Bread-baking was gone. Gone forever.

Mildred pursed her lips thoughtfully. No, that wasn't quite true. There actually was somebody in Darling who practiced many of the old crafts. Somebody who had a loom in her living room, and who actually *did* make her own sauerkraut. She baked bread, too.

And when Mildred thought of *her,* she thought that she might just have solved the problem. For Saturday, anyway.

CHAPTER TWELVE:
"DON'T GET
YOURSELF KILLED"

Charlie Dickens had fled Darling when he was a young man, survived the trenches of the Great War, then spent a couple of years as an itinerant stringer for the Associated Press, hoofing it through Europe and the Balkans. After he returned to the States, he began a newspaper career with the *Plain Dealer* and the *Baltimore Sun,* with a special interest in stories about fraud, graft, influence peddling, and corruption. His reporting, some of it done undercover, had put several big-time politicians in jail. Now, he was living a settled life as a Darling newspaper publisher and job printer. But at heart, he was still the investigative reporter he had once been.

Which is why Charlie had been so eager to agree to what Sheriff Buddy Norris asked him to do, in spite of the obvious danger. He knew a good story when he smelled it. In fact, given the subject — murder and its

172

possible cover-up by an award-winning state official — it might even be a Pulitzer-caliber story. He also knew that Buddy, young as he was, had the instincts of a good lawman. The sheriff wouldn't have asked him to do this if he weren't perfect for the job.

And even though he might be a little out of practice, Charlie liked the idea of testing himself in a tight situation. Sure, he was nervous, nervous as a cat on a hot stove. Who wouldn't be, heading into the lion's den? But nerves were a reliable measure of just how much was riding on this investigation. It was good to be nervous. Nerves kept a man alert and watchful. Nerves kept a man alive.

It had been unexpectedly easy to get permission to visit the Jericho State Prison Farm. All he'd had to do was say that he wanted to interview the warden about his recent award for prison management and the exemplary way the prison was run, and the invitation was forthcoming.

"Warden Burford will be happy to see you," said the young man who telephoned to make the appointment. "How about Friday morning at ten?"

Except for the few local men who were employed out there as guards, the prison farm had always been off limits to Darling folk. They had no special interest in going out there, anyway. Their chief acquaintance with the farm occurred via a practice called contract leasing. In this system, prisoners were farmed out to harvest cotton at local plantations, cut trees for one of the big timber operations, or repair a road washout or rebuild a bridge taken out by a flood. So people got used to seeing small groups of men in black-and-white striped uniforms dragging cotton sacks through a field or shoveling gravel along a road, overseen by a mounted armed guard.

But other than the occasionally visible evidence of the prisoners-for-rent program, Jericho didn't call itself to the attention of Darling's residents. Isolated and almost completely self-supporting, it didn't rely on supplies or services from the local community. The prisoners grew and processed their own food, cooked and served their own meals, produced their own clothing, operated their own laundry, built their own buildings and roads, and repaired and maintained their own vehicles. Jericho even generated its own electricity with its own power plant, which also powered a small furniture factory. It was a closed shop.

And remote. It was some twenty miles outside of town, down a bad road. The compound was surrounded by a seven-foot chain-link fence topped with curls of razor wire, with a twelve-foot-high wooden tower at each corner. If anybody was foolish enough to try to escape, he'd be gunned down by the watchful guards.

But there was no point in attempting an escape. The farm's far-flung pastures and fields were bordered on the west by the muddy Alabama River and the notorious Briar Swamp on the south, both forbidding barriers. What's more, Warden Burford was often heard to say that if he had to go to the trouble of sending out trackers and dogs, they should let the dogs have the escapee for lunch rather than go to the trouble of bringing him back. Most prisoners preferred a bed, regular meals, and a roof over their heads to swamp gators, copperheads, and Burford's dogs. Jericho had the lowest escape rate in the state.

Seen from the point of view of the Alabama Board of Prison Administrators in Montgomery, Jericho was a model prison, and Grover Burford was a model warden. The BOA judged the state prison farms on their profitability as well as their self-sufficiency and their ability to manage prisoners. The bigger the profit the better, and under Warden Burford, Jericho generated an impressive profit from its cash crops — lumber, corn, sorghum, cotton, cattle, pigs, and chickens. And prisoner labor, which was also a cash crop. One admiring BOA official had been heard to remark, "If all our wardens had Burford's management skills, our budget problems would be solved."

In recognition of his stellar contributions to the state's bottom line, the BOA paid Warden Burford a sizable bonus for productivity and efficiency. He had recently collected the check and an imposing gold-colored trophy at the annual banquet of prison officials in Montgomery. And now Charlie was on his way to interview him for an article in the *Dispatch*. At least, that was his cover story.

What else he was there for . . . well, that wasn't quite so clear. Buddy had told him that the bullet that killed Bragg wasn't fired from the gun that had been found with his body, which meant that Bragg had been murdered. The sheriff's instructions, such as they were, were comprehensive but sketchy.

"Get whatever you can about Bragg's death. And then get some more. But for God's sake, don't get yourself killed in the process."

Friday morning's pale December sun came out briefly as Charlie climbed into his old green Pontiac and started south on the Jericho Road, past the Cypress Country Club, the county fairgrounds, and Darling's unused airfield. As he drove, he saw that the gaudiness of a few weeks before — the burnished golds and coppers of the maples, the rich bronze of the bald cypress, the regal red and purple of the sweet gums — had faded. The hills and river bottoms were clad in somber browns and grays, as though they had repented themselves of their October flamboyance and were determined on a more puritan course for December. But still, the landscape was beautiful, and its muted shades matched Charlie's uneasy mood.

By the time he reached the compound, the sun had ducked back into its shelter of clouds, the sky was the color of dull pewter, and a cold north wind was snapping the Alabama flag that flew over the gate. He was stopped by a swarthy, broad-shouldered guard who curtly ordered him out of the car, frisked him, and sneered at his press card. The guard made a telephone call, then directed him to the administration building with a jerk of his head and a warning.

"Second building on the right, fifty yards

down the road. But don't park in the warden's space, or you will get your butt
nailed." The guard gave him a hard look.
"And don't go no further without an escort.
You got that?"

"Sir, yes, *sir,*" Charlie said with barely
suppressed sarcasm, and shifted into gear.

The administrative offices were in a single-
story wood-frame building on the north side
of a neatly mowed quadrangle. It was
painted forest green with brown trim. Other
frame buildings — the prisoners' and
guards' barracks, the mess hall and kitchen,
a recreation building, and a hospital — were
painted the same colors and arranged
around the east and west sides of the quad.
On the south were sheds for shops, equipment repair, and vehicle maintenance, as
well as the power plant and a small furniture
factory. In the dull light, the place looked
exactly like what it was: a prison.

Charlie parked on the gravel apron in
front of the administration building, noting
that the warden's spot was empty. He got
out of his Pontiac, pulling his overcoat
closer around him against the whipping
wind and jamming his felt fedora on his
head so it wouldn't blow off.

The front door opened into a small, chilly
lobby that intersected with a hall running

the length of the building, painted a poisonous green. Charlie walked past a Negro prisoner on his hands and knees, scrubbing the floor with a brush and a bucket of soapy water that smelled strongly of lye. Another, on a ladder, was slapping more green paint on the already painted wall. Both returned Charlie's greeting with sullen stares.

The door to the warden's outer office was closed. Charlie opened it tentatively. At a desk sat a slight, thin-shouldered young man with gingery hair and round, wire-rimmed glasses, typing rapidly. The name tag on his khaki uniform shirt pocket identified him as Corporal Casey, and Charlie remembered that the guards held quasi-military rank.

The young man looked up when Charlie came in. "Mr. Dickens?" he asked with an eager smile.

"That's me." Charlie returned the smile, wondering where he had seen Corporal Casey — who seemed hardly more than a boy, really — before. Without being asked, he lowered himself into the chair in front of the desk and pushed his hat to the back of his head. "Dickens, from the *Dispatch.*"

"The warden had to go out to the barns to deal with a problem with one of the tractors," the corporal said. "He just left, and

I'm not sure when he'll be back. I hope you don't mind waiting." He pushed his chair back. "Can I get you some coffee?"

"Coffee would be swell," Charlie said, thinking that the boy looked glad to have some company. He probably felt as out of place as he looked. "Black. And hot."

"Hot and black." Casey smiled. "Coming right up, Mr. Dickens." He was back in a moment with two mugs.

Charlie unbuttoned his coat, grateful for the heat — such as it was — coming from the small oil heater in one corner of the room. As he leaned back in his chair, chilly hands wrapped around his coffee mug, it came to him.

"Say, I think I recognize you. Aren't you Hamp Casey's boy, Wilber?"

Hamp Casey owned a gravel pit near Darling and had just finished a term as county road commissioner. He farmed part of the old Delaney plantation — and he swung a lot of weight in Cypress County. Which might be why his nephew had this job.

"Hamp is my uncle," Wilber said, his freckled face brightening. "I'm Melton's son. Maybe you knew my dad."

"I did," Charlie said, adding, "Sorry about the accident." Melton Casey had died the previous Fourth of July when, emboldened

180

by Bodeen Pyle's tiger spit, he'd thought he could beat an L&M locomotive across the tracks. "Your dad was a fine man. Straight as an arrow." Well, apart from the occasional bender.

"He sure was," Wilber said gratefully. "Him and that train — it was hard to handle, I'll tell you."

"I went to school with both your dad and Hamp," Charlie went on, which was true. But then he stretched the connection a bit more than the facts warranted. "We used to play hooky and go swimming on Pine Mill Creek." He shook his head, smiling a little. "You don't want to know what kind of trouble the three of us got up to when we were young, Wilber. Well, not serious trouble. Just things boys do when they think nobody's looking. Your dad was one smart kid. And nobody could hit his fast ball."

He was making this up as he went along, thinking it might be good to have a friendly connection inside Jericho — given the real purpose of his trip. His story had the desired effect.

"Dad had a fast ball?" Wilber asked wonderingly, shaking his head. "I never even knew he played baseball. Gee, thanks, Mr. Dickens. It's a small world, isn't it?"

"It is. And I'm sure your father would be

181

very proud of you, Wilber." Charlie put down his mug and nodded at the nameplate on the desk, which identified Corporal Wilber Casey as assistant to the warden. "You've got a pretty important job for a young fella," he added. "You've been working out here long?"

"Three years come spring," Wilber said, but not proudly. "I was hired right after high school."

Charlie did a quick calculation. The boy was twenty-one, then. He didn't look it.

Wilber couldn't suppress an involuntary sigh. "Prison work wasn't exactly what I was looking for. But jobs are awf'lly hard to get these days, and like my Uncle Hamp says, you gotta start somewhere, even if it's not where you want to be for the rest of your life. I was grateful when he found me a job here, in accounting. Otherwise, I don't know where I might've ended up. The gravel pit, maybe."

Charlie had seen some of the farmed-out prisoners working in Hamp Casey's fields and his gravel pit. Wilber's uncle — as crooked as his brother had been straight — no doubt had an inside track with the warden. In an admiring tone, he said, "Accounting. Say, you must be good with numbers. That's a swell skill to have. Going to college?"

"I hope, maybe. Someday." Wilber gave him a shy smile. "But not in accounting. Journalism is what I want to do. I edited our high school newspaper for three years. I read the *Dispatch*, every issue, front to back."

"Do you," Charlie said. "That's good to hear."

"I do." The smile got bigger. "Whenever I run across something that interests me, I write it up like a page one story, the way I would if I was a real newspaperman."

"Huh," Charlie said, now more interested.

"Sometimes I have to do quite a bit of research to get it right." The boy took a breath and added, "My real goal is to be a reporter, like you."

Charlie stared at him. Suddenly, a light bulb went off in his brain, and he thought of Ophelia's defection to the CCC camp. Might Wilber do a few of her jobs? But there was more. Sitting where he was, at Jimmie Bragg's desk, the boy might know a little something about Jimmie Bragg's death. At the very least, he was eyes and ears inside the prison's closed shop, which was a good thing. A useful thing that he, Charlie, could exploit.

"So you want to be a reporter," he mused.

"Well, I'm mighty pleased to hear that. Reporting is a challenging profession. Requires a man with an ability to smell a story and the guts and determination to follow wherever the hell it leads him. If you're that kind of man, and if you can write, you'll do well."

Wilber sighed wistfully. "Thanks, Mr. Dickens. It means a lot to me to hear you say that. I've been saving my money. I was all set to go to college last fall and get started on my journalism degree. But that has to wait, I'm afraid. Now that Dad's gone, Mom needs me at home."

"That's admirable, Wilber." Charlie leaned forward. "But you don't need a journalism degree to work on a newspaper, you know. Not if you've got the skills, and the story." He paused for emphasis. "And the right connections." He repeated it, just to be sure. "Connections, Wilber. Connections. That's what's important."

Wilber got the point. "You *mean* that, Mr. Dickens?"

"I mean it," Charlie said. If he felt guilty for dangling a carrot in front of this young eager beaver, he didn't let that bother him. "A degree is good. I'm not telling you it isn't, if you've got the time and the money. But a man who can write, a man with a nose for news — why, once a man like that has a foot in the door, he can do just as well without college. All he needs is a strong story. A story with legs, it's called in the biz. Find that story, Wilber, and it's good as gold. It's your ticket to wherever you want to go."

Wilber let out a long breath. "A story, huh?"

"That's right, a *story*. The bigger the better." Charlie paused, watching the boy deal with that for a moment. Then he decided it was time to redirect the conversation. He made a point of glancing down at the nameplate on Wilber's desk.

"I notice that you're not clerking in accounting now," he said approvingly. "You got promoted. To the *warden's* office, no less."

"Yeah." Looking pleased, Wilber ducked his head. "When Warden Burford found out I could type and spell pretty good, he moved me over here. There are three hundred thirty-two men in this prison, but most of 'em can't read, let alone type. The guards can't, either."

"The warden made a good move. Congratulations, Wilber." Charlie took out his Camels, shook several cigarettes loose, and leaned across the boy's desk, holding out the pack with a man-to-man gesture. "Smoke?"

Wilber brightened and leaned forward. "Oh, yeah, sure. Thanks, Mr. Dickens." He took a cigarette and Charlie flicked his lighter to it, then lit his own.

"So you've got Bragg's old job," Charlie said conversationally, leaning back in his chair and drawing on his cigarette. "The guy who shot himself a few weeks back, I mean. Jimmie Bragg. He was assistant to the warden, wasn't he?"

Wilber looked troubled. "Yeah. I've got his job," he said. "Matter of fact, this was his desk." He cleared his throat. "Matter of fact, I was there that afternoon. When it happened."

Charlie felt his stomach muscles jerk. Of all the things he might have expected to hear, this was the most surprising. "You were, huh?" He lowered his voice. "You saw Bragg shoot himself? You were an *eyewitness*?"

The word startled the boy, and Charlie wished he could take it back. But there it was, blinking in the air between them like a neon sign.

"Well, I —" Wilber swallowed. "Not exactly." He dropped his eyes and his voice flattened out. "I happened to come along a minute or two after Sergeant Richards found Mr. Bragg behind the maintenance shed. Mr. Bragg was dead, and there was the gun, right there, on the ground."

"Just a minute or two?" To Charlie's ear, the report sounded rehearsed, as if Wilber had given it several times before. To the sheriff, maybe? To the warden?

Wilber flashed him a sidelong glance. Charlie saw the apprehension in it, and the desire, and waited, hoping there would be more. But there wasn't.

The boy hesitated. "Yeah. A minute or two. That's right. Mr. Bragg was dead."

Charlie stared at him. He knew the boy was lying. There was more to the story than he was letting on. But this wasn't the time or the place to prod him. So he only said, in a mild tone, "Holy moly, Wilber. Must have been quite a shock, stumbling across a dead body."

"Yeah, that's what it was, all right. A shock. Real unexpected." Wilber hesitated. And where a competent liar would have ended the matter and let it rest, he couldn't resist adding, "Kinda crazy, too. At least, that's what people are saying."

"Crazy?" Charlie asked. "You mean, it didn't make sense?"

"Yeah." Wilber pulled too hard on his

cigarette, then coughed and sputtered. When he could talk again, he said, "Mr. Bragg was . . . well, he was cocky, swaggering, you might say. He liked being the boss's right-hand man, and he always had to let everybody know it. He liked to swing his weight. People — guards, I mean, and the prisoners who were acquainted with him — are saying he didn't seem like the type to kill himself." There was a noise out in the hall and he paused warily, as if he expected the door to open. When it didn't, he went on, in a lower voice, "That's the scuttlebutt, anyway. The fellas around here like to gossip. There's not much else to do."

"That's interesting, Wilber." Charlie leaned forward confidentially "I have to agree with the scuttlebutt. I ran into Jimmie Bragg myself, just a few hours after the accident that killed Whitworth. He certainly didn't act like a guilty man at that point — much less like somebody who would be so overwhelmed with guilt that he would shoot himself the very next day. I'm still asking myself about that." Pointedly, he added, "I just keep thinking there's a story here somewhere."

"You . . . do?" Wilber asked uncertainly, tilting his head to one side.

"I do," Charlie said with an emphatic nod.

"If you had actually seen it happen, of course, the story would be bigger. Eyewitness accounts are the heart of any piece of reporting."

He let that sink in for a moment, then leaned back again and smiled encouragingly at the boy. "Actually, I envy you, Wilber. Working in the warden's office puts you in the catbird's seat. Gives you a chance to see how the system works when nobody's looking, I mean. Am I right? Is that pretty much the case?"

"Pretty much," Wilber said, clearly flattered. "I handle the warden's mail, type his letters, fill out his reports. A lot of things you'd never in the world think about come over this desk every day." Lowering his voice, he added, in a troubled tone, "To tell the truth, Mr. Dickens, stuff goes on in this prison that you couldn't guess in a million years. Things aren't always what they seem — to folks on the outside, I mean." He glanced apprehensively toward the door. "I suppose that's true for most prisons, but somehow this . . . Well, it seems like a special case."

"Oh, I'll bet," Charlie said sympathetically. "Jericho is tough, and here you are, right in the thick of it."

Bragg had been in the thick of it, too, he

remembered, and a different thought occurred to him. Maybe that's why he was dead and Wilber was sitting behind his desk. Had the boy considered that possibility, he wondered. Was the threat of it keeping him awake at night?

But he only smiled. "Tell you what," he said easily. "This conversation is giving me an idea. Like I said when I called to set up the appointment with the warden, I'm here to interview Burford for an article about that award he got for running a tight shop." He gave the boy a thoughtful look. "But now I'm thinking that I should get your perspective as well, Wilber. You could give me a better idea about the way things really work here — an inside look at the bigger picture, so to speak. No need to go on the record if you don't want to," he added reassuringly. "You'd just be filling in the background, so I wouldn't quote you. Unless you tell me to, that is." He met Wilber's eyes. "If you're willing to go on the record, there could even be a story in it for you."

Wilber's eyes widened. "For *me*?"

"Yeah. But that depends."

"On . . . on what?"

"On what kind of a nose for news you have. And how much guts you've got. It takes balls to dig into tough stories —

stories like the ones you're likely to find at Jericho." He regarded the boy. "How about if we sit down together and talk some more about this?"

"Yeah, maybe," Wilber said uneasily. "Yes, I think I could do that." He lowered his voice. "But we can't do it here. It's not smart for people to see me talking to you. They might get the wrong idea, you know."

"Sure thing," Charlie said. "You got a free evening this weekend? We could maybe get together over a beer and a cigarette somewhere."

Wilber picked up a pencil and tapped it nervously on the desk, seeming to give the matter some thought. "Well, I might could do it tonight, I guess. I was going to take Evelyn — she's my girl — to the Cotton Gin Dance Hall, over on the other side of Monroeville." He made a face. "But when she let slip where we were going, her mother decided they would drive up to Montgomery, to visit a sick aunt. So our date's off."

"Too bad about that," Charlie said. He wasn't surprised that the girl's mother didn't want her to go dancing at the Cotton Gin. But it would be a good place to meet Wilber. The roadhouse was dark and noisy. People would be so busy dancing and flirting that they wouldn't pay any attention to a couple of guys having a private conversation at a back-corner table. What's more, it was twenty-some miles away, which meant that they were much less likely to be recognized.

"The Cotton Gin is fine with me," he added. "How about if I meet you there tonight, say, nine o'clock?"

Wilber's face brightened. "Yeah, sure. Tonight'll be good. Maybe I'll even bring —"

Out in the hallway, they heard the warden's irate voice. "What in the *hell* do you think you're doing, you idiot? I told you to paint the *other* end of the hall, didn't I? *Didn't I?* You painted this end last week. You're painting the same damn patch all over again!"

Wilber hunched his shoulders as if against a blow. "Sounds like the warden is back. And he's not in a real good mood."

"Sounds like," Charlie agreed, glad that he and Wilber had made their arrangements before the boss walked in. With a grin, he pushed back his chair and stood up.

"It's been real nice talking to you, Wilber. I'm looking forward to tonight."

He was, too. Meeting Wilber had been an unpredictable, unexpected, but very welcome stroke of luck. The boy had a story to tell, perhaps about Bragg's death. He might try to appear reluctant, but Charlie had the feeling that he was ready to tell it.

And Charlie was more than ready to listen.

CHAPTER THIRTEEN:
"WE COULD WIND UP DEAD"

The morning light was pale outside the window of Buddy Norris' office, and the elm tree's bare branches shivered in the wind. The oil heater near his desk kept his feet minimally warm, but the rest of the place was chilly enough that the people who came in and out usually didn't take their coats off. Buddy was wearing an all-wool union suit beneath his jeans and flannel shirt, with two pairs of wool socks inside his boots. He was still cold.

Buddy laid aside the state report he was reading — "Crime in Alabama: Statistics for 1933" — pushed back his chair, and went into the waiting room to check the Musgrove's Hardware thermometer on the wall. Fifty degrees, and that was *indoors.* It must be close to freezing outside.

He went over to the old Warm Morning parlor stove that they had inherited with the house, opened the top lid, and stirred up the fire inside. When the stove was regularly fed, its cast iron sides and black stovepipe radiated heat and raised the temperature. But the bucket beside the stove was empty, so he took it out to the shed on the alley and filled it with chunks of coal, glad that Tater Brinkley had delivered a load before the cold spell hit. The cost had gone up again, though. Coal was now just over eight dollars a ton, delivered, almost a full dollar more than this time last year. At that price, some folks might not be able to afford it.

But it wasn't a good day to skimp on coal or let the fire go out. WALA, down in Mobile, had warned that tonight's temperature might fall as low as fifteen, which was downright *frigid.* Darling's December temperatures averaged around forty degrees, although once when Buddy was a kid, it had fallen to five degrees just before Christmas. It had snowed that week, too — the only time he'd ever had a chance to use his father's rusty old sled that hung in the barn, along with the horse harnesses and haying tools and fishing poles. He'd made good use of it that week, though. He'd taken it out on the hill behind the house every chance he got. Snow was a kid's heart's desire.

When he'd added more coal and punched up the fire so it was burning brightly, Buddy stuck his head into his deputy's office, where Wayne Springer was hunched over his desk, updating his report of recent calls for Charlie Dickens' Police Blotter section of next week's *Dispatch*.

It had been a normal week. A dog reported stolen had turned up in a neighbor's chicken coop with feathers on his muzzle, incontrovertible evidence of criminal behavior. Mr. Turnell's bull had gone on the rampage and trampled Mrs. Stewart's rhubarb patch. A threatened brawl among the colored patrons at the Red Dog over in Maysville ended peacefully when the joint's manager brandished his granddaddy's Union sword and began singing "Mine Eyes Have Seen the Glory."

"Yo, Wayne," Buddy said, "It's going to be cold tonight. If you want to set up your cot beside the stove in the waiting room, feel free."

Wayne looked up from his typewriter. "I'll do that," he said. "The pantry got pretty chilly last night." He leaned back in his chair. "I heard on the radio that it was down to eighteen in Gainesville. They're saying it froze the Florida orange and tangerine crop."

"Too bad," Buddy said. "It's looking like it could be that cold here. Be sure and bring

196

in enough extra coal to keep the fire going over night."

The deputy's salary was barely enough to hold body and soul together, so Buddy let Wayne live in the sheriff's office rent-free. He cooked in Mrs. Crumpler's old kitchen and slept on a folding cot in the pantry — which Buddy thought was a pretty good plan. Since Wayne was sleeping on the premises, he was handy to answer the telephone or go to the door if a citizen showed up with a problem in the middle of the night. And Buddy could now tell the county commissioners that the Cypress County Sheriff's Office was staffed around the clock.

Which was a good thing, because he was planning to ask for a fifteen percent increase in the sheriff's department budget at the next commissioners' meeting. Free rent or not, he really ought to raise the deputy's salary. Buddy still couldn't figure out why a good man like Wayne had been willing to give up the decent money he was earning in Birmingham to come to Darling. It was a mystery.

And he would really like to have more money himself. If he got a raise, he might even ask Bettina Higgens to marry him. He was getting pretty uncomfortable at Mrs.

Beedle's rooming house, where his five dollars a week got him a bed, breakfast five days a week, a hot bath on Wednesday night, and laundry on first and third Mondays. But his room wasn't any bigger than Wayne's pantry and unheated. Worse, if there was an emergency nighttime situation, the call came in on the hand-crank telephone on the hallway wall, which woke everybody up — not only at Mrs. Beedle's (four longs), but at the five other households on the party line, where people got up to listen in and find out what was going on. He couldn't expect Mrs. Beedle to go to the expense of a private line just because she was renting the sheriff a five-dollar-a-week room.

Buddy went to the kitchen, poured himself a cup of coffee from the percolator on the back of the stove, and returned to his office. He glanced at the clock with a flash of worry, wondering how Charlie Dickens was making out at the prison farm that morning, and hoping he wasn't getting himself into trouble.

It wasn't an idle worry. He had awakened in a cold sweat in the middle of the night, thinking that it had been a very bad idea to send a civilian to do police work — an undercover fishing trip, fishing for information. It was flat-out dangerous, that's what it was. A man had been killed out there at Jericho and the murder made to look like a suicide. Anybody who would do a thing like that would do just about anything. What if Dickens got himself killed?

But Charlie'd had plenty of experience in investigative reporting. He had a cool head and he'd proved, on a couple of previous occasions, that he could use it.* And Buddy hadn't had any other choice, had he? Jericho was a closed shop, and neither he nor Wayne could get any answers out of it. Charlie could — if he was smart. Careful. And lucky.

He looked at the clock. It was nearly eleven. If he hadn't heard from Dickens by lunchtime, he'd call the Dispatch office and see what was going on.

He had just sat down at his desk again when the front door opened and somebody came into the waiting area. Through his open office door, Buddy could see the visitor. He was surprised. It was Bodeen Pyle, bundled up in a sheepskin coat, a black

* For example, in *The Darling Dahlias and the Eleven O'Clock Lady,* where Charlie's connection with a spy at the CCC camp put a clever swindler out of business.

199

knitted cap pulled down over his ears.

"Hey, Bodeen," Buddy called. "Come on in and get warm. It's cold outside."

"You said it, man," Bodeen replied with a shiver. "That wind is like a knife." He pulled off his leather gloves. "Don't suppose you've got any coffee."

"Sure thing," Buddy said. "There's a pot on the kitchen stove. Help yourself." He pushed his chair back and stood up. "I need to check on something with my deputy. Be with you in a minute."

A few moments later, they were in Buddy's office with the doors shut, and Bodeen was seated in the chair on the other side of the sheriff's desk, close to the oil heater. He was a well-built man, broad-shouldered and narrow-hipped, with a firm jaw, a direct look, and the sharp edge of a man who'd been around long enough to know all the tricks. Bodeen Pyle wasn't somebody you wanted to mess with. If you did, you'd better know what you were doing. His bark could be pretty bad, but his bite was a damn sight worse.

Looking over his coffee cup, Buddy wondered how many times Bodeen had sat on the other side of the sheriff's desk. The Pyle brothers — Randall, Beau, and Bodeen — didn't have much truck with law enforcement unless they were on the business end of an arrest. Randall, the oldest, was in jail in Atlanta. Beau, the youngest, was out on bail here in Darling, charged with pulling a knife on a guy who'd had the bad sense to beat him at a game of pool.

And Bodeen, the middle son, ran the biggest bootleg liquor operation in Cypress County. Buddy knew for a fact that he had five blackpots out there in Briar Swamp, and that he was running at least one hauler — a fast car loaded with twenty or more gallons of whiskey — every night. Twenty gallons at twelve dollars a gallon. Two hundred forty dollars a night. Every night. Buddy also knew that sooner or later, he'd have to arrest Bodeen. If that pesky revenue agent, Chester P. Kinnard, didn't beat him to it.

But in the meantime, Buddy and Bodeen had an agreement — or rather, Bodeen was operating under the assumption that they did. Buddy understood the matter differently, but that didn't change this awkward and even potentially dangerous situation.

It had happened this way. Some weeks before, Buddy had dropped in on Bodeen's moonshine operation in Briar Swamp to question him about the automobile crash that had killed Whitney Whitworth. During the conversation, Buddy learned that Whitworth had been Pyle's partner, and that Whitworth's investment was allowing him to expand. Whitworth was, in effect, the goose that was laying Pyle's golden egg. Pyle had been rattled — and blindsided — by his death.

But even more startlingly, Buddy had learned that Roy Burns, his highly respected predecessor in the sheriff's office, had been operating what amounted to a protection racket. For years, Burns had been accepting regular payments from Bodeen, Mickey LeDoux, and the smaller moonshiners in the county in return for the promise that he wouldn't arrest them.*

This had come as a disquieting surprise to Buddy, although on reflection, he wondered why it hadn't occurred to him before. He had admired Burns, that's why. He'd been naïve. It had just never entered his mind that such a fine man, with so many friends and supporters throughout the county, could be as crooked as a dog's hind leg. But he *should* have seen it, and he blamed himself for being deceived by friendship and admiration for the older man.

* For the story of Buddy's unsettling discovery, read *The Darling Dahlias and the Unlucky Clover.*

Surprised by Bodeen's assumption that he was in on Burns' racket, Buddy had let him think that he was carrying on the former sheriff's venerable tradition of extortion. Now, some might think that the current situation was different than it had been during Prohibition, when Burns was turning a blind eye, and in some ways, it was. Repeal had happened the year before, and Alabama had gone local option. While Cypress County was still dry, it was likely to go wet at the next election, unless the churches and the Temperance Union swayed the vote.

But even if the county went wet, Bodeen and the local shiners wouldn't be off the hook. In fact, they would be as outlawed as ever. The only lawful booze a man could drink now came in bottles that bore Uncle Sam's tax stamp, proving that the fed had already taken its cut — about two dollars on every twelve-dollar gallon of whiskey. Bootleggers didn't pay taxes. Their liquor was illegal. If Roy were alive, he'd still be collecting his protection fee.

It had been Bodeen himself who sprang the news of Burns' racket on Buddy. At the same time, he had let the new sheriff know that he was expected to take the same deal Bodeen had had with the old sheriff. Ten dollars a week for "protection," plus five dollars for every carload of white lightning that left Bodeen's still (which by rights ought to be more like twenty-five, considering that every car was carrying some two hundred fifty dollars' worth of illicit booze).

"So we've got a deal, right?" Bodeen had demanded.

Buddy had been caught between a rock and a hard place. The infamous Franklin County moonshine conspiracy trial had begun up in Virginia, and Charlie Dickens was running the ongoing story almost every week in the *Dispatch*. Nine Virginia county officials had been indicted by a federal grand jury for running a protection racket. Buddy understood the potential criminal consequences of taking Bodeen's money, but until he got things sorted out and understood the situation, he felt he had to accept it. First, though, he had made something clear.

"Yeah, we've got a deal, Pyle — for the moment, anyway. But that doesn't mean you get a free pass in town. Long as you do right, stay out of sight, and don't give me any heartburn, we're pals. Give me or my deputy a bad time, and the deal's off."

Bodeen had accepted his condition and had abided by the terms of the agreement, and Buddy, reluctantly, had made no move to break up the Briar Swamp operation. Something else was motivating him, although he wasn't sure he was doing the right thing.

Now, Bodeen reached into his pocket and took out a wad of bills. "Owe you some money," he remarked casually and tossed it across the desk. "This is the weekly ten, plus five for every carload that left my still."

Without counting the bills, Buddy swept them into the top drawer of his desk. "You shouldn't oughtta come here to deliver money," he growled. "Matter of fact, you shouldn't oughtta come here at all, Pyle. I'll go out to the moonshine camp to collect. And if you want to talk, send me a message. We'll meet where there's nobody to listen in."

"Understood," Buddy said defensively, "but I had to come today. It can't wait."

"What can't wait?" Buddy asked, scowling.

Bodeen leaned forward. "One of my haulers works part time out at the prison farm. He's seen something out there that you are gonna want to know about. In fact, you are gonna want to shut it down fast as you can — seein' as how we're *partners*." He gave Buddy a straight, hard look. "And if you already know about it, and it's on your protection list, I'm tellin' you to take it off. Now."

"Is that right?" Buddy asked, hearing the threat. He pulled a Lucky Strike out of the pack on his desk and lit it, to cover his confusion. "So what is this operation I'm supposed to shut down?"

"It's Jericho," Bodeen said, reaching for his own cigarettes. "The warden out there is cookin' shine."

Buddy choked on his lungful of smoke and began to cough. "Jericho?" he managed at last.

"Yeah." Bodeen flicked a match to his boot, then held it to his cigarette. "My guy says that the warden out there has got his first big batch of mash started."

Stupidly, Buddy's mouth dropped open. "Burford is running a . . . *still*?"

"Ain't that what I just said?" Bodeen demanded impatiently. He gave Buddy a dark look. "You know I been sellin' to the prison farm, Sheriff. They're my biggest customer in the county. When Burford gets his production goin', he's gonna stop buying from me. Even with Mickey gone, that will be a big chunk of business for me to lose. For *us*," he added significantly. "Partner."

Finally, Buddy understood what Bodeen

206

was getting at. For years now, two local boys had been making the bulk of the moonshine in Cypress County. Mickey LeDoux had run a highly professional moonshine production and distribution business out of a wooded hollow on Dead Cow Creek — under the "protection" of Sheriff Burns, Buddy now knew. Then Agent Kinnard had put the still out of business, and Mickey had been packed off to the Wetumpka State Penitentiary.

Now, Bodeen had Mickey's customers to supply, so losing the prison farm wouldn't cripple him. But it would be a big loss. *If* this was true — this story about Burford setting up a still. Maybe it was, maybe it wasn't. Maybe this was some kind of cockamamie test that Pyle had cooked up to see if the sheriff was in his pocket. Maybe —

"What's more," Bodeen went on, "if I know anything about this business, Burford ain't intendin' to just make liquor for Jericho. He's growin' his own corn out there, and he can buy sugar through the state system and truck it in without anybody the wiser. Plus, he's got all the free labor he needs, and he don't have to worry about somebody stumbling on his operation and turning him in to the law. In fact, he's got so much muscle, he might even buy off

Agent Kinnard. Even easier, he could sic him on *me*." He blew out a stream of smoke. "Give Burford a month to get up to full production, and he'll be the biggest operator in this part of Alabama." He paused and added emphatically. "And because he can make it cheap, he'll undersell me — undersell *us* — everywhere."

"Ah," Buddy said, still trying to grasp the situation. "And you're telling me this because . . ."

"Because I expect you to close Burford down."

Buddy just managed not to cough again. "Close him . . . down?" If this was a test, it was a damned dangerous one. Burford had all the power he needed to break a local sheriff. Slice him up into little pieces and grind him under his boot heel.

"Yeah. What I said. Close him down. Arrest him. Break up his still. Whatever it takes to put him out of business and keep him there." Bodeen's voice became sarcastic. "You think you can do that without asking Kinnard to help? We don't want the feds coming into the county and nosin' around. Kinnard might take it into his stupid head to come after *me,* and I can't buy him off."

Buddy swallowed. Even if this was true (and maybe it wasn't), now was *not* the time

208

to make a move on Burford's bootleg operation. He had to get the Bragg murder settled first. "Well, I hear what you're saying, Pyle, but I —"

"Something else here, too, Sheriff," Bodeen cut in. "When Whitworth died in that car crash a few weeks back, it was Jimmie Bragg who ran him off the road. Right?"

Buddy was taken aback by the change of subject. But yes, if there was one thing he was sure of in all this confusion, it was that Bragg had been responsible for running Whitworth off the road and killing him. He could be confident of that because a witness had seen what had happened and identified Bragg as the driver. And it was no surprise that Pyle knew this, because it had been in the *Dispatch*.

"Right," Buddy said. "So?"

Bodeen leaned forward, his face intent through the smoke that curled out of his cigarette. "So my guy says that the scuttlebutt out there at the prison is that Bragg didn't kill himself, the way everybody thinks."

"I'll buy that," Buddy said cautiously.

"You mean, you *know* that?" Bodeen asked, narrowing his eyes again.

Buddy thought of the ballistics evidence

209

Wayne had assembled, and weighed his answer. "Yes," he said finally. "I won't tell you how, but I pretty much know that."

Bodeen straightened his shoulders. "Well, if you know so damn much, Sheriff, maybe you know who killed him." There was a sullen look on his face. "And why."

"I'd rather hear the information you've got," Buddy said quietly. He let the challenge come into his voice. "Maybe *you* have a name?"

"Matter of fact, I do," Bodeen said. "And since we're partners, I'm going to tell you who it is. When you go out there to question him, you can bust that still. I intend to keep on supplying that farm," he added belligerently. "I don't want no competition from Burford."

Buddy gave him a fixed look. "The name?"

"Richards. Sergeant Horace Richards. He's a guard out there."

"The man who claimed he found the body," Buddy said. The man who claimed to have found the fatal gun. The gun that had *not* shot Bragg.

"I don't know nothin' about that," Bodeen said. "And I reckon, if the guard did it, it'll be hard as hell to prove. There weren't any witnesses. Just rumors is all."

Buddy didn't reply to that. "You got any

information about *why* Richards might have killed Bragg?"

"Only that he did it on the warden's orders. Rumor is that Burford thought Bragg was too rough on Whitworth, like he didn't need to do what he did. Or maybe Bragg was just gettin' too big for his britches." Bodeen grinned mirthlessly. "Burford don't like nobody workin' his side of the road."

Buddy considered that. Both were possible. Also possible, and perhaps more likely: that Bragg — who had been the warden's assistant — knew too much about what was *really* going on out there at Jericho, which now appeared to include an illicit distillery. Maybe he had asked for something in return for his silence. What he got instead was a bullet. Yes, Buddy thought. That was more likely.

Pyle levered himself out of his chair, put his hands palms down on Buddy's desk, and leaned forward, thrusting out his lower jaw like a bulldog. His breath smelled of cigarettes and garlic. "I'm paying you good for your protection, Sheriff. You close down Burford's still, I'll pay you better. We'll double the per-haul payment to ten dollars. You like that?"

Buddy stood up, thinking that those who

danced with the devil invariably ended up with singed eyebrows and a real bad burn. "Thanks," he said with a small smile. "I'll get in touch with you later."

Bodeen straightened up. "Make it sooner, not later," he said. "Make it real soon." He took his gloves out of his pocket and turned to leave. "Partner."

Buddy stood by the window, watching, as Bodeen strode down the path to the street, pulling his black cap down over his ears. He got into his black Ford, parked out front, and drove off, spinning his wheels.

Without turning or raising his voice, Buddy said, "You there, Wayne?"

Buddy's office had two doors, one that was open to the waiting area. The other, closed, led to the kitchen. That door opened, and Wayne stepped in, carrying a notebook.

"Here, boss," he said.

Buddy turned. "Did you get it all?"

"Pretty much word for word," Wayne said, raising the notebook. "I'll type it up and we can both sign it." He paused. "How much did he hand you this time?"

Buddy opened the drawer and took out the wad of bills Bodeen had given him. "You count," he said, pushing them across the desk.

The deputy peeled them off. "Looks like

two hundred fifty." He chuckled. "The wages of sin."

Buddy was not amused. He rummaged in his desk drawer and found an envelope. "Interesting that Bodeen's worried about competition from Burford."

"Now *that* was a surprise," Wayne said. "A working still, out there on the prison farm."

"Maybe." Buddy picked up the bills and put them into the envelope. "But when you stop to think about it, it makes all kinds of sense. They're producing everything else they need. Why buy corn whiskey when they can cook it themselves? Burford's got thousands of acres of wilderness, as many acres of corn as he can grow, and the men it takes to run his moonshine operation around the clock. And it's all off the books. When he sells his liquor, the money goes right into his pocket. He'll make a mint — and he'll buy off anybody who's tempted to spill the beans. He'd even buy off Kinnard, if he could. He's got the perfect setup."

"You said it." Wayne crossed his arms. "It's going to be kinda hard to shut him down, don't you think? When it comes to doing what has to be done, I've got as much guts as the next guy. But a couple of local lawmen walking into that prison out there —" He shook his head. "We could wind up dead real easy."

Buddy licked the envelope flap and sealed it. "I agree with you. It's a job for the feds. They get paid a helluva lot better than we do." He paused. "But it's complicated, Wayne. Kinnard and his agents are pretty ham-handed. Bringing them in to close down the still could throw a monkey wrench into our investigation of Bragg's murder."

"Where are we on that?" Wayne asked.

"You heard Pyle. Sergeant Richards sounds like a pretty good bet. And Charlie Dickens went out there this morning to have a look around. I'm hoping he'll bring us a lead." On the outside of the envelope, across the sealed flap, Buddy wrote, *$250 received from Bodeen Pyle for 'protection,'* dated and signed it.

"You sign it too," he said, pushing the envelope across the desk to Wayne, and watched while he wrote his name. "When you get your notes typed up," he added, "we'll take them to Moseley."

Wayne raised an eyebrow. "Both of us?"

"Both of us. He may have some questions for you, as a witness to this transaction. I'll call Liz to be sure, but I think she said he'd be back in town today."

The office of Cypress County attorney — the same thing as the district attorney in other court systems — didn't take more than a few hours a week of anybody's time. So it was rotated among Darling's three lawyers. Benton Moseley had the job right now. Which meant that if any indictments came out of this case, he would be handling them.

Buddy had already given Mr. Moseley the envelope containing the first seventy dollars Bodeen Pyle had paid him and explained where the money came from. Now, with Wayne's notes and the deputy himself as a witness, he felt a hundred percent better about the situation. The earlier conversation had taken place out at Briar Swamp, with nobody but Pyle's men around. By taking money from a bootlegger (especially one he hadn't arrested yet) he had put himself in a vulnerable position. Now, with Wayne's verbatim notes and Pyle's second payment to hand over to the county attorney, he felt he was in the clear. His judgment might be questioned. But he couldn't be convicted of corruption.

The phone rang on Buddy's desk. "Want me to get that?" Wayne asked.

But Buddy had already picked up the receiver. "Sheriff's office," he said. He listened a moment, then said to Wayne, "It's Dickens. I'll handle it. How long will it take

215

you to type those notes?"

"Give me twenty minutes," Wayne said, and left.

Buddy sat down behind his desk. "How did it go out at Jericho this morning? You still in one piece? Got any holes in you?"

"No shots fired." Charlie chuckled mirthlessly. "Big news: I've found somebody who has an inside track out there and might be willing to talk about it. He's a kid, really, but he seems to have a pretty good head on his shoulders. I'm hoping to ask him some questions and get some answers — at nine tonight, over near Monroeville, at the Cotton Gin Dance Hall. I'd invite you, but he's got ants in his pants. Understandably so, given where he works."

"That's swell, Charlie," Buddy said enthusiastically. "Anything I can do?"

"There might be," Charlie said. "I'll know more after I've talked to this guy. What are you doing first thing in the morning — say, around eight?"

"Meeting you," Buddy said promptly. "Where?"

"The apartment," Charlie said. "Fannie will fry you up some griddle cakes to go with your bacon and eggs."

Buddy hung up with a smile. Griddle cakes, bacon, and eggs for breakfast —

something to look forward to, maybe served with a side of answers to some important questions.

Maybe.

Chapter Fourteen:
"Somebody Is Threatening to Steal Our Cupcake?"

On Friday morning, Lizzy was awakened by the lusty crowing of Mrs. Freeman's rooster, who supervised his harem of colorful hens a few doors down the block. Rowser (the rooster's apt name) made it his duty to ensure that, as soon as the morning sun peeped over the eastern hills, the entire neighborhood rolled out of bed and welcomed the day as enthusiastically as he did.

Lizzy snuggled deep into her down-filled comforter, hoping to get just a little more sleep, but she knew it was futile. Daffy was already awake, patting her cheek with his paw and inquiring about his breakfast. Mr. Moseley was due back in the office this morning, and the day was going to be busy — and complicated. It was time to get up.

But the air outside her warm nest was frosty, and the goosebumps popped up on her arms as she got out of bed. She pulled her winter flannel nightgown over her head and hurriedly put on her brassiere — a "bra," as the *Ladies' Home Journal* was calling it now. The flapper era was over, thank God, and women were allowed to have breasts again. She had even read that one company was proposing to make bras in different cup sizes — A for small and D for very large — so they would fit better. But Lizzy had the feeling that it would be a while before an innovation like that made it to Mann's Mercantile, or even the Sears, Roebuck catalog. Like tampons. She'd read that a doctor had patented a tampon with a cardboard applicator, but how long before you could actually *buy* one was anybody's guess. Until then, it was Kotex and an elastic belt.

Shivering, she quickly stepped into a fresh cotton and wool knee-length union suit with sleeves to her elbows and buttoned it up the front. The women's magazines might consider it an old-fashioned, even amusing undergarment. But there was only one coal stove in Mr. Moseley's office, and when the winter wind blew, the old building was downright frigid. Lizzy appreciated all the extra warmth she could get, so she pulled a white flannelette slip on over her head. Then she went to her closet and took out the warmest outfit she owned: a navy pinstriped wool mohair one-piece dress with a pleated skirt. Over that, she added a navy sweater and a string of pretty white beads. She felt like dressing up a little. Mr. Moseley had been away for a week. She wanted to look nice.

With that in mind, she sat down at her dressing table and deftly applied an eyebrow pencil and a soft pink lipstick. Firehouse red was smart these days for lips and nails, and her dark-haired friend Verna wore it dramatically. But Lizzy preferred a more feminine look, framed by the soft brown hair that rippled around her face.

Which didn't mean that she was a softie, she reminded herself, studying her reflection in the three-panel mirror. She saw a face with wide-spaced, steady gray eyes, prominent cheekbones, and a resolute mouth — not quite pretty, by the standards of the Hollywood movie magazines. She tilted her chin, giving her reflection a small smile. She liked to think it was the face of a woman who knew her mind and stood her ground.

But her smile faded as she thought of Grady's telephone call the night before, inviting her to dinner this evening at the Old Alabama Hotel. The Old Alabama was widely acknowledged as Darling's most fashionable dining spot, which only made it more fashionable than the Darling Diner, where you had your choice of a seat at the lunch counter or a table. Or the Dine-and-Dance, where you stood in line for spareribs or pulled pork sandwiches, then found your own table.

But Lizzy had not been at all tempted by the prospect of dining on a snowy white damask tablecloth with ice cubes in her water glass and Mrs. Vaughn playing dinner music on the grand piano in the lobby. And Grady sitting on the other side of the table, being sweetly nice and doing everything he could to win her over. Surely it was better not to put either of them in that uncomfortable position.

But instead of saying "No, thank you, and don't ask me again, please," she had said "I'm sorry, Grady. I have other plans." Which was true. She and the other Puzzle Divas were getting together that night to try to improve their teamwork on the new puzzle she'd rented from Mr. Lima at the drugstore — this one, a complicated poinsettia puzzle with 750 pieces.

But true or not, the *other* truth — that she didn't want to give Grady any reason to believe she might consider a serious relationship with him — was far more important. She should have told him that, instead of making her voice sound almost regretful. She had been soft and spineless. As she often was when she had to confront her mother's demands, she had been weak.

But Daffy was twining himself around her ankles, reminding her that breakfast was on the menu, and the sooner the better. With one last frown at herself in the mirror, she stood up and went downstairs. The morning was chilly, and she was looking forward to a breakfast of scrambled eggs and toast, with a bowl of warm Cream of Wheat and a hot cup of coffee.

And when she got downstairs, there was something to make her smile: that lovely red poinsettia on the kitchen table, and the note from Ryan Nichols.

Not that Mr. Nichols' poinsettia — or Mr. Nichols himself, for that matter — had anything at all to do with her refusing Grady's invitation. Her relationship with Mr. Nichols was entirely professional, and their meeting two months before had been very brief and businesslike. At least until the end, when he'd handed her the four-leaf clover he found in the grass in her front yard.

"When I got out of the car in front of your house," he'd said, "I happened to look down and noticed this." His voice had softened. "It was growing in your yard, so it belongs to you. But since I'm the one who found it, maybe it means good luck for both of us." Lizzy had pressed it between two small squares of wax paper and stuck it in the corner of her dressing table mirror, where she saw it every day.*

Ryan Nichols was with the WPA — the Works Progress Administration, the New Deal's answer to America's enormous unemployment problem. He had dropped in to let her know that the WPA was developing a new program called the Federal Writers' Project. The program aimed to support teams of writers and editors who would publish travel guides for each of the forty-eight states, as well as other things. For instance, writers might also be assigned to record local history and folklore or do social research. At this point, the program seemed fluid and open ended. But most importantly, it would employ women, something that the current WPA programs (the Civilian Conservation Corps and the many road and bridge construction projects) couldn't

* You can read about Lizzy's unexpected visit from Ryan Nichols in *The Darling Dahlias and the Unlucky Clover.*

easily do. Mr. Nichols had come to see her because — once it was funded — the project would need program directors and administrators, some of them part time, others full time. And Lizzy's agent and editor had both recommended her!

At the time of their conversation, Lizzy had been working full time for Mr. Moseley, and she told Mr. Nichols that. He'd promised to stay in touch, though. And now that Mr. Moseley had cut her hours, the income from a part-time job with the Writers' Project might be very welcome — as long as it left her time to work on her book.

Anyway, she was glad to hear from Mr. Nichols again and hoped that his project was still a possibility. He was a Yankee, yes, but courteous and soft-spoken, in a comfortable way that made him seem to be a friend from the moment he'd walked through her front door. Plus, he was quite nice-looking.

But if there were any other feelings tucked away in the corners of her heart, Lizzy wasn't ready to pull them out and look at them.

Mr. Moseley came in a little after ten, having driven down from the state capital at Montgomery. "It is *cold* out there," he said, shrugging out of his navy blue overcoat and hanging it and his felt hat on the coat tree beside the office door. "The heater in the car isn't working right, either. My feet are just about frozen. Is the coffee hot, Liz?"

"Coming up." As always, Lizzy was glad to see him. His presence in the office made things feel . . . well, complete again. "I brought you a couple of Raylene's dough-nuts. They're on your desk."

"Ah, wonderful," he said. "You take such good care of me, Liz. Makes me wonder why I ever leave Darling." He smoothed back his dark brown hair. "The capital is a circus when the legislature is in session. So much political infighting going on, especially with Senator Long campaigning up a storm all across the South. You'd think the presi-dential election is tomorrow, instead of nearly two years away. Long is going to give the president a real test in thirty-six — if FDR runs again, that is."

Lizzy was surprised. Mr. Moseley was well connected, politically, and usually knew what was going on. At Thanksgiving, he'd spent a day with FDR and some of his advi-sors at the Little White House, at Warm Springs, over in Georgia. "You think the president won't run for a second term?" she asked.

"He says he won't, although I'm not sure I believe him." Mr. Moseley blew on his cold fingers and rubbed his hands together. "But enough of that political stuff. I'm glad to be back home in Darling, where nothing exciting ever happens." He grinned. "Bring the coffee to my office, Liz. While I take care of Raylene's doughnuts, you can fill me in — if there's anything to tell, that is. As I say, this is Darling."

Sitting across from Mr. Moseley with a cup of coffee in front of her and her steno notebook in her lap, Lizzy didn't waste any time. She got right into the phone call from Mr. Price, the lawyer in Los Angeles, and the threat against Cupcake.

But she had only managed a few words when Mr. Moseley held up his hand. "You're telling me that somebody is threatening to steal *our Cupcake*?" he asked incredulously. "I don't believe it!"

"I'm afraid it's true," Lizzy said ruefully. "According to Violet, Neil Hudson — Mr. Price's client — is Cupcake's real father. Raylene thinks he's planning to take her to Hollywood and try to get her into the movies."

Mr. Moseley rolled his eyes. "Okay," he said. "Take it from the top, Liz. Chronologically and in detail. Don't leave anything out."

He loosened his tie, lit his pipe, and smoked while Liz — who prided herself on her ability to tell a coherent story — recounted the whole thing, beginning with Cupcake's birth in Memphis. She ended with Raylene's report of Neil Hudson's appearance at the dance recital, his amazement at the discovery of his daughter, and his plan for turning himself and Cupcake into a Hollywood dancing duo.

"On the order of Shirley Temple and James Dunn, in *Stand Up and Cheer*," she added. "Remember the song-and-dance number, 'Baby Take a Bow'?" She and Mr. Moseley occasionally went to the movies, and that was one they had seen together.

"Ah," Mr. Moseley said thoughtfully. "Ah, yes. Shirley Temple. The shiniest little star in Hollywood. I'm sure he thinks there's money to be made. Give me a moment to think about what we should do." He turned his chair around and looked out the window.

Benton Moseley was a good listener who never failed to hear what was said — as well as what wasn't said, but was meant. In his early forties, he was a slender, attractive man with neatly clipped brown hair, regular features, and brown eyes behind dark-rimmed glasses. He looked, Lizzy thought, a lot like Gary Cooper, puffing away on his pipe.

She also thought, just for an instant, how glad she was that he was back in the office and how *relieved* she was that she could turn this latest crisis over to him. She didn't ask herself whether there was anything else behind her pleasure, although if she had, she would have refused to admit it. That silly old business had been settled a long time ago, when she had outgrown her schoolgirl crush on her boss. All that was behind her, in the past.

After a moment, Mr. Moseley turned his chair back around and looked at her over the rim of his glasses. "Thank you," he said. "That was a very clear recap, Liz. Now, tell me how *you* see this situation. Both sides of the issue, please."

Lizzy pressed her lips together. Mr. Moseley frequently asked her opinion about his cases, and always asked her to see both sides. This time, though, that was difficult to do.

"Well," she said hesitantly, "On Mr. Hudson's side, I'd have to say that it doesn't seem right to keep a little girl from her father. He would certainly have a stronger claim than a mere aunt. I'm supposing that his legal claim is valid — that he can *prove* he's her father. There's a birth certificate, I suppose — but is that enough? And Violet says he's the father. But if the case went to court, she probably wouldn't testify to that."

She stopped, thinking about it. "Actually, Violet can only testify that her sister was the child's mother — she can't say with certainty who the father was. And since her sister and this man weren't married . . ." Her voice trailed off.

"Very good, Liz," Mr. Moseley said encouragingly. "Go on."

"In fact, Violet wasn't even with her sister when she got pregnant, so her testimony on that issue would be meaningless." Lizzy blushed. This was a rather delicate subject. "We're talking about proving paternity. I'm not sure how Mr. Hudson might do that, if it were contested. I've read that blood tests aren't conclusive."

"That's right, Liz," Mr. Moseley said. "Yes, the courts have decided that the blood typing system that was developed in the 1920s — Type A, Type B, Type O — isn't accurate enough to determine paternity. There are some new serological tests, but none of them can be relied on." He gave an ironic chuckle. "In fact, *I* could claim to be the girl's father, and the current tests couldn't exclude me. It would be nearly impossible for Hudson to prove paternity to a court. Now, what arguments do you have on the other side?"

Lizzy tilted her head. It was easier to argue for her friends. "Cupcake has *two* loving mothers and a grandmother, and lots of friends here in Darling. She has a stable home in an established community. And while Hollywood might be alluring, what would happen to her if she and her father don't make it in the movies? Would he go back into vaudeville? Is a traveling vaudeville troupe any place for a child to grow up?"

"And what happens if they *do* make it in the movies?" Mr. Moseley asked, in a rhetorical tone. "Shirley Temple may be enormously popular now. But a child star can't count on staying popular. A star for a few years, three or four at the most, and then she outgrows the part. Suddenly she's a has-been." He puffed out a ring of blue smoke. "Remember Baby Peggy?"

"Oh, I *do*!" Lizzy exclaimed. Along with Jackie Coogan, Baby Peggy had been a hugely popular child star in the silent movies of the 1920s. "She made an enormous amount of money, didn't she?" She tilted her head. "But then she dropped out of the picture."

"That's right," Mr. Moseley said. "Ten years ago, the newspapers dubbed Baby Peggy the Million Dollar Baby. That was the year she earned a million and half dollars." He pulled on his pipe. "After that, it was all downhill. She tried for a comeback recently under her real name, Peggy-Jean Montgomery. But it was no surprise when that didn't work out."

"And if it's a question of custody," Lizzy went on, "the court ought to be interested in Mr. Hudson's ability to provide for the child — beyond a long shot at Hollywood. He wasn't around to take care of Cupcake's mother in her last days, and he was willing to give the baby to an orphanage. What's different now? Can he provide a stable home for the little girl, a place to live comfortably, have friends, go to school? These are things that Violet and Myra May can provide, here in Darling."

"Very good," Mr. Moseley said. "A judge awarding custody would have to consider all those issues." He sat up straight in his chair and put his elbows on the desk. "It's likely that Hudson — and that lawyer of his, Price — have already thought about all this. That phone call sounds to me like a bullying strategy. They're hoping to scare Violet into giving them the girl without getting a court order." His eyes narrowed. "Hudson might even be thinking that if there's any resistance on this end, he'll just swoop in and *take* the child." He gave Lizzy a hard, direct look. "Is there any way you can ensure her safety, Liz?"

"There might be," she said slowly. In fact, she had thought of several possibilities as she walked to work that morning. "How about if we —"

Mr. Moseley held up his hand. "Don't tell me what it is. If Cupcake disappears and I'm questioned, I want to be able to say 'I don't know' without telling an outright lie. It's called deniability." He gave her a narrow-eyed look. "If you have an idea — a *good* idea — you should act on it. The sooner the better. Got that, Liz?"

"Yes, sir," Lizzy said firmly. "Got it."

"Fine," Mr. Moseley said. "I suggest that you get started on that little project today, since we have no idea whether — or when — Hudson may show up in Darling." He picked up a pencil and tapped it on his desk. "I want to make a telephone call. In the office directory, you'll find the number of a private detective out in L.A. by the name of Jake Gillis. See if you can get him on the phone. He's kind of a shady character, which is perfect for what I want him to do." He turned his pipe over and tapped it into the ashtray. "When you put in the call, I don't want any of the switchboard girls — especially Violet — listening in. The fewer people who know about this, the better."

Lizzy stood and picked up their empty coffee cups. "I'll make that call now."

"Thanks." Mr. Moseley smiled at her. "I'm glad to be back, Liz. Montgomery might be where the action is, but this office is home. I think it's because I . . ." His voice trailed off, and he gave her a searching look.

"Because?" Lizzy prompted. Her skin prickled. Why was he looking at her like that?

He reached into his drawer and took out a pipe cleaner. "Oh, just because," he said carelessly. He sniffed. "Is that camphor I'm smelling? Couldn't be my Santa Claus suit, could it?"

"That's what it is," Lizzy said with a light laugh. "Suit and cap and snowy white beard. It's hanging in the closet, ready and waiting for the big day. Verna Tidwell promises that there'll be a plenty of kids at the party."

"Ho ho ho," Mr. Moseley muttered. "Close the door when you leave."

Chapter Fifteen:
"Watch Me Eat My Words"

Fifteen minutes later, Mr. Moseley had finished talking to Jake Gillis. Lizzy, who had placed the call and got off the line as soon as Mr. Moseley got on, was curious about what was going on. But she had learned not to ask Mr. Moseley about his conversations. If he wanted her to know, he would tell her.

She was bent over a filing cabinet drawer, getting out a file Mr. Moseley would need for court the following week, when the door opened. Buddy Norris came in, followed by his deputy. Both were wearing winter coats, wool caps, and mufflers. The cold blew in with them.

"Why, hello, Sheriff," Lizzy said cordially. "And Deputy Springer." The sheriff had called earlier to say that he wanted to see Mr. Moseley on urgent county business — something that involved the Whitworth case and an ongoing investigation at the prison farm. "He's expecting you, but let me see if he's available."

But before Lizzy could knock at his door, it opened. "Gentlemen, come in," Mr. Moseley said. "I want to hear what's going on." To Lizzy, he added, "You, too, Liz. We'll need good notes."

Which was why Liz found herself seated in a corner of Mr. Moseley's office, taking rapid shorthand notes as Mr. Moseley smoked his pipe and listened while Buddy Norris made his report. She had known that Jimmie Bragg's death had been reported as a suicide — everybody who read the *Dispatch* knew that. So it came as a great surprise to hear that the sheriff was now saying that Bragg had been murdered (thanks to some firearm research conducted by Deputy Springer). And that Bodeen Pyle had heard a rumor that the murder was committed by a guard at the prison farm, on the order of Warden Burford.

What's more, Pyle (himself the biggest bootlegger in Cypress County) had told the sheriff that the warden had set up a still and was making corn liquor. To try to get some insider information, the sheriff had sent Charlie Dickens out to the prison as an "undercover agent," on the pretext of interviewing the warden about his latest award.

Tonight, Charlie was supposed to have a confidential talk with an informant he had met at the prison. He would report to the sheriff first thing Saturday morning.

And then (as if all that wasn't enough!) the sheriff reported that Bodeen Pyle had given him a large sum of money to keep him from breaking up the still at Briar Swamp and arresting him — a "protection racket" that had apparently been going on with the widely respected former sheriff, Roy Burns! The sheriff handed over an envelope containing the latest payment of the money, along with Deputy Springer's notes on the conversation.

"I'll feel a heckuva lot better now that you have this," he said. "I sure don't want anybody pointing the finger at me and accusing me of accepting a bribe to look in the other direction." He shifted his weight uneasily. "Matter of fact, I *am* looking the other direction, as far as Pyle is concerned. I'm going to have to shut him down, though, sooner or later. Which will make a lot of folks unhappy hereabouts."

For Lizzy, this was an altogether unsettling series of revelations. As she quickly recorded the conversation — the sheriff's report and Mr. Moseley's questions — she felt as if she had been given an unwelcome and deeply unsettling glance into the dark underside of Darling. She had never thought of herself as naïve. After all, she had worked in a lawyer's office for a good many years, and the view from her desk had sometimes been unpleasant. She had seen some unseemly things that other Darling citizens knew nothing about and heard some stories that were much too ugly to make it into the *Dispatch*. And she had learned that the rules only *seemed* black and white, the law only *appeared* solid, and it was the very elasticity of justice that made it work.

But to learn that a trusted Jericho prison guard might be a murderer, a respected warden a moonshiner and a bootlegger, and Darling's beloved former sheriff a *crook* . . .

Well, it was almost too much for Lizzy to manage all at one time. But she tried to conceal her feelings of disillusionment and went on making notes as if all this was business as usual. As perhaps it was, if she just looked a little closer.

Finally, Mr. Moseley sat up straight in his chair, dropped his pipe into the ashtray, and said, "Thank you for that report, Buddy. You, too, Wayne. Good work, both of you." He paused. "I could wish that you hadn't involved Charlie Dickens, but I understand why you felt you had to. Charlie's done a fair bit of investigating in his career as a reporter, and he's smart enough to stay out of trouble." He stood. "You say you're meeting him tomorrow morning?"

The sheriff and the deputy stood, too. Lizzy kept her seat and continued to take notes. The sheriff said, "Yeah. For breakfast. You going to be around?"

"I'll be here in the office early," Mr. Moseley said. "If Dickens turns up anything interesting, come in and report. I want to know what's going on."

"I'll do that," the sheriff said. "About the moonshine operation that the warden is planning —"

"All you've got is Pyle's say-so," Mr. Moseley said. "I'm not sure he can be trusted. This is tricky business, Sheriff, and there may be more going on out there than just the distillery. Before we make a move, you need to pull together as much hard evidence as you can. Witnesses, documents, whatever you can dig up. Maybe use that inside source Dickens has located."

"Maybe." The sheriff sounded dubious. "Of course, we have no idea whether he's reliable. The source, I mean."

"Or vulnerable," Mr. Moseley said softly. "Remember what happened to Bragg."

The sheriff nodded. "Yeah. There's that, too."

"Well, go as far as you can with it," Mr. Moseley said briskly. "Once you've got enough probable cause to impress Judge McHenry, we can get a warrant. I'll also have a phone conversation with my contact at the Board of Prison Administrators. And with Agent Kinnard. Jericho is state land, and shutting down an illegal still at the prison is a job for state and federal agents — a whole passel of them."

He looked from the sheriff to his deputy. "Don't get me wrong. I'm not suggesting that you two gentlemen couldn't handle this on your own. But the warden's distillery is not the county's business. *Murder* is, and it has priority. If you get a firm line on Burford's involvement in Bragg's death, I want to be in on the questioning."

"You will be," the sheriff said. "Thanks for your help, Mr. Moseley." He grinned and added, with unexpected frankness, "A county attorney who knows his way around sure makes this job a lot easier."

"That's what I'm here for," Mr. Moseley said matter-of-factly, but Lizzy thought he sounded pleased. "Deputy Springer, that was good forensic work on that weapon. That's going to be persuasive evidence

239

when we get to court. *If* we get to court," he amended. "We've still got a long row to hoe."

When they had gone, Mr. Moseley wrote his name and the date on the envelope containing the money that had come from Bodeen Pyle and handed it to Lizzy. "This goes into the safe," he said. "When you get your notes typed up, add them to the report Buddy submitted, and put them into the safe, too." He regarded her curiously. "Well? What do you think?"

"I guess I'm pretty surprised," Lizzy confessed. "I always believed that Sheriff Burns was an honest lawman. And I never suspected that a prison warden and a guard might be implicated in something like bootlegging — or murder."

Mr. Moseley stuck his hands in his pockets. "What was that I was saying just this morning? Nothing exciting ever happens in Darling?" He chuckled. "Watch me eat my words."

CHAPTER SIXTEEN:
"HAIR-RAISING IS
MORE LIKE IT"

It was almost two o'clock on Friday afternoon when Mildred realized that she was never going to bake her way out of her dilemma and thought of someone who might help. She brushed the flour out of her hair, put one of the loaves from her final batch into a bag, and set out for her destination, which was only a couple of blocks away.

Aunt Hetty Little's small frame cottage on Cherry Lane was painted a rosy pink, its shutters and front porch a sprightly apple green. All through late spring and summer, spires of old-fashioned gladiolas, hollyhocks, foxgloves, and larkspur brightened the small front yard, and sweet peas and moonflowers festooned the fence. Aunt Hetty collected old-fashioned flowers the way some people collect teapots.

But the summer flowers were taking their winter nap, and the border was alight with pots of the scarlet poinsettias that Aunt Hetty always "darkened off" (as she put it) in her bedroom closet. From early October until a couple of weeks before Christmas, she kept them in the dark for at least twelve hours every day. This period of extended darkness stimulated the plants to produce their brilliant red flowers — which were really not flowers at all, but modified leaves called bracts. (The actual flowers were the inconspicuous yellow blooms in the center of each red leaf cluster.)

"Why, Mildred, hello!" Aunt Hetty exclaimed, when she opened the door to Mildred's knock. She was wearing a red apron over a blue cotton dress printed with tiny red strawberries. A bright red sweater set off her silvery hair. Her blue eyes were sharp and piercing behind silver-rimmed glasses. Aunt Hetty didn't miss much.

"You're just in time to give me a hand, dear," she added. "I was on my way to bring the poinsettias indoors. They're originally from Mexico, you know — in the tropics. This chilly wind makes them want to drop their leaves. Will you help, please?"

"Sure thing," Mildred said warmly. So she put down the bag she had brought, and for the next little while, she helped Aunt Hetty bring in the potted poinsettias and line them up on the window sills. By the time they were done, the little house had a distinctly Christmassy appearance.

"I'm curious," Mildred said, looking around the small parlor, where Aunt Hetty's loom took up an entire corner. "How did you get so *many* poinsettias? You must have —" She turned, counted the window sills, and did a quick calculation. "Why, you must have a dozen!"

"Thirteen, actually. There's one in the bathroom." Aunt Hetty pointed to a particularly brilliant plant. "That's the mama. Isn't she splendid? Bessie Bloodworth gave her to me for Christmas years and years and *years* ago. Every spring, I've taken cuttings and rooted them, so these are all her babies. I give several away every Christmas." She tilted her head, her eyes bright. "Maybe you and Earlynne would like two or three for that grand opening of yours."

"We would love that," Mildred said promptly. "I'll use them in our Christmas window. I've been working on that window — I really want to win the contest."

Aunt Hetty was smiling. "Well, then. Let's sit down and have a hot cup of tea and you can tell me how you girls are getting on with your bakery. It's really quite exciting, you know. Darling's very own bakery!"

243

"Exciting isn't the word for it," Mildred said ruefully, picking up her bag and following Aunt Hetty down the hall. "Hair-raising is more like it."

Aunt Hetty laughed. "That's always the way with new things, isn't it? A surprise around every corner, and some of them not so pleasant."

A few moments later, the two of them were seated in Aunt Hetty's charming old-fashioned kitchen. The room was dominated by the wood-fired cast iron kitchen range that took up most of one wall, its gleaming stovepipe making a sharp elbow bend and disappearing into the wall a foot below the ceiling.

Most Darling women had begun cooking with gas after the Great War, because gas stoves were much cooler in the summer. And when Darling got its newfangled electrical system in the early 1920s, the rest began using modern electric stoves, like the one Mildred had at home. She had been thrilled when she could give up the old-fashioned iron range, which she thought was a monstrosity.

But while Aunt Hetty kept a small electric stove on the back porch for cooking in July and August, she refused to part with her kitchen range. On this December day, its radiating warmth was as comforting as a favorite woolly sweater. A cast iron kettle steamed on its cooktop, and a bowl of rising dough, covered by a yellow-checked cloth, sat on the wall shelf behind the range. Against the opposite wall stood a gleaming white Hoosier cabinet, with a sifter-bin for flour, another bin for sugar, and shelves that held jars of dried herbs from Aunt Hetty's garden, all neatly labeled. A dark oak icebox with polished brass fittings stood next to the old-fashioned porcelain sink. The oilcloth-covered table was set with a pair of delicate porcelain cups and saucers, a small white china teapot, and a cherry-red glass plate laden with slices of warm gingerbread. Mildred put her bag under a chair, feeling herself relaxing and thinking how good it was to take a step back in time. And if the electricity went down for a day or two or more (as it often did, especially in the winter), Aunt Hetty could carry on as usual.

Aunt Hetty picked up the teapot and poured cups of fragrant mint tea. "Now tell me," she commanded with a twinkle, "how you and Earlynne are getting along with your project. I walked past this morning on my way back from the post office and saw your Christmas window, with the cookies and those gingerbread houses. It's very attractive, Mildred. I've been telling all my neighbors about the grand opening, and everyone is looking forward to it. Are you ready?"

"I certainly hope so," Mildred said fervently. "We've been working practically night and day. The shop is cleaned and painted, and we installed a big glass display case and fixed the oven in the kitchen. Scooter Dooley repaired the leaky faucets, and I drove to Mobile and bought a load of baking supplies. And Earlynne is baking up a storm. All kinds of pastries — scones and croissants and sticky buns and tarts and cookies and —" She stopped. "Too many, if you ask me."

"Earlynne has always been a first-rate baker." Aunt Hetty stirred a spoonful of sugar into her tea, glancing at Mildred over the tops of her silver-rimmed glasses. "And you've got a good business head on your shoulders. Between the two of you, I'm sure the bakery will be a great success."

"I hope you're right," Mildred said, trying to sound more confident than she felt. "There's just one little thing —" She stopped, feeling quite foolish, and busied herself putting sugar into her tea. "Well, I suppose it isn't really a *little* thing, Aunt Hetty. Actually, it's probably pretty important." She took a breath. "To tell the truth, it turns out that neither of us is very good at baking . . . well, bread."

"You're not very good at baking —" Aunt Hetty gave an amused chuckle. "I really must look into getting a hearing aid, Mildred. I thought I heard you say that you and Earlynne aren't very good at baking bread."

Mildred sighed. "That's what I said, I'm afraid. When it comes to bread, we are absolute duds, *both* of us." She took a deep breath, feeling her cheeks growing warm. "I've brought a loaf from one of the batches I baked this morning. My best loaf, actually." She took her bag out from under her chair, pulled out a misshapen loaf of bread and set it on the table. "Do you have a knife?"

Aunt Hetty eyed the lopsided loaf warily, but she got up and took a knife out of a drawer. "This is the one I use to slice my bread. The serrations make it easy."

"Nothing will make this easy," Mildred said grimly, and demonstrated. Sawing hard, she finally managed to cut a slice from the brick-like loaf and handed it to Aunt Hetty.

Aunt Hetty gazed at it in surprise. "This is your *best* loaf?" She wrinkled her nose,

247

broke off a corner, and put it into her mouth. She chewed for a moment, then made a wry face. "Tastes like sawdust. I don't think your customers would come back for seconds."

Mildred nodded regretfully. "You're right. I only brought it to show you where we are. Earlynne and I should have planned better. We should have discussed who was going to do what — in detail."

"But you didn't." Aunt Hetty pushed the loaf away.

Mildred shook her head. "Unfortunately, I just assumed that Earlynne was as expert with bread as she is with carrot cake and meringues and scones and such. In fact, I didn't find out about the bread until yesterday afternoon. She baked some loaves for me to sample and they were . . . well, pretty awful. I couldn't eat them. She's giving them to Liz for her chickens."

"Oh, dear," Aunt Hetty murmured. She pushed the plate of gingerbread toward Mildred. "Have a slice, do. It'll make you feel better. This is AdaJean LeRoy's gingerbread. She sent me her recipe and told me to tell you that you and Earlynne could use it for your shop."

"Thank you." Mildred took a slice of gingerbread and nibbled on it, then took another bite. It was certainly tastier and had a nicer texture than the gingerbread they'd been making. She'd be sure to get the recipe.

But she felt she had to tell the whole story, so she hurried on. "When I understood the problem, I knew I had to do *something*. So I got to work this morning and —" She sighed. "But it turns out that when it comes to bread, I'm no better than Earlynne. I paid attention to the recipe and did everything it said, as carefully as I could. But it was an utter fiasco. I made a mess of everything, including the kitchen — and the neighbor's cat."

"The cat, too? Gracious sakes alive," Aunt Hetty said softly. "I *am* sorry to hear that, child."

Now close to tears, Mildred clenched her fists. "Aunt Hetty, bread is a bakery's staple item. If we can't sell a decent loaf at a reasonable price, all the splendid scones and Danish and fruit tarts in the world won't save us. The Flour Shop is *doomed*!"

To Mildred's ears, her words sounded a bit . . . well, melodramatic, and she feared that Aunt Hetty would think she was exaggerating. But she meant every single syllable. She was panicked.

Aunt Hetty pursed her lips. "I'm not sure

I totally agree with you, my dear. But I can certainly see why you're upset." She picked up a slice of gingerbread. "And I'm wondering. Why have you come to *me*?"

"Who else would I go to?" Mildred demanded passionately. "Everybody knows that you bake the very best bread in Darling. You always win blue ribbons at the Cypress County Fair. So I was . . ." She gulped. "Well, I was hoping you might bake a few loaves for our Saturday grand opening. Just a few," she added hurriedly. "Maybe five or six loaves. Or a few more," she said in a lower voice. She bit her lip. "As many as possible, that is."

Aunt Hetty put down the gingerbread. "But that won't solve your problem, Mildred," she said sternly. "You'll surely need more than a few loaves for the opening. And if you plan to operate a bakery, at least *one* of you ought to be able to bake a decent loaf."

"I know," Mildred said wretchedly. "But what can we do?"

"You can stop being such a namby-pamby. You can *learn,* for pity's sake." Aunt Hetty's sharp voice softened a bit. "But I'll help. I'll bake a couple of batches for your Saturday grand opening, and I'll see if I can round up a few other ladies who can pitch in."

Mildred let out her breath. "Oh, Aunt Hetty, that's wonderful! You are an angel!" She leaned forward eagerly. "You're an answer to our prayers. You've *saved* us!"

"Not yet." Aunt Hetty held up her hand. "I'll do this — but on one condition."

"Anything," Mildred said. *"Anything."* She paused and added apprehensively, "What is it?"

"You and Earlynne agree to come over here right after church on Sunday. I'm going to teach you how to bake a decent loaf of bread."

Mildred pulled her brows together. "It won't help," she said. "Neither of us have the knack." At the look on Aunt Hetty's face, she added, "I'll come. But I can't speak for Earlynne."

Aunt Hetty folded her arms. "*Both* of you, or you'll get no bread from me. And don't be so down in the mouth. Mrs. Noah was baking bread on the ark, and she didn't have a modern oven like mine. And heaven only knows how she managed, with all those animals in the kitchen." There was a smile in her blue eyes, and her voice lightened. "Of course you can learn, Mildred. There's no mystery to baking bread. *Anybody* can learn, with the right teacher."

"If you say so," Mildred replied, still un-

251

convinced. She was sure that Earlynne would balk. But at the moment, she didn't see any alternative. "Well, okay. I'll be here on Sunday morning. And I'll do my best to see that Earlynne is here, too." Hesitantly, she added, "So you'll bring a few loaves to The Flour Shop early Saturday morning?"

"What time do you open?"

"Nine o'clock."

"Look for me at eight forty-five." With a benign smile, Aunt Hetty picked up the teapot. "Are you ready for another cup of tea, dear? And I'll get a couple of pots of poinsettias for you. They're just what you need to brighten up that window of yours."

CHAPTER SEVENTEEN:
"DON'T LEAVE WITHOUT YOUR COOKIES"

A dusky winter twilight was falling on Friday evening when Lizzy started out for Magnolia Manor, where she was meeting the Puzzle Divas for another practice session. The brisk wind, flavored with fragrant woodsmoke from neighborhood chimneys, had a wintry bite to it. But Lizzy was wearing her warm wool coat and green knitted cap, muffler, and mittens, and the unaccustomed chill only stirred her blood and made her alert to everything around her.

The trees stretched their bony arms up to the dark gray clouds while fallen leaves danced and whirled around their feet. In a driveway, two little girls were skipping rope, and a small boy wearing a striped engineer's cap and red mittens was riding a tricycle, ringing the bell on the handlebar and shouting "Choo-choo!" In the windows of several homes, lighted Christmas trees seemed to symbolize a perennial faith in the enduring

253

tradition of giving and sharing. In others, lamps glowed with a golden warmth, and Lizzy caught sight of mothers and fathers and children sitting down to dinner — a reminder that while the Depression had fractured so many American hopes, it also pulled families closer together in their brave efforts to hold onto today and create a brighter tomorrow.

A few blocks down Robert E. Lee, Lizzy ran into Verna, who was on her way to the same destination. At the next corner, they turned right and walked down Camellia Street to Bessie Bloodworth's Magnolia Manor, a large, two-story white-frame residence, not quite so elegant now as it had once been.

They went up on the front porch and Verna rang the doorbell. It was one of the old-fashioned ones with a brass handle that you twisted — probably, Lizzy thought, originally installed by Bessie's paternal grandfather, the much-admired local doctor who had built the house sometime before the War Between the States. Bessie (who was also Darling's local historian and knew all the old stories) enjoyed pointing out that the bullet holes in the painted wooden porch pillars had been put there by the Union troops that stormed through Darling in the last days of the War. If you seemed interested, she would also show you the hidey-hole behind the fruit jars in the cellar, where her grandmother had hidden the Bloodworth silver to keep the damn Yankees from carrying it off.

Back in those days, however, the Bloodworth house was not called Magnolia Manor. Bessie (who had never married) gave the house its current name after her father died and she had to go into the boardinghouse business in order to keep the place.* She had been afraid that people might start calling it Bessie Bloodworth's Home for Old Ladies (like Mrs. Brewster's Home for Young Ladies on West Plum or Mrs. Meeks' Rooms for Single Gentlemen over on Railroad Street) — which would not do at all!

So she put a wooden sign in the front yard and an ad in the Darling Dispatch: "Wanted: Older unmarried and widowed ladies of refinement and good taste, to occupy spacious bedrooms at the Magnolia Manor. Fine meals and pleasant parlor (with radio) included." And then she was in business.

It was true that the bedrooms were spa-

---

* You can learn why Bessie has never married in *The Darling Dahlias and the Naked Ladies.*

cious and the meals were exceptionally fine (thanks to Roseanne, the Manor's colored cook and housekeeper). The parlor was pleasantly convivial, especially during the long winter evenings, when Bessie's boarders gathered to play cards or knit or listen to the radio. The ladies loved the The National Barn Dance, the A&P Gypsies, and The Major Bowes Amateur Hour. They especially enjoyed the Amateur Hour because the host, Major Edward Bowes, chatted with the contestants and they got to hear their personal stories. And because the show encouraged its listeners to believe that any ordinary somebody — even your average Darling Joe or Jane — might have a remarkable hidden talent that would one day be discovered and make them famous. (Just look at little Shirley Temple, for instance, who was only three years old when she was discovered at her dancing school!) In a time of national gloom, the possibility that anyone could become a rising star buoyed everyone's spirits.

The Manor, however, was not what you'd call a profitable business, for while the ladies were certainly refined and genteel, none of them had much money to speak of. In fact, all were enthusiastic supporters of FDR's idea for "social security" — pension payments to retired people over sixty-five. They only wished the president would stop shilly-shallying and make Congress vote it into law, effective immediately. If he didn't, they thought Huey P. Long would make a better president. They had gathered around the radio when the senator gave his famous "Every Man a King" speech, and they were all in favor of his plan for "sharing the wealth." Bessie even had a little red, white, and blue sign — "Huey P. Long for President in 1936!" — taped to the front window, and she kept a copy of his speech in the drawer of her bedside table, where she could take it out and read it when she felt down-hearted.

Currently, there were four boarders, with room for one more. Mrs. Sedalius was better off than the other Magnolia Ladies (as they liked to call themselves), for her son was a doctor in Mobile. He was too busy to visit but sent a monthly check for his mother's room and board — whenever he (or his secretary) managed to remember. Leticia Wiggens had a widow's pension of thirty dollars a month from her late husband's service as a Confederate company commander in the War Between the States, but the pension was paid by the state of Alabama only when there was money in the state treasury. Miss Dorothy Rogers earned six dollars a week as the Darling librarian. The Darling City Council was usually a month or two late with her salary, however, and for the past two months, hadn't paid her at all.

The situation was a little better for Maxine Bechtel, who owned two rent houses over in Monroeville. But her renters didn't always pay with cash money. Recently, for example, they had brought four fat hens that Roseanne cooped up in the garage and turned into chicken and dumplings every Sunday for a month, with the carcasses served up as a tasty chicken and vegetable soup on Wednesday night. Bessie would have preferred the cash — the property taxes were due at the end of December and she wasn't sure where the money was coming from. But it all came out in the wash, she reminded herself, or nearly so. The chickens saved on the bill at Hancock's Grocery, and everybody enjoyed their Sunday dumplings and Wednesday soup.

Verna (always the impatient one) gave the Manor's doorbell another hard twist. "Bessie knows that we're meeting here tonight, doesn't she?" she asked.

"Yes, she's expecting us," Lizzy said. She turned as someone came up the path behind them. "Oh, hello, Aunt Hetty. Glad you could make it tonight."

"Cold enough for you?" Aunt Hetty asked, clutching her brown felt hat to her head. Her cheeks were pink. "That wind fair takes your breath away, don't it?"

At that moment, the door opened and Bessie said, breathlessly, "Sorry to keep you waiting, ladies. I was talking on the telephone. It looks like I'm going to have another boarder!" She stepped back and held the door open. "Come on in, please. You must be frozen!"

"It's a bit on the chilly side tonight," Lizzy agreed, as the three of them went into the pleasant front parlor. She saw that Bessie had set up the card table for their puzzle practice in front of the fireplace, where a bright fire was burning. Under a draped pine swag, the mantel was hung with decorated Christmas stockings for everyone in the house, a tradition at Magnolia Manor, Lizzy knew. And there were holiday refreshments — an antique china platter with a selection of Christmas cookies and a silver chocolate pot filled with hot cocoa and wrapped in a red and green quilted cozy, set up on the library table against a wall.

"Another boarder?" Verna asked.

Bessie clasped her hands ecstatically.

"Isn't it *wonderful*? Just when I was wondering how I was going to pay the property taxes! She's moving in next week."

"Where is she from?" Lizzy asked, taking off her coat. "Is she anybody we know?"

"How old is she?" Aunt Hetty asked, taking off her hat and unbuttoning her coat. "Is she a widow? A spinster?"

Bessie pulled her brows together. "Her name is Emma Jane, and she's from Birmingham. I didn't think to ask about the rest, I was just so excited by the idea of another boarder to help pay the bills." Her expression cleared. "But she sounded very nice on the telephone. I'm sure we'll find out all about her when she's settled in."

Verna looked around. "Where are the Magnolia Ladies? I was expecting to see them this evening."

"It's bingo night at the Oddfellows Hall," Bessie said, taking their coats. "The neighbor from across the street drove them. So it's just the four of us." She pointed to the sideboard. "There's some hot chocolate over there. It'll warm you up."

It was just as well, Lizzy thought, that the other ladies were gone. She and Verna had something to talk over with the others, and it would be better if it were kept confidential — at least until they were ready to put their plan into action.

"Here's the puzzle I rented from the drugstore," she said, taking the box out of the bag she'd been carrying. She put it, unopened, in the middle of the table. The picture on the cover showed a large poinsettia in a ceramic pot, decorated with a silver ribbon against a variegated blue background.

"Poinsettia!" Aunt Hetty crowed, bending over the box. "My favorite winter flower! Did you know that the Aztec Indians used to make a red dye from this plant? It was also medicinal — they treated fevers with the sap."

"Really?" Bessie asked curiously. "I wonder how they made the dye. It would be fun to try, don't you think, Hetty?"

"We could experiment after the holidays," Aunt Hetty replied. "Let's do it, Bessie."

Verna glanced down at the puzzle box. "This one is seven hundred and fifty pieces. Do you think we can do it all tonight, Liz?"

"We can try," Lizzy said. "I decided to get a bigger one because we did so well with the five-hundred-piece puzzle we practiced with the other day. I thought this might stretch us a bit."

"That's a smart idea," Bessie said approvingly. She moved the floor lamp to one corner of the table. "If we can finish this one in less than four hours, the contest puzzle ought to be easy. That one is supposed to be just five hundred pieces."

"But we don't have to actually finish it tonight," Lizzy said. She looked at the grandmother clock on the wall beside the door, its gold pendulum swinging steadily back and forth. It was seven o'clock. "At the contest, we'll have just two hours, you know. So why don't we work until nine o'clock and see how far we get."

Bessie adjusted the lamp so it cast a bright light over their working surface. "I wonder what the contest puzzle will be."

"Why don't you ask Miss Rogers?" Aunt Hetty said with a teasing smile. "She's your boarder, Bessie. Can't you get it out of her?"

"Not a *chance,*" Bessie said. "The contest is the most important thing that's happened in her life for months and months. She's not going to give me a single clue."

"Mr. Lima knows, too," Lizzy replied, "since he's helping Miss Rogers collect the puzzles. But it wouldn't be right for him to tell me." She took a chair to the left of Aunt Hetty. "Divas, if you're ready, we can get started turning the pieces face-up and sorting them. Who wants what colors?"

"I'll take red and yellow," Aunt Hetty said

promptly, putting her elbows on the table. "Those red petals are bracts, you know. They're really leaves, not petals." She pointed at the box cover. "And that little yellow thingy in the center is really the flower."

"The ceramic pot for me," Bessie volunteered, from the other side of the table. "And the silver ribbon. But there's a *lot* of red, Hetty. I'll help you with that."

"I'll do the blue background," Verna offered, taking the empty chair to Lizzy's right.

"Which leaves the frame for me," Lizzy said, opening the box and dumping the puzzle pieces in the middle of the table. "If you see any straight-edged pieces, push them in my direction. The sooner we get the frame in place, the better." She hesitated. "But I wonder — can we sort and talk at the same time? Verna and I have something we need to discuss with you."

"Can we sort and talk?" Aunt Hetty repeated, turning pieces right-side up. "That's like asking if we can chew gum while we're baking an apple pie. Nothing to it." She pulled a red piece into the little pile in front of her. "What are we talking about?"

Lizzy pulled two border pieces out of the pile. "It's about Cupcake. Violet and Myra

263

May's little girl."

"Oh, that *precious* child," Bessie said with a smile. "Have you seen her dance? Why, she is as good as little Shirley Temple. Here, Hetty — two red pieces for you. And a blue one for you, Verna." She glanced apprehensively at Lizzy. "*What* about our Cupcake? She's not sick, is she?"

"No, nothing like that," Verna said, pushing a straight-edged piece to Liz. "But she's in a very difficult situation. We're afraid it could even be . . . dangerous."

" 'Dangerous?' " Bessie rolled her eyes. "Verna, you always dramatize *everything.*"

"Look! I've found a blue corner," Aunt Hetty exclaimed. "Here you are, Liz. I think it goes at the top right." She scowled at Verna. "What on earth can you mean, Verna? 'Dangerous'?"

"Well, if you'll give us a chance, we'll tell you," Verna replied, fitting two blue pieces together. "You begin, Liz. You're the one who got the phone call from that lawyer."

So, while they turned and sorted and began assembling their individual sections, Lizzy and Verna told them how Violet had brought Cupcake home to Darling after her sister's death — and then about Neil Hudson's appearance at Cupcake's dance recital, the lawyer's telephone call from Los Angeles, and Raylene's belief that Hudson (a vaudeville song-and-dance man) wanted to take Cupcake to Hollywood.

"Hollywood!" Bessie exclaimed excitedly. "Well, if you ask me, our little Cupcake could give Shirley a run for her money. Have you heard her sing 'Baby Take a Bow'? I would *love* to see her in the movies. Wouldn't you?"

"But Hollywood wouldn't be any kind of life for Cupcake," Aunt Hetty objected. "Not for *any* child, in my personal opinion." She sniffed. "Nothing goes on out there but the three Ds."

"The three Ds?" Lizzy asked.

"Dancing and drinking and divorce," Aunt Hetty replied with a sniff. "Hollywood marriages are finished faster than you can say Jack Robinson. Why, just take Joan Crawford and Douglas Fairbanks, Junior. They were married for less than three years! Whatever happened to until-death-do-we-part? How can you bring up a child in a place like that?" She moved a section of several red pieces into the puzzle frame Lizzy was constructing. "I think this goes about here, Liz, but you can move it if that's not right."

"Hollywood or no Hollywood," Verna said firmly, "none of us want Neil Hudson to take Cupcake away from Violet and Myra

May and Raylene. That would be *criminal*. Aunt Hetty, please hand me that box cover."

"Mr. Moseley is looking into the matter from the legal angle," Lizzy said. She had completed the top of the puzzle now, with only two or three short gaps on the right side. "He thinks Mr. Hudson doesn't have a very strong claim to the girl."

"It must be a very *weak* claim," Verna replied decidedly. "After all, the man was ready to give his brand-new baby to an orphanage, wasn't he? How can he possibly think that all he has to do is show up and demand her and she'll be handed over?" She stood up. "Why don't we trade places for a few minutes, Liz? That'll give me a different view of this."

"How do we know that he's the child's father?" Aunt Hetty asked, working busily at her red puzzle pieces.

"Violet says so," Lizzy replied, moving into Verna's chair.

"But how does *Violet* know?" Bessie asked, arching both eyebrows. "It's easy to tell who the mother is — unless the baby is born in a hospital and accidentally gets switched. But sometimes not even the mother knows who the father is."

"Bessie!" Aunt Hetty was scandalized. "Really! The things you say!"

266

"Well, it's true, Hetty," Bessie replied evenly. "Remember when Tom Benson said he was the father of Billie Jean Winkler's baby and Roy Parkins stepped forward and claimed *he* was? They never did get that one figured out. Nobody knows what goes on in people's bedrooms — married or not." She looked around. "Who's got the box lid? I need to see the picture again."

"And you can't go by peoples' say-so," Verna said, handing the box cover to Bessie. "Do you remember when Maisy Lipcock declared that Bernie Jamison was the father of her little boy, and he swore on his grandmother's Bible that he wasn't and refused to marry her, even when Maisy's father got his shotgun and went looking for him? To this day, the Lipcocks and the Jamisons won't speak to one another. And Maisy married Larry Tombull and now has another little boy who is the spit and image of his older brother. They could be twins."

Lizzy nodded. "Mr. Moseley says it's hard to make a paternity case that can stand up in court. They can do blood tests, but they're not reliable. He says Mr. Hudson likely wouldn't risk going before a judge." She paused and looked around the table. "He might just try to kidnap the child."

"Kidnap her?" Aunt Hetty cried, horrified. "Take her away from Darling? Oh, no!"

Bessie's eyes widened. "What can we do, Liz? We have to do *something*. We can't let anybody steal our Cupcake!"

"At Mr. Moseley's suggestion," Lizzy said, "I discussed this with Violet and Myra May this afternoon, and we came up with a plan. Here's what we think." She leaned forward, crossed her arms on the table, and outlined the scheme.

"Sounds like it'll work," Aunt Hetty said when she was finished. "I'll certainly be glad to do my bit. Won't you, Bessie?"

Bessie agreed warmly, adding another two pieces to the part she was working on. "I'm sure the ladies will be absolutely delighted to help." She sat up straight. "There! Just one more piece and the pot is finished!"

"Count me in, too, Liz," Verna said. "Weekends are the best for me. Earlynne and Mildred are probably too busy with their bakery to volunteer, but you might ask Ophelia and Lucy." She grinned. "Everybody will want to do her bit, you know."

Bessie began assembling the ribbon pieces. "When do you want to start?"

"The sooner the better," Lizzy said. "We don't know when he'll show up — or even *if* he'll show up. He might leave everything in the hands of his lawyer, and this could be

268

entirely unnecessary. But just in case . . . ."

"All you have to do is tell us what and when and where, and everybody will be glad to chip in," Aunt Hetty said.

"Thank you," Lizzy said, greatly relieved. looking around with a big smile. "I knew we could count on you. I'll draw up a schedule and let everybody know. But remember, not a word to anybody outside of the Dahlias. We can't risk the secret leaking out. I don't think anybody in Darling would intentionally give us away. But it might happen inadvertently, if Mr. Hudson shows up and starts asking questions."

There was a moment's silence, as everyone thought about that. Then Bessie pushed back her chair and stood. "There's more chocolate," she said, and brought the pot to the table to refill their cups.

"Speaking of helping," Aunt Hetty said, as they went back to their puzzle sections, "I'm sorry to report that Mildred and Earlynne have baked themselves into a corner with that new enterprise of theirs."

"Why am I not surprised?" Verna said dryly.

"I love the name they chose for their shop," Lizzy said. "The Flour Shop. For a pair of Dahlias, it's perfect."

"And they have a very nice display of

cookies and sweet little gingerbread houses in their window," Bessie added, assembling several more pieces. "So tempting. It's a first-rate advertisement." She glanced up at Aunt Hetty. "You said they've baked themselves into a corner. What's their problem, Hetty?"

Aunt Hetty chuckled. "You won't believe this, girls, but their problem is bread."

"Bread?" Lizzy blinked. "How in the world can *bread* be a problem?"

"They've run out of flour and need some more?" Bessie guessed. "Here at the Manor, we buy by the fifty-pound sack. I'll be glad to loan them a few pounds."

"Or maybe they've figured out that they can't make it cheaply enough to compete with store-bought," Verna conjectured. "Mrs. Hancock sells Wonder Bread for nine cents a loaf. And every loaf is perfectly sliced — wrapped and sealed to keep it fresh. People like that, you know."

"But not everybody thinks Wonder Bread is so wonderful," Bessie objected. "It doesn't taste anything like home-baked. At least, not like Roseanne's bread," she added with a little smile. "She bakes eight loaves a week for us — more, if we have French toast on the weekend instead of pancakes. The ladies love it."

"Your ladies are lucky to have Roseanne," Lizzy said.

"And don't we know it," Bessie replied comfortably. She put four more pieces into the puzzle. "She's a treasure."

"Mildred and Earlynne haven't run out of flour," Aunt Hetty said. "And they understand that they can't compete with Mrs. Hancock on price. They're selling their bread for eleven cents a loaf."

"I'd be more than glad to pay an extra two cents for The Flour Shop's bread," Lizzy said, filling in a section of the puzzle's blue background. "If I didn't bake my own," she added. Lizzy usually baked two loaves every Saturday, enough to make breakfast toast and sandwiches for herself all week. But she had to admit that while Wonder Bread was a little too soft-textured (some might call it doughy), its perfect slices were . . . well, perfectly uniform. They couldn't be beat for sandwiches.

Verna coughed. "If Mildred and Earlynne have all the supplies they need and they're not concerned about competition, what *is* their problem, Aunt Hetty?"

Aunt Hetty fitted two red pieces together and added them to the section she was working on. "Their problem," she said with a sigh, "is that they don't know how to bake

271

bread. They have tried, both of them, and they've failed."

"They don't know how to bake bread?" Bessie's eyebrows disappeared under her gray bangs. "They don't know *how?*" she repeated incredulously.

"Then why in the world did they go into the bakery business?" Verna asked, open-mouthed.

"Are you sure about this?" Lizzy asked, frowning. "It can't be true."

"Oh, it's true, all right," Aunt Hetty said ruefully. "Mildred showed me her best loaf. It had the texture of a brick. And it tasted like sawdust."

"Oh, *no.* That's terrible!" Lizzy stared at Aunt Hetty. "What are they going to *do?*"

"They can sell cakes," Verna suggested. "And cookies and tarts and scones. I know for a fact that Earlynne is an excellent baker where those are concerned."

"They can do that," Aunt Hetty agreed. "I gather that Earlynne thinks that's the best solution. Mildred, on the other hand, has the idea that they don't have a *real* bakery unless they can sell bread."

"I agree with Mildred," Bessie said emphatically. "People may not be able to afford cakes and cookies and such, but bread is a basic. Without it, that bakery won't last

272

more than a few months."

"Well, then," Lizzy repeated, "what are they going to do?"

"The question is, what are *we* going to do?" Aunt Hetty replied. "That's why I wanted to talk to you girls. I told Mildred that I would bake a couple of batches for their opening, if they would agree to let me teach her and Earlynne to bake a decent loaf of bread. They're coming over on Sunday to learn how."

"But a couple of batches won't likely be enough," Verna pointed out. "And it takes a while to learn how to bake bread. It's not something you can learn to do overnight." She put three more pieces of blue background together and added them to the puzzle.

"You're right, Verna," Aunt Hetty said. "So that's where all of you come in." She turned to Bessie. "How many loaves can Roseanne produce by nine o'clock tomorrow morning?"

"It depends on how early we get up, I suppose," Bessie said. "Ten loaves, maybe a dozen?"

"And you, Liz?" Aunt Hetty asked.

"I'm not sure," Liz replied doubtfully. "I can bake four loaves at a time in my oven." She calculated. "If I baked three batches, I could produce a dozen by noon, probably."

"When Walter was alive, I used to bake once a week," Verna said. "I'm sure I could do it again."

"Could you bake a dozen loaves?" Aunty Hetty asked.

"Oh, I think so," Verna said, in an off-hand way. "If I have enough flour, that is."

"If you don't, I can give you some," Bessie said.

"Well, then," Aunt Hetty said, with a satisfied smile. "If the four of us can come up with a dozen loaves tomorrow, that's a total of forty-eight loaves. That should be enough for the grand opening, don't you think?"

"And they don't need all four dozen loaves at nine in the morning," Bessie pointed out. "As the first batch sells out, they'll need more, throughout the day." She pulled her brows together. "But what about next week? Do you really think Mildred and Earlynne can learn to bake a decent loaf in time to start baking for customers on Monday?"

"Probably not," Aunt Hetty agreed. "But I can ask the other Dahlias. If we all contribute, I'm sure we can keep them stocked until they're able to do it themselves." She straightened resolutely. "After their first lesson, there'll be more. Lessons, I mean."

Bessie had to laugh at that. "Mildred and

Earlynne don't know what they're in for."

At that point, the grandmother clock whirred and began to chime, and Lizzy looked up. "It's nine o'clock, girls. If this were the contest, our two-hour time limit would be up."

"And we're more than two-thirds done, aren't we?" Bessie asked, surveying the puzzle. "All the blossoms are finished, and the pot is missing just one piece."

"And the background is nearly done," Verna said. "If we hadn't been talking so much, I think we might have finished the whole thing inside our two hours. And this is a bigger puzzle than we'll have for the contest."

"But we had important things to talk about," Lizzy reminded them. She pushed back her chair. "If you don't mind, I think I'll call it quits for tonight. If I'm going to have a batch of loaves ready for The Flour Shop's nine o'clock opening, I'll have to get up very early." She smiled. "Even before my neighbor's rooster."

"Me, too," Verna said.

"Same here," Aunt Hetty agreed. "And you'll keep us posted, Liz? About Cupcake, I mean."

"Oh, absolutely." Lizzy began to break up the puzzle and put the pieces back in the box. "I'll call everybody tomorrow and we can work out the schedule."

Bessie stood up. "Let me get some bags and you can take Roseanne's cookies home with you. She'll be hurt if nobody eats them, you know."

With an effort, Aunt Hetty pushed herself out of her chair. "Bless your hearts," she said, looking around the table. "And thank you very much."

"What for?" Verna asked, helping Lizzy put the puzzle back in the box.

"Why, for being Dahlias, of course." Aunt Hetty reached for her cane. "Dahlias, and friends."

"Amen and praise the Lord," Bessie said over her shoulder. "And don't leave without your cookies."

CHAPTER EIGHTEEN: "ONE PIECE OF THE PUZZLE HERE, ANOTHER PIECE THERE"

Charlie's old green Pontiac didn't have a heater, which meant that on a very cold night, the driver's hands and feet were pretty well frozen by the time he got to wherever he was going. This wasn't much of a problem, usually, given the southern Alabama climate. But tonight it was, since the Cotton Gin Dance Hall — where he was supposed to meet Wilber Casey — was a half hour away, near Monroeville, and the temperature was hovering near freezing. Charlie couldn't help wishing that he had the money for a new Ford V-8. He'd read that the Fords finally had a car heater that actually kept you warm without grilling the soles of your shoes.

But there had been another problem. When he got home that afternoon, Fannie had reminded him of their Friday night movie date, which he had entirely forgotten in the excitement of the prison farm story.

Red Dust, starring Clark Gable and Jean Harlow, was playing at the Palace, catty-cornered across from their apartment. And Fannie (who was crazy about Clark Gable) was eager to see it.

Charlie was too, as a matter of fact, because while he didn't care much for Clark Gable, he'd heard that Harlow took a bath in the movie — not a scene he was likely to see again. The prudish new Hays Code, promoted by the National Legion of Decency, banned such "vile and unwholesome" scenes from Hollywood movies and turned every movie (in Charlie's view) into moralistic pabulum. Even the cartoon character Betty Boop had been censored, transformed from a sexy, flirtatious, short-skirted flapper into a demure career girl in a modest, unrevealing dress. Charlie was pretty sure that he wouldn't have another chance to see Harlow in a bathtub.

So when Fannie reminded him of their date, Charlie flinched. "Aw, gee," he said. "I'm meeting a kid tonight at the Cotton Gin, over at Monroeville. At nine."

"Oh, for heaven's sake, Charlie." Fannie pouted. "Do you *have* to?"

"Afraid so, honey," Charlie replied ruefully. "The boy's name is Wilber Casey — Hamp Casey's nephew. I'm writing a story on the prison farm for the *Dispatch,* and he works in the warden's office. I'm hoping he's going to tell me some things I want to hear."

This was true. Charlie hadn't learned anything he didn't already know from his interview with Warden Burford, so as an undercover assignment for the sheriff (who was coming for breakfast the next morning) the trip to Jericho was pretty much a bust. But Wilber had been a surprise, and a good one. Charlie was convinced that the boy knew something about Bragg's murder — *if* he could get him to talk. It was a big if.

"Well, then, how about if we take in the early show?" Fannie suggested.

"We can do that." Charlie glanced down at his watch. "It's just five-thirty. How about if we walk over to the Diner for supper? Don usually starts running the newsreel at six-thirty. We ought to be out by eight."

But the movie projector at the Palace was old and balky, and Don Greer (the theater's owner) had trouble getting it running. Then the film broke halfway through the third reel and again in the sixth, which cost Charlie an extra box of popcorn. But the bathtub scene (Jean Harlow taking a bath in a barrel), was worth the wait, Charlie thought. Other men thought so too, for there were plenty of whistles and a few admiring ooh-la-las. The women mostly looked shocked, although Leona Ruth Adcock gave an offended *harrumph* and made a big point of walking out. She could be heard in the projection room, threatening to report Mr. Greer to the National Legion of Decency.

It was going on nine by the time Charlie and Fannie left the theater, and Charlie saw that he was going to be late for his meeting with Wilber Casey. "Sorry, honey," he said, and gave her a quick kiss. "I hope I'll be home by midnight. Don't forget — the sheriff is coming for breakfast. I told him you'd make griddle cakes."

Fannie rolled her eyes. "You're meeting some shady character at a dance hall tonight and the sheriff is having breakfast with us tomorrow morning? Something is going on, Charlie. What is it?"

Charlie saw the opening he'd been waiting for. "I'll tell you about it when you tell me what's going on at Warm Springs," he said.

Fannie sucked in her breath. "At Warm . . . Springs?" she said faintly.

"Who is J. C. Carpenter?"

Fannie's eyes were large. "How did you find out?"

"I'm late," Charlie said. "Let's talk about

280

it tomorrow." He gave her a quick kiss and dashed for his car, which was parked behind the apartment.

He was twenty minutes late to the Cotton Gin, which he was sure that the National Legion of Decency would censor if it had a chance. During Prohibition, the roadhouse had earned a racy reputation as a place where you could bring your own bootleg booze. Now, there was a fully stocked bar (although Charlie had heard that Bodeen Pyle was the chief supplier of corn whiskey), and customers were discouraged from bringing their own. They did anyway, but they drank it in the parking lot.

The large, ramshackle old barn had once housed a real gin, where plantation owners and sharecroppers brought their cotton to have the seeds removed before it was baled and sent off to market. Invented by Eli Whitney some 140 years before, the cotton gin was responsible for the explosion in production — and the explosive increase in the number of slaves — that had transformed cotton into an enormously profitable cash crop. By the middle 1800s, Alabama led the nation in "King Cotton" and had evolved into a kingdom run by a class of landed gentry with immense fortunes built on the backs of the slaves. In Charlie's opinion (he fancied himself something of a historian), cotton was the fuel that had fired the Civil War.

But Lincoln had freed the slaves, the plantation economy failed, and it was no longer easy to make a killing in cotton. The boll weevil had migrated north from Mexico before the Great War, devastating the South's cotton fields. In the 1920s, other countries got into the cotton business, and America lost its monopoly on the international market. Now, under the New Deal, the government paid farmers to plow under a third of their cotton crops and keep the fields fallow. There was only one working gin left in Monroeville and another one in Darling. And from the number of cars and trucks parked around the Cotton Gin, Charlie could reasonably suppose that there was a lot more money to be made in the roadhouse business — especially post-Prohibition — than in growing cotton.

It was crisp and cold outside, but inside the rickety old building, the air was hot and steamy, heavy with the odors of cheap booze, sweaty bodies, and cigarette smoke. Charlie also caught a distinctive whiff of marijuana smoke: illegal as sin and just as ubiquitous, in spite of the efforts of the Federal Bureau of Narcotics and the state of Alabama to shut it down. Tables were crowded around a wooden dance floor, where pairs of Lindy Hoppers — more energetic than graceful, and most of them half-drunk — were flinging each other around. In one corner, a jukebox was blaring Bix Beiderbecke's recording of the "Davenport Blues," its volume turned up full blast to compensate for the dancers' pounding feet, loud voices, and raucous laughter. The place was badly lit, what there was of the light pooling in the middle of the large room, leaving the corners shadowed.

It took a moment for Charlie's vision to adjust to the darkness. When it did, he looked over the heads of the crowd to see a long, mirrored bar across the back of the room. He pushed his way through the sea of moving bodies, bought a mug of frosty root beer (he'd stopped drinking to please Fannie), and began looking for Wilber. He finally saw him sitting by himself in a dark corner, his back to the wall, nursing a can of Jax. Charlie almost didn't recognize him, for the boy had traded his prison employee uniform for a white shirt with an open collar and the sleeves rolled up. His ginger hair was rumpled, and he wasn't wearing his glasses.

"Busy night," Charlie said, pulling out a

chair. "Noisy, too."

"Hello, Mr. Dickens." Wilber looked relieved to see him. "I thought maybe you'd decided not to come."

"Now, why would I do that?" Charlie asked. "I promised my wife I'd take her to a movie tonight. Figured we'd be out in plenty of time, but that didn't happen. Sorry."

"Don't be." Wilber grinned. "I like to watch people, and this is a good place to do it. Kinda wish my girl was here, though. I'd rather look at her." His grin faded. "I had to run an errand while you were talking to Warden Burford so I missed you when you left this morning. How did your interview go?"

Charlie shrugged. "Burford gave me a bunch of bull — but that's par for the course. I'll use what's usable and dig some more." He sipped his beer. "That's the name of the game when you're working on a story, you know. You get one piece of the puzzle here, another piece there. You just keep asking questions until you get the whole picture."

Wilber leaned forward, his brown eyes intent. "Mr. Dickens, were you serious when you said that a guy could break into the newspaper business on the strength of a good story?"

"I was." Charlie regarded the boy, then pulled out the carrot again. "Somehow, I have the feeling that you might have a story like that, Wilber. Want to tell me about it?"

Wilber looked down at his beer. "I might," he said guardedly. "But after we talked this morning, I started wondering. Say I know about something that's going on at the prison farm — something that nobody outside the farm knows. Something that's against the law."

"Then you tell me about it on background," Charlie began, "and your name won't —"

"No." Wilber held up a hand, stopping him. "Say I write the story, under *my* name. Say you print it in the *Dispatch*. Then say I get fired at Jericho. What happens next? To me, I mean."

Charlie was taken aback. Wilber hadn't snatched the carrot. He was weighing and measuring it and proposing substitutions.

"Well, there are a lotta variables here," he said slowly, trying to come up with an honest answer. "It depends on the size of the story, the nature of it, the people involved, your skill as a reporter and a writer. It's a crap shoot. The story could die in the *Dispatch,* or it could get picked up by one or more of the wire services. At this point, nobody can say for sure. But beyond all that, it depends on what you want to do with your life, how much you're committed to becoming a newspaperman."

"Oh, I'm committed, all right," Wilber said fiercely. "I'm not staying in that prison for the rest of my life."

"Well, there are other things to consider." Charlie turned his mug in his fingers, making snail trails in the condensate on the glass. "That girl of yours, for instance. And didn't you say that your mother depends on you? It sounds like you've got some personal ties holding you in Darling."

"Yes, to both," the boy said. "I want to marry Evelyn, and I need to make sure my mom is taken care of." He paused uncertainly. "But . . ." His voice trailed off.

"That 'but' tells me a lot right there," Charlie said. "What happens if your story gets picked up and you get a job offer from the AP over in Atlanta? Or up in Chicago. I've seen it happen." Now he was being truly honest. "Are you free to go where the work takes you?"

"I could, I guess." Wilber folded his arms on the table. "But the truth is, I'm a small-town fella. Big cities leave me cold." He gave Charlie a hopeful look. "I was sorta thinking that maybe I could — well, you know. Work with you. At the *Dispatch.* You could teach me the business — reporting, how to run a newspaper, the whole works."

"Ah." And there it was. Only now Charlie wasn't sure who was dangling the carrot.

"If you like my writing, I mean," Wilber added earnestly. "If you think I'm good enough." He reached down and took a manila folder out of a leather bag beside his chair. "I brought you some pieces. It's mostly stuff I wrote for our high school paper, but some of it's more recent." He put the folder on the table between them, adding quietly, "It's okay if you tell me it stinks, Mr. Dickens. I know I've got a lot to learn, but I'm a quick study. I want you to teach me."

Taken aback, Charlie stared at the boy for a moment. He felt in his shirt pocket, took out his Camels, and lit one, pushing the pack across the table to Wilber. Then he put on his glasses, opened the folder, and began to leaf through the papers.

The dim light made reading difficult, but he could see that the pieces were neatly typed in standard-width newspaper columns — the boy knew how to do that, anyway. He skimmed several quickly, stopped here and there to reread, and was impressed.

Whole sentences, grammatically correct. Details in the right order and complete. Sentence length and syntax, no problems. Vocabulary appropriate. Even an interesting turn of phrase here and there. Nothing exciting in terms of content, but that was Darling for you. Nothing ever happened in Darling.

Except, Charlie reminded himself, that Ophelia was deserting him, and he was short a reporter, an advertising manager, and a Linotype operator. He closed the folder.

"This is good stuff for where you are now, Wilber," he said slowly. "I'm a pretty decent judge, and in my opinion, you've got the skills it takes to get started. From there, you can build the rest of what you need." He tipped up his mug and emptied his root beer. But he didn't come here looking for a replacement for Ophelia. He was after something else — and the sheriff was depending on him. He gave the boy a straight look.

"There's a story that's not in this folder, though. The one about Bragg."

"Yeah." Wilber looked troubled. "About Bragg, and . . ." He pushed Charlie's cigarettes back across the table and took a new pack — Lucky Strikes — out of his pocket and clumsily began to open it. "And there's more, Mr. Dickens. I've been thinking about this all day — how much I should tell you, I mean. There's a lot more. I just don't know what to do with it, or how." He fished out a cigarette and lit it with a match.

Charlie stared at the boy for a moment. *More? More than Bragg?* Feeling that it was time to take charge of the situation before it got completely out of his control, he leaned closer.

"Okay. Here's what I'll do. Wilber. You write the story you've got, and I'll take a look at it. If it's ready to go, I'll tell you. If it needs more work, I'll tell you that. I'm your editor, remember? And I'm your publisher. Got that?"

"Wow!" The boy's eyes were shining. "Oh, yes, Mr. Dickens! Yes, sir. I got that. I —"

"Hang on," Charlie said. "While you're writing your story, I'll be writing mine. When I say it's time to publish, *I'm* the one who decides whether we go with my story or yours. If we go with yours, it'll have your name on it. If we go with mine, you can decide whether you want to be named as a source. Either way, there'll be a job for you at the Dispatch. It'll pay peanuts, and include advertising and subscription sales, Linotype and press operation, as well as job press stuff. But you'll get a fair crack at reporting."

Wilber was exuberant. "A job at the Dispatch! Mr. Dickens, I can't tell you how much I —"

Charlie held up one finger. "One condition. Before you write, I have to hear what you've got. And depending on what it is, we may have to involve the sheriff."

"The sheriff?" Wilber frowned.

"As in the law," Charlie said firmly. "We're dealing with a crime here. Right?"

"Well, yes." Wilber's mouth firmed. "More than one."

"I don't think you want to be an accessory after the fact," Charlie said. "I know *I* don't. So you tell me what you've got and we'll take it from there."

Wilber squirmed. "It sounds like you're holding all the cards. I gotta trust you to be square."

Charlie grinned mirthlessly. "That's the way the world works, Wilber." He picked up his mug, saw that it was empty and put it down again. He was remembering what the sheriff had told him about the ballistics test.

"Now, how about we start with what you know about Bragg. Like, he didn't shoot himself with that Colt revolver, did he?"

The boy shook his head. His voice was

very low. "No. Richards shot him, with his own gun. Richards' gun, I mean. He had another that he threw down beside Bragg. That one was the Colt."

"Ah." Charlie took a deep breath. "You *saw* this?"

Wilber nodded mutely.

"Did Richards see you?"

Wilber shook his head. "I know I should have told the sheriff right away, but I was . . . well, I was scared."

"I can't imagine why," Charlie said ironically. "Your word against Richards'. And you're just a kid. Right?"

"Right." The boy gave him a grateful look. "The prison is . . . well, it's got its own laws, and the warden is his own sheriff. I figured I could end up dead real easy, just like Bragg. But then you showed up and I began to think about using the *Dispatch* to go public with what I know. And quitting my job at the prison. Which would make it harder for them to go after me." He chewed his lower lip. "Maybe. Am I wrong?"

Charlie hesitated, wanting to be straight with the boy. "You're not *wrong*," he said slowly. "Bragg was an easy target. But you're not entirely right, either. It depends on how much you know and what the downside is for them. And how fast the sheriff can act."

Certainly, Buddy Norris would be pleased. With an eyewitness, he would be able to get a warrant for Richards' arrest — *and* his gun. The sheriff might be momentarily ticked off that Wilber had been so slow in coming forward, but he would appreciate the boy's predicament. And in the long run, since the case was just coming together, the delay wouldn't make much practical difference. Nobody had been indicted yet.

"All right," he said, looking around for an ashtray, "that's Bragg. But I'm guessing there's more." Not finding one, he dropped his cigarette on the floor and stepped on it. "What else have you got?"

Wilber leaned forward, lowered his voice, and told him, in detail. It took a few moments, while the music from the jukebox slowed to "Mood Indigo" and dancers crowded onto the floor until they were packed as tight as dill spears in a pickle jar.

"Well, I'll be damned," Charlie said when the boy had finished his story. Now he really *was* surprised. "How long has this been going on?"

"I haven't been out there, but I know they're pretty far along. I've overheard the warden and the others talking about it, and I've seen the invoices for supplies and equipment. I even know where they're doing it — a place out by the river they call the Back Forty. I can draw you a map if you want." He paused. "Do you want to hear more?"

Charlie stared. "There's more to tell?"

"Oh, you bet," Wilber said grimly, and lit another cigarette.

CHAPTER NINETEEN: "THE DAHLIAS TAKE CARE OF THEIR OWN"

Saturday, December 22

"Well, it's finally here." Mildred unlocked the back door of The Flour Shop. "Opening day." Never mind that it was pitch black outside on a bone-chilling December morning when everybody else in Darling was warmly cocooned in their beds, with another hour or more to sleep.

"I can't believe it." Earlynne's breath was a steamy cloud. "It's happening at last. It seems impossible!"

"Seems entirely possible to me," Mildred said grumpily. She pushed the door open, fumbling for the light switch. "Especially given all the elbow grease we've used on this place. All the hours it took to scrub and paint. All the repairs —"

She switched on the overhead light and gasped loudly, frozen in place.

"What's wrong?" Behind her, Earlynne gave her a hard push. "Don't stand in the door, Mildred. Don't —" She gasped, too. "Oh, no! No, no, *no!*"

When they left just before midnight the night before, the old kitchen had positively sparkled. The green linoleum was scrubbed within an inch of its life, the counters and sink and refrigerator and stove and large oven gleamed, the white-painted walls shone, and the new shelves were neatly stacked with sacks of sugar and flour and jars of home-canned fruit, as well as bowls of rising dough and trays of shaped pastries in their second rising, ready to be popped into the oven first thing this morning.

But the sparkling kitchen was now a wreck. There were drifts of flour and sugar everywhere. Bowls of rising dough had fallen onto the floor and broken, spilling the dough in soft, spongy heaps. Large shards of broken Mason jars lay amid puddles of canned apples and peaches. A tray of rising dinner rolls lay upside down on top of two of Earlynne's cookbooks. And in the shadowy darkness of the top shelf, just above eyelevel, sat a fat, fluffy, furry creature, mostly black with a wide white streak —

"Skunk!" shrieked Earlynne, wrapping her arms around herself as if she were about to be attacked. "Mildred, get the broom!

You've got to get that skunk out of here before it —"

"Wait," Mildred commanded. Picking her way through the litter of broken crockery and mounds of sticky dough, she advanced cautiously toward the animal.

It looked down on her with amber eyes and politely inquired, "Meow?" Beside it on the shelf was a large gray mouse, headless and very dead.

"Mrs. Hancock's cat, from the grocery store," Mildred said, much relieved. "His name is Smudge." She reached up and took him down. With the cat in one arm, she picked up the dead mouse by the tail. "He must have come in after this mouse, and the two of them had a tussle."

"Put that cat out!" Earlynne cried, with a stamp of her foot. "I never want to see the wretched creature again!"

"Thank goodness he isn't a skunk," Mildred said, showing Smudge and his mouse the back door. "That would have been worse."

Helplessly, Earlynne threw up her hands. "But just *look* at this mess!" she wailed. "Broken glass and china all over the floor, all that wonderful dough and those lovely peaches and apples, all totally lost! We'll never get it cleaned up in time to —"

"We won't as long as you stand there sniveling," Mildred snapped, taking charge. "I'll get a box for the glass. You clean up a counter space where you can start making replacements for the batches we lost. But first —" She headed for the electric coffee maker on the shelf beside the stove. "Coffee," she muttered. "I will not survive this debacle without coffee."

It took a full thirty minutes of frantic work to clean up the mess, fueled by several cups of hot, black coffee. But at last the floor was clean again, the sacks of flour and sugar (partly depleted) were replaced on the shelves, and Earlynne had finished mixing up the dough to replace the batches Mrs. Hancock's cat had spoiled. And Mildred had found out how Smudge had got into the kitchen in the first place, via a loose vent cover in the wall, which she fixed with a few turns of a screwdriver.

Earlynne had turned on the oven and headed for the pastry case in the front room of the shop, where she slid open the glass doors and pulled out two trays of oven-ready croissants that had been resting overnight, the yeasty dough plumping up, safely away from the marauding cat. She carried them into the kitchen.

"Aren't they *gorgeous*?" she asked, as she

slid the trays into the hot oven. "I'm glad I put them into the display case, where that beastly animal couldn't get to them." She sighed. "Oh, I hope people will love them!"

For once, Mildred couldn't think of a single quibble. Indeed, Earlynne's croissants were gorgeous, and yes, she hoped people would love them — especially because she knew the amount of love and attention Earlynne had invested in the croissant dough, rolling it out, rolling the chilled butter out to the right size, then stacking the butter and the dough together, turning and folding it like a book. And then doing it again and again, until at last she cut the rolled dough into neat little triangles, shaped the triangles into croissants, and finally baked them.

Mildred knew that for Earlynne, this was a labor of pure love — love of the dough, love of the process, and love of the people who would enjoy the flaky perfection of each perfect croissant. And for the first time in their decades-long friendship, she allowed herself to see how Earlynne's patient dedication to her craft made her the person she was — and to appreciate that. She faced the day with a new understanding of her friend.

After she repaired the damage Smudge had caused in pursuit of his mouse, Mildred had turned on the lights in the shop and began getting ready for their first customers. She put a mat on the floor in front of the door, because the radio weather forecast predicted rain and cold temperatures. She installed a new paper tape in the cash register and put thirty dollars in bills and coins into the cash drawer. She set their new scale on the counter next to the register, to weigh bulk items or things they might sell by the pound. She stowed paper bags and boxes under the counter, along with string to tie up the boxes. She put fresh white paper doilies on the shelves in the glass display case, to make their baked goods — scones and gingerbread and cinnamon buns and orange nut bread and lemon tarts — look even prettier, and a large glass bowl of holiday cookies on the top of the case, with a neatly lettered sign that said "Free! One to a customer, please."

And finally, she placed one pot of Aunt Hetty's bright red poinsettias on the counter and the other in the front display window. Along with the Christmas tree and the cookies and little gingerbread houses she had decorated, the poinsettias brought a note of wonderful Christmas cheer to the shop. As she paused to take a look around, checking to make sure that everything had been done, she found herself smiling happily. The shop looked wonderful, absolutely wonderful, she thought, as she put on a fresh white apron and got ready to greet their first customers.

But there was still the difficult matter of bread.

Mildred had told Earlynne about her desperate visit with Aunt Hetty the day before, and Aunt Hetty's generous pledge to help them out with a couple of batches of fresh loaves — in return for their promise to go to her house on Sunday for a lesson on how to bake bread.

To put it mildly, Earlynne had not been enthusiastic. "I hate for Aunt Hetty to see what an utter bumbler I am about bread-baking," she said. "What's more, Henry and I were planning to visit his parents on Sunday." She turned down the corners of her mouth. "I think it's a waste of time. But if you insist —"

"It's Aunt Hetty who's insisting," Mildred interrupted. "And since she has offered to help us out with the opening, I think we have an obligation. Don't you?"

Earlynne sighed and rolled her eyes, but she finally said yes. So when Aunt Hetty walked through the front door promptly at eight forty-five, bearing a box filled with a dozen beautiful loaves of home-baked bread, Mildred could tell her to expect both her new students right after church the next day.

"Wonderful!" Aunt Hetty held out the box. "Why don't you put these loaves into that lovely new display case of yours while I look around and see which of Earlynne's pastries I'd like to buy. I know you're not open yet, but —"

"Oh, please!" Mildred said. "Choose whatever you'd like, Aunt Hetty. It's on the house. We're just so grateful to have this wonderful bread!"

Mildred arranged Aunt Hetty's beautifully browned bread in beautifully neat rows, with a small sign that said "Baked FRESH this morning! Only 11¢ a loaf." By the time she was finished, Aunt Hetty had picked out a lemon tart, a sticky bun, and a scone.

"Are you sure this is all you want?" Mildred asked, putting the items into a bag. "Wouldn't you like to have a few —"

"No, thank you," Aunt Hetty said. "I do my own baking, you know." She added, enigmatically: "If you sell out of my bread, don't despair. There's more on the way."

Mildred was too busy to give that mysterious comment much thought. Soon after Aunt Hetty left, she placed the "Open" sign in the front window, the little brass bell over the front door began to tinkle, and Darling people started flocking in. They came by ones and twos, sometimes by threes — so many at one time that Earlynne had to put on a clean apron and come to the front to help out for a while.

Mildred had always liked talking to people, and standing behind the counter of her very own shop gave her an unexpected thrill — especially since almost all of the Darling folks came with a smile and a warm "Congratulations on your opening!" Several brought cute handmade cards, two of the Dahlias brought winter bouquets of chrysanthemums and asters, and Mildred's neighbor Mrs. Rooker brought a cute little painted-rock doorstop and a flyswatter decorated with ribbons, to be used in warmer weather. As the gifts accumulated, The Flour Shop began to seem more and more homelike.

And the baked goods simply flew off the shelves. Bob Denny's wife Clara bought a loaf of bread and a small carrot cake. Henrietta Conrad, a telephone operator at the Darling Exchange, bought four doughnuts and a loaf of bread. Bettina Higgens, Beulah Trivette's associate at the Beauty Bower, bought a loaf for herself and one for

Beulah, plus a half-dozen scones for the ladies who were getting their hair done that morning. Mrs. Lima (the wife of Lester Lima, who owned the drugstore) bought eight cupcakes, a gingerbread house for her grandson Little Elmer, and a loaf for herself and another for Little Elmer's mother. Pauline DuBerry, from the Marigold Motor Court, bought two loaves and two sticky buns. Everybody complimented Mildred on her window display and said how Christmassy the shop looked. And when Mildred said, "Please come back," each one said, "Oh, I will!" or "You can count on it," or "Sure thing!"

And so it went, in spite of the chilly wind and dreary skies — not the best kind of day for a grand opening, Mildred thought. Around ten that morning, when Earlynne brought in more trays of sweet and savory baked goods to fill the empty spaces in the display case, every single one of Aunt Hetty's beautiful home-baked loaves had been sold. Mildred was making a small "Out of bread — SORRY!" sign for the empty spot in the display case, when Bessie Bloodworth came in, carrying a shopping bag.

"A dozen loaves from Roseanne and me, as a grand opening present for The Flour

Shop," she said, putting the shopping bag on the counter.

Mildred stared at her. "A . . . dozen loaves?" she managed. "Oh, my goodness! Why, that's . . . that's *wonderful,* Bessie! However can we thank you?"

"Thank Aunt Hetty," Bessie said. "It was her idea." She smiled. "You don't get to be eighty-something without having a passel of good ideas."

And at that point, a light bulb went off in Mildred's brain, as she understood Aunt Hetty's mysterious remark. "Ah," she said. And then, "Who else?"

"Liz and Verna, that I know of," Bessie said. "And maybe more, next week. The Dahlias take care of their own, you know." She leaned over the display case. "Oh, what *cute* Christmas cupcakes, Mildred! I'll take six, for my dear Magnolia Ladies, plus Roseanne and me. And give me six of those gorgeous croissants, too. Earlynne is quite the baker, isn't she?"

"No, it's on the house," Mildred said, as Bessie opened her pocketbook.

"Not on your life, dear," Bessie said sweetly. "The bread is a gift. Let's not make it a trade."

With a grateful smile, Mildred went to arrange Roseanne's bread on the shelf — just in time for Mrs. Hart, from Hart's Peerless Laundry on the other side of the square, to buy two loaves, as well as cupcakes for all the little Harts, some gingerbread, and two croissants.

"We've been so *busy* at the laundry," Mrs. Hart told Mildred, speaking in her customary italics and exclamation points. "I just don't have *time* to bake the way I *used* to, and I know my poor family must feel *utterly deprived*! It's so *lovely* to run over here and pick up a few sweet treats for Mr. Hart and the kiddies." She waved her hand at the shelves in the display case. *"Everything* looks so *tasty,* just like home-baked. You tell Earlynne I said Darling *needs* you! *Both of you!"*

"Thank you," Mildred said. "I'll tell her."

They had just sold out of Roseanne's bread (which was every bit as pretty as Aunt Hetty's) when Liz Lacy appeared just before noon. She had a shopping bag in one hand and was holding a little girl's hand in the other. The child wore a bright red wool coat, red and green stockings with black patent leather Mary Janes, and a red wool bonnet over her strawberry blond curls.

"I've brought you more bread," Liz said. Glancing at the display case, where Mildred had just stuck the "Out of bread — SORRY!" sign, she said, "Looks like you've already sold out. Now, you can take your sign down." She handed over her sack.

"We sold out twice," Mildred said. She peeked into the sack. "Oh, just look at that wonderful bread. Liz, you are an angel!"

Liz smiled. "I know I speak for all your friends when I say how much we want you to succeed, Mildred. Darling needs a bakery!"

Mildred came around the corner and gave her a hug. "You have no idea how much your support means to us — you and all the other Dahlias." She bent down and gave the little girl a kiss. "My goodness, Cupcake, you are as cute as a bug's ear today. Where are you going, all dressed up in that pretty red coat?"

"To Aunt Opie's house," Cupcake replied excitedly, bouncing up and down. "Aunt Liz and I are playing 'Hide the Cupcake.' It's like hide and seek, only better!"

Liz put a finger to her lips. "Sssh, honey. You know, if you tell people where you're hiding, they might find you!"

"Oops!" the little girl said. Blue eyes sparkling, she clapped her mittened hand over her mouth. "I forgot! The game is supposed to be a *big* secret! So please don't tell *anybody*, Aunt Mildred. Please?"

"I won't," Mildred said. "But to celebrate

your secret game, you should take some holiday cookies to Aunt Opie's house. Let me get you some." She filled a sack with a dozen of the prettiest ones and handed it to Liz, lowering her voice. "Is something going on here?"

"I'm afraid so," Liz said. "But I'll have to tell you later. Cupcake, we need to be on our way. Say thank you to Aunt Mildred for the lovely cookies."

"Thank you, Aunt Mildred," Cupcake said, and made a little curtsey.

"You're welcome, Cupcake," Mildred said, and waved goodbye as they left the shop. She was curious about the secret game they were playing, but she didn't have time to think about it. Mrs. Hazelwood (the Baptist minister's wife) came in and bought the last carrot cake and two loaves of the bread Mildred was putting into the display case.

"Wonder Bread is fine with me," she said, "but Reverend Hazelwood's favorite story is the miracle of the loaves and fishes. He will be so pleased when he sees this home-baked bread. You'll be selling it from now on?"

"We certainly hope to," Mildred said, tempted to tell Mrs. Hazelwood that they had experienced their very own miracle of the loaves that morning. But she didn't. It was just the sort of story the Reverend would love to tell his Sunday School class, and before long, it would be all over Darling.

Liz's bread lasted until just before two. When it was gone, Verna Tidwell came in with enough to take care of the rest of the day's customers. When all was said and done and Mildred had put the Closed sign into the front window, she calculated that they had sold forty-six loaves (there were only two left on the shelf in the display case), all of them contributed by the Dahlias' Puzzle Divas: Liz, Verna, Bessie, and Aunt Hetty.

As well, they had sold all but a few of the sweet and savory pastries and treats that Earlynne had baked. Mildred put what was left on a tray and took it to the kitchen, where Earlynne was finishing the prep for early Monday morning. All signs of Smudge's mouse-killing spree had been cleaned up, and everything was back in its place. Happily, Mildred passed along Mrs. Hart's compliment, Verna's remark, and the good words of other customers, and reported on their sales.

"Forty-six loaves of bread!" Earlynne exclaimed, her eyes wide. *"Forty-six?* You're sure? Mildred, that's amazing! Why, that's over five dollars, just in bread!"

"I told you so," Mildred murmured, but not very loud.

Still, Earlynne heard her. "Yes, you did," she said contritely. "And I have to tell you that I was wrong. You said bread would be our best seller, and it was. I apologize." In a lower voice, she said, "There's no two ways about it. I am going to have to learn to bake bread. When we go for our lesson tomorrow, I'm going to put my heart into it."

Mildred shook her head. "Bread might have been our single best-selling item. But almost your entire stock of baked goods has disappeared." She gestured at the tray. "People loved your croissants, Earlynne. And the cupcakes and the carrot cake and the gingerbread and the cookies. I was wrong when I said that you were baking too many different items. I'm sorry."

"It's very nice of you to say that," Earlynne replied softly. "But I —"

Mildred stopped her. "No, let me finish. All day, I watched people hesitating among their choices. Everything was so tempting that they couldn't decide what to buy. So they bought two or three or even four or five *different* things instead of just one or two. They said they were sampling, and everybody promised that they would be back for more of what they liked. You are right to insist on putting out a wide selection. People might come into the shop for bread, but they leave with lots more."

Mildred paused for a moment, thinking how remarkable it was that she and Earlynne had just traded apologies — unrehearsed, impulsive, and spontaneous apologies — almost without noticing.

And that it actually felt *good*.

CHAPTER TWENTY:
"AS SERIOUS AS IT GETS
IN DARLING"

While Darling folk were getting their first taste of The Flour Shop's irresistible bakery goods, Sheriff Buddy Norris was having a different kind of day.

It had begun at seven-thirty that morning at the Dickens' second-floor flat over Fannie Champaign's hat shop, next door to the new bakery. Breakfast was prepared by Fannie herself, who (in addition to being a well-known milliner and Charlie Dickens' wife) had a reputation as a pretty darned good cook. On the table in the apartment's small kitchen, she had put a king-sized platter of griddle cakes, fried ham, and fried eggs, a china pitcher of red-eye gravy, a basket of biscuits, a small pottery jug of maple syrup and a jar of raspberry jelly, glasses of orange juice, and cups of coffee.

"Wow," Buddy said, blinking. "This is nothing like Mrs. Beedle's breakfasts. What a feast! Thank you."

"Coffee pot's on the stove," Fannie said briskly. "You boys help yourselves when you're ready for more. I'm going downstairs to work on a hat." And then she had left the room so Buddy and Charlie could have a private conversation while they ate.

That was when Buddy learned about Wilber Casey, who had taken Jimmie Bragg's job as Warden Burford's assistant at Jericho. Charlie had met the young man at the Cotton Gin the night before and had plenty to report. Like any experienced newspaperman, Charlie had practically perfect recall of the details. Listening, Buddy was more and more surprised — and satisfied. By the time he'd used the last bit of biscuit to sop up the last delicious bit of red-eye gravy, he was shaking his head in genuine wonderment.

"Holy cow," he said reverently. "The kid actually *saw* Sergeant Richards shoot Jimmie Bragg? With the sergeant's own gun?"

Mr. Moseley was going to like this news, Buddy thought. Now that they had an eyewitness, they could get a warrant for Richards' arrest. They could get his gun, too, and Wayne could test it. Maybe also send it off to Chicago for a test that would stand up better in court.

"There's more," Charlie said. "Wilber says

that Richards was ordered to kill Bragg — by Warden Burford. He says he can document that, too. He didn't go into detail, and I haven't seen his evidence. But I believe him."

Buddy whistled. "Better and better." Now they were talking conspiracy, in addition to the other charges.

"Yeah." Charlie lathered jam on a biscuit. "Wilber is a smart kid. He'll be a pretty convincing witness when the case goes to trial. Too bad he didn't come forward earlier, huh?"

"Some crimes don't get wrapped up overnight," Buddy said, sounding wiser than he felt. But knowing *who* didn't answer all the questions. Thoughtfully, he added, "We still need to know why." If the warden had ordered the killing, why did he do it? Why did he want Bragg dead?

But there was more. It turned out that young Wilber Casey had a secret hankering to be an investigative reporter. He had begun paying attention to some of the more intriguing items that crossed his desk on their way to and from the warden. As a result, the boy was now privy to some enterprising skullduggery on the part of Grover Burford, who — it was becoming clear — was hardly the model manager the state prison board thought he was.

According to Wilber, the warden treated the prison as his own personal profit center. His sins ran the gamut from overcharging for prison labor and prison-raised crops and products (the profits going into Burford's personal checking accounts in out-of-state banks), to smuggling in girls of questionable moral character for weekends at the warden's residence, recently renovated to include a fancy spa and a well-stocked wet bar. And operating a bootleg corn whiskey still in a remote corner of the prison farm informally called the Back Forty. When he heard this, Buddy couldn't help breaking into a big smile. It was confirmation of the rumor that Bodeen Pyle had heard.

What's more, Wilber hadn't been content to simply raise an eyebrow as these criminal evidences slid across his desk. He had made notes of names, dates, invoice numbers, amounts, and (where he thought it might be useful) copied the information into a small pocket notebook. Buddy was glad to hear this, although he fervently hoped that most of it would turn out to be somebody else's enforcement problem.

"Bootlegging was the thing I couldn't quite get my head around," Charlie said. He pointed to the last pancake on the platter. "You want that, Sheriff?"

"No, thanks," Buddy said, pushing back his plate. "I am full up to the gills." He took out a cigarette and lit it. "What is it you don't quite get about making shine?"

Charlie poured syrup on the pancake. "It just seems, well, stupid. I mean, it's one thing to set up a small still and make enough whiskey to keep the local boys happy. But it's another thing altogether to go into the distillery business — with a plan to distribute it all over the state."

Buddy was surprised. "Is that what the kid told you?"

"Pretty much. And according to him, he's got documentation. Supplies, plans, stuff like that. He even knows where the still is located, more or less. Or says he does." He hesitated. "Is that something you have to act on?"

Remembering his conversation with Mr. Moseley, Buddy shook his head. "The Jericho still — if there is one — isn't the county's business. I'll probably be working with Agent Kinnard."

Charlie finished the pancake. "Well, if you ask me, Wilber is putting himself into some personal danger." He looked up, his expression serious. "Bragg may have been killed because he knew too much about what was going on out there at the prison farm. The same thing could happen to Wilber, couldn't it?"

"It could," Buddy said slowly. It was certainly true that young Casey was putting himself in jeopardy. And Richards was, too. If Burford had had anything to do with the Bragg murder, was there anything to keep him from silencing Richards, permanently? He could probably get away with it, too. Bury his body in some distant corner of the farm, and nobody would be the wiser.

Buddy stubbed out his cigarette in the ashtray Charlie had put on the table. "I owe you a big one, Dickens. You got a helluva lot more information out of that trip to the farm than I figured. After I leave here, I'm walking across the street to let the county attorney know about this. I'm thinking we ought to get moving on this in a hurry. It might save us some time if you were there to answer Moseley's questions. What do you say?"

"Sounds like a plan." Charlie stood up and began collecting their plates. "Give me a few minutes, though. I have a deal with Fannie. When she cooks, I wash the dishes."

"Fine with me," Buddy said. "If you'll find me a towel, I'll dry."

■ ■ ■ ■

After a brief strategy session with Mr. Moseley, Buddy and Charlie drove to Wilber Casey's mother's house outside of Darling, where they invited the young man to have a conversation with the county attorney. He was reluctant at first, but Charlie persuaded him that they needed him to clinch the case and that it would be a good idea if he co-operated.

"Moseley can get a warrant for those notes of yours," Buddy said. "But it would be better if you'd hand them over voluntarily."

Charlie added, "If you're still interested in being a reporter for the *Dispatch,* that is."

Wilber looked from one of them to the other, apprehension written on his face. "This is serious, huh?"

"It is," Buddy said quietly. "There are two cases here, Wilber. One is Bragg's murder, which will be tried here in Cypress County. The other is Burford's corrupt private empire, which the state will investigate. You're key in both of them."

"And you're in a hot spot, my boy." Charlie's tone was sympathetic. "Not to put too fine a point on it, but if the warden

317

figures out just how much you know, you could get what Bragg got."

Wilber squared his shoulders. "I'll come," he said. "And bring my notes."

Back in Darling, Charlie headed for the Dispatch office, while Buddy took Wilber upstairs to talk to Mr. Moseley. The attorney questioned the young man in a low-key, nonthreatening way. Moving quickly from one point to another, he confirmed that Wilber claimed to have actually seen Richards shoot Bragg as he was ordered to do by the warden, and that he knew about and had documented many of Burford's corrupt extracurricular activities. Nodding approvingly, he scanned Wilber's notes, then got up from his desk and locked them in his safe.

Coming back to his desk, he said, "You've done a good job, Wilber. Your documentation will help us decide what charges to file, and you'll be a valuable witness when both of these cases come to trial. But if I were you, I think I'd take a little trip out of town. Do you have a friend you could stay with for a little while? Just to be on the safe side, until we get this thing wrapped up."

Nervously, the boy pushed his glasses up on his nose. "Well, my Uncle Hamp has a place up on the Alabama River —"

"I've got a better idea," Mr. Moseley interrupted. "There are some papers I need to have delivered to my office in Montgomery. How about if you take them up there for me, today? I'll get my associate, Mr. Jackman, to fix you up with a place to stay. You can see the sights and take in a few shows."

"Montgomery?" Wilber asked excitedly. "Gee, Mr. Moseley, that would be *swell*. Thanks!"

"Thank *you*." Mr. Moseley gave him a straight look. "By the way, it might not be a good idea to tell your uncle where to find you. No point in spreading the news."

Wilber frowned. "You don't think —"

"I don't *know*," Mr. Moseley said. "So let's just keep it quiet, shall we?" He put a piece of paper and a pencil on his desk. "Before you go, I'd like you to draw us a map that will take us to Burford's still."

"Sure thing," Wilber said confidently. "It's not hard to find, if you know where to look. And how to get there."

Mr. Moseley chuckled. "That's true about a lot of things." He turned to Buddy. "Sheriff, I'll write up a warrant for you to take to Judge McHenry. I want you and Wayne to pick up Richards this morning. Get that gun, too. We need the gun."

"Yes, *sir,*" Buddy said. "What about Agent Kinnard?"

"I talked to him yesterday." Mr. Moseley grinned. "Don't worry, Sheriff. You won't have to handle it on your lonesome."

"I'm happy to hear *that,*" Buddy muttered.

Mr. Moseley's grin faded. "But before you go, you and I need to have a little talk." To Buddy's inquiring glance, he added, "It's about Violet Sims' little girl."

"Cupcake?" Buddy asked. He was very fond of the child and looked forward to seeing her dance when he stopped at the Diner for lunch, usually on Wednesdays (when Raylene served fried chicken) and on Fridays (when Euphoria's meatloaf topped the menu). "She's not sick, is she? I would sure hate to hear that."

"No, she's not sick," Mr. Montgomery replied. "But there's trouble all the same. I may need your help, Sheriff. In your official capacity."

"You got it," Buddy said fervently. "I'd do just about anything for that sweet little girl."

"Glad to hear that," Mr. Moseley said. "You may have to."

Judge McHenry was still in his bathrobe, sitting beside the living room fireplace with his feet in a pan of warm water and Epsom salts, reading the *Mobile Press Register*. The old man was close to eighty, with a head of shaggy white hair and white bushy eyebrows above piercing blue eyes. He peered over his glasses as Buddy explained why he had come, handed him the warrant for Horace Richards' arrest, and asked him to sign it.

"First degree murder, huh?" the old man said, reading over the warrant. "Seems like you young fellas are makin' a habit of pokin' your noses into other folks' business. Don't recall Roy Burns ever asking me for a warrant to arrest a Jericho guard."

Sheriff Burns probably knew better, Buddy admitted to himself. "It's an unusual situation," he said aloud. "Mr. Moseley said that if you had any questions, just pick up the telephone and give him a call. But now that we've located an eyewitness —"

"Who isn't named here." The judge thumped the warrant. "Is this character somebody who knows what he's talking about? Is he goin' to be a credible witness if this case goes to trial?"

Buddy swallowed. "He's Hamp Casey's nephew, Judge. He works in the warden's office. And now that we've located him, we figure we'd better move fast on Richards. There are other —"

The judge broke in. "Wonder what old Hamp is gonna do when he finds out about this. Him and that warden play a lot of poker together, I understand."

"Yessir," Buddy replied. "But as I was saying, there are other considerations —"

"There gen'rally are." The judge said gave Buddy a narrow look. "You reckon on serving this today, boy?"

"As soon as I can."

"Then you'd better stop wastin' time talkin' to me and get on with it," the judge said, and signed the warrant with a flourish of his pen.

Buddy found his deputy reading a *True Detective* magazine at his desk in the sheriff's office. "Come on, Wayne," he said. "We've got a job to do."

Wayne closed his magazine and put it into a drawer. "What kind of job?"

Buddy went into his office. Over his shoulder, he said. "We're arresting Sergeant Horace Richards, the guard at Jericho. On suspicion of murder."

Wayne whistled between his teeth. "Sounds like we'll be earning our pay today. Such as it is," he added ironically.

With a sigh, Buddy reached for his gun belt, which was hanging on the back of the door. He buckled it on and took his .38 out of the safe in his office. He had considered not wearing his gun when they went to pick up Richards, on the theory that if he wasn't armed, he'd be less likely to shoot somebody and maybe less likely to be shot. But Buddy had met the man once, on the day that Bragg was murdered. He was about as big as an elephant. He wasn't exactly cordial, either, and Buddy thought he would likely be aggravated when he was arrested. It was a reasonable assumption.

So like it or not, he figured he'd better go armed. Anyway, Wayne always wore his gun, and it wasn't fair to depend on his deputy to shoot and be shot at while he stood by with his hands in his pockets.

When he came out of his office, Wayne eyed his holster. "Hey," he said, raising both eyebrows. "Looks like we're in for some serious business today."

"As serious as it gets in Darling," Buddy said. "You ready?"

Wayne took out his .38 Special and spun the cylinders — the way, Buddy thought, they did it in the movies. "All set," he said cheerily. "You driving or am I?"

"I am," Buddy said. "We're bringing back a prisoner."

That was the plan, anyway. When he was

a deputy, he had ridden his Indian Ace motorcycle, which had got him pretty much anywhere he wanted to go. Now that he was sheriff, he drove Roy Burns' black Model T. He had converted it into a patrol car by installing a strip of hog wire between the front seat and the back. Now, he could haul a prisoner without worrying whether the fellow was going to grab him around the neck and try to throttle him or snatch his gun.

Buddy hitched his holster around so that it rode better on his hip. "Come on," he said. "Let's get this damned thing over with."

Wilber Casey had told Buddy that Sergeant Richards stayed in the Jericho guards' barracks only during the week. He spent weekends at his place out past the cemetery — a house and barn and a few acres of scrub timber — which was where he was likely to be on a Saturday morning. Buddy was glad when he heard this. He hadn't been thrilled by the thought of arresting the man at the prison, where the odds were something like four hundred to one, and not in his favor. Including Wayne didn't markedly improve the odds, either. Four hundred to two wasn't much better.

Richards' house was about five miles west of Darling. It was a rundown frame building, no more than four rooms, with an open porch across the front and a screened porch on the back. There was a bucket of coal beside the front door, an ax and a two-man crosscut saw propped against the wall, and chickens — black-and-white Barred Rocks, a rooster and a half-dozen hens — scratching in the front yard. A brick chimney, leaning slightly to the left, leaked smoke, and as Buddy got out of the car, he could smell bacon frying.

"Seems like our man is at home," Wayne said.

"Yeah," Buddy said, without enthusiasm. He had parked behind a dense stand of bushes that screened the car from the house. "You go around to the back door, Wayne. Just in case he decides to make a break for it out the rear." He thought Richards was man enough to tough it out, but he couldn't count on it. "If I yell, you come on around front."

He waited until he thought Wayne had time to get set at the back of the house, then walked up the dirt path to the screen door, opened it, and rapped smartly on the closed wooden door.

"Richards," he called, making his voice

sound deeper than it usually was. "Horace Richards, this is Sheriff Norris. We got to have a talk. You come out here on the porch so we can do this peaceable-like."

Inside the house, a dog barked. It sounded, Buddy thought, like a *big* dog. He rapped on the door again, louder this time. "Come on out, Richards, hands on your head. I have a warrant for your arrest."

What happened next happened fast. A slamming door somewhere inside the house. A flurry of excited barks and heavy running footsteps, elephant-sized footsteps. Another slamming door, at the back of the house. Then Wayne's voice, rough and angry.

"Stop, police! Stop, you sonuvabitch! Stop!"

Then a gunshot.

Buddy pulled his gun and sprinted around to the back of the house. Richards was face down on the path, Wayne astride of him. On the path lay a revolver.

"What happened?" Buddy asked breathlessly.

"He came barreling out the back door and I tackled him," Wayne said. "He's out. Must've hit his head when he fell. And pulled the trigger. Gunshot went wild." He unclipped a pair of handcuffs from his belt, jerked Richards' arms around behind his

326

back, and cuffed him. He stood up and nudged the revolver with his toe. "Smith and Wesson .44. What do you want to bet it'll test as the gun that killed Bragg?"

"I hope," Buddy said. He tried not to feel too relieved that there hadn't been any serious shooting. "You stay here. I'll pull the car around and we can put him in the back seat. With luck, he won't wake up until we get him back to the office."

He did. But he was cuffed and his ankles were securely tied, so there wasn't a heckuva lot he could do except curse. Which he did. A blue streak.

Buddy was amazed. He thought he had a pretty wide vocabulary. But listening to Richards, he felt like a babe in the woods.

Mr. Moseley (who as county attorney would prosecute Richards when his case went to trial) came over to the sheriff's office to talk to the prisoner. He sat behind Buddy's desk, Richards in a chair front of him. In one corner, Wayne took notes. In the other corner, Buddy sat with folded arms, watching and listening.

Richards was now dressed in the gray jail coverall provided by Cypress County, but it was a size too small, and the buttons strained across his chest. He hadn't shaved for a couple of days, his dark hair hung down in his face, and his face and neck were sweaty, even though the office was about as cold, Buddy thought, as the inside of Mrs. Beedle's icebox. He was also surly and uncommunicative, until Mr. Moseley told him that an eyewitness was willing to testify that he had seen him shoot Jimmie Bragg. And that his Smith and Wesson would be subjected to a ballistics test that would prove that it was the gun that had fired the fatal bullet — the bullet that had *not* been fired by the Colt that Richards had left at the scene.

"What the *hell*?" he shouted. "An eyewitness? You're lying! Wasn't nobody around to —" He stopped abruptly.

"First degree murder gets you twenty to ninety-nine years," Mr. Moseley said in a conversational tone. "On the high side, I reckon, since you attempted to conceal your crime by throwing down that Colt. And no possibility of parole."

"You're tellin' me somebody seen it?" Richards' eyes narrowed. "Who, man?"

Mr. Moseley took out his pipe. "On the other hand," he went on, "I might consider manslaughter. Two to ten." He fished a pouch of tobacco out of his shirt pocket and began filling it. "Up to you, Mr. Richards."

Richards hunched his shoulders. "What do you mean, up to me?"

Mr. Moseley let the silence lengthen as he tamped down the tobacco in his pipe. At last he said, "I doubt that you killed Jimmie Bragg on your own personal say-so." He put the pouch back in his pocket. "Did you?"

Richards was silent.

Mr. Moseley took out a book of paper matches and lit his pipe. "You tell us who put you up to it, and I might let you plead to a lesser charge."

Richards shifted uneasily. "Lesser . . . charge?"

"Manslaughter." Mr. Moseley pulled on his pipe. "Ten years. Possibility of parole."

"Immunity. Give me immunity and I'll tell you everything I know." As an afterthought, Richards added, "Anyway, I want a lawyer."

"Fine." Mr. Moseley pushed his chair back and stood. "You get yourself a lawyer. I can recommend Tommy Knight. He's won a couple of cases this year. But you *killed* a man, Mr. Richards. Immunity is not an option."

"It wasn't my idea!" Richards protested. "I just —" He mopped his sweaty forehead with the back of his hand.

"The plea deal is a one-time offer," Mr. Moseley said. "Nonrenewable. In fact —"

329

He looked at his watch. "It's on the table for two minutes only. Starting right now." He turned and walked to the window, standing with his back to Richards.

"Who is this so-called eyewitness?" Richards demanded.

Mr. Moseley put his hands in his pockets. "Looking damned cold out there, isn't it?" he said, to nobody in particular. "Wonder if it's going to snow."

"Might could," Buddy allowed. "Snowed once when I was a kid. Got down to five above, too." He shivered.

"Who is he?" Richards was belligerent. "I want to know. I got a right to know who's accusin' me, don't I?"

"Time flies when you're having fun." Mr. Moseley looked at his watch. "A minute thirty."

There was a silence. Then, "Five years, damn it," Richards growled.

"Ten." Mr. Moseley spoke without turning.

"Seven. Bragg was a low-life scum who deserved what he got. He killed Whitworth, didn't he?"

"Nine." Mr. Moseley turned away from the window. "Who ordered you to do it?"

Richards was silent.

Mr. Moseley looked at his watch. "Fifty

seconds."

"Eight," Richards said. "I'll plead, if it's eight."

Mr. Moseley's face hardened. "Who?" His voice was steely. "Who told you to kill Bragg?"

Richards let out a long breath. "Burford," he said, very low.

Mr. Moseley looked at Wayne, hunched over his notebook. "I heard you say that Warden Grover Burford ordered you to shoot Jimmie Bragg," he said distinctly. "Is that correct, Mr. Richards?"

"Yeah," Richards muttered. "It was Burford. All his idea."

"Louder, please."

"Burford," Richards said. "Eight years, Moseley. I know the system. Eligible for parole in two."

"Why?" Mr. Moseley sat down again. "Why did Burford want Bragg murdered?"

Another silence. Then, finally, Richards said, "Burford was pissed that Bragg killed Whitworth by ramming him off the road. He was only supposed to scare him. Bragg was a cocky little bastard. Didn't know when to stop. Didn't like to take orders."

"Why did Burford want to scare Whitworth?"

"To show him what would happen if he

invested any more money in Bodeen Pyle's bootleg business."

"Why did Burford care what Whitworth did with his money?"

"Cause Burford is goin' into the moonshine business. He was aiming to shut Pyle down."

"Just a matter of a little local competition, huh?" Mr. Moseley said. "Was there anything else?"

Richards sighed. "Bragg threatened to blow the whistle on some of the other stuff Burford was doin'. But Burford don't like nobody gettin' in his face. So he told me to take him out."

"What other stuff?"

"Oh, man." Richards rolled his eyes. "There's a lot. I don't know —"

Mr. Moseley turned to Buddy. "This prisoner needs some paper and a pencil. See that I get a list of that 'other stuff' the warden is doing. All of it." To Richards, he said, "That's it for now, Mr. Richards. I may have more questions later."

"Eight years," Richards said.

"I'll want that list by —" Mr. Moseley looked at his watch. "Three this afternoon."

Wayne closed his notebook and stood up. "I'll take him to his cell. Jed Snow will keep an eye on him."

332

When they had gone, Mr. Moseley turned to Buddy. "I talked to Agent Kinnard on the phone yesterday. He's bringing two men with him. You and Wayne will make five — that ought to be enough to break up that still. They'll get here in an hour or so."

"That's good news," Buddy said, letting out his breath. He didn't much like Kinnard, who was famous for his smash-and-grab raids, leaving stills in smoking ruins and shiners in handcuffs. But the man had busted stills all over Alabama and Georgia. He knew his business.

Mr. Moseley took a folded map out of his pocket and laid it on the desk. "I've transferred Wilber Casey's sketch of the still's location to this map of the prison farm area. It'll give you a good idea of the layout of the Back Forty and where to look for the still. But you'll have Burford with you. He ought to be able to tell where to go, if you ask him nicely. When you're finished breaking up his still, bring him back here and we'll have a little talk." He straightened up. "About Bragg's murder."

"Richards' word is enough to hold him, then?"

"It'll do for a start. But I had a quick look at Wilber's documentation. Burford was dumb enough to put Richards in for a pay raise right after the shooting. In a note in the file, he said that Richards was getting the raise for 'the prompt execution of an order.' A nicely ambiguous phrase that Burford will have to explain when I put him on the stand." Mr. Moseley glanced up at the rack on the back of the office door, where Buddy had hung his gun belt.

"Better wear your weapon, Sheriff," he added. "Somebody might shoot at you, and you'll want to shoot back."

CHAPTER TWENTY-ONE:
"SAFE AS A BABY LAMB"

True to her word, Lizzy had gotten up before Rowser woke the neighborhood on that Saturday morning. She had to bake several batches of bread for The Flour Shop's grand opening. There was the Cupcake problem to deal with. And she was hoping to spend some time at her typewriter. She *had* to finish her Garden Gate column, or she would miss Charlie Dickens' deadline.

So she dressed quickly in tan slacks, a blue plaid blouse, and a blue cardigan. The bread was easy and fun, and by late morning, Lizzy had filled a large shopping bag with loaves, some of them still warm. While the batches were baking, she had been on the telephone with several of the Dahlias. The day before, she had told Mr. Moseley that she had an idea to keep Cupcake safe, someplace where her father couldn't snatch her up and make off with her. Now, she was making the final arrangements for what she was calling "Hide the Cupcake." It would begin today and go on as long as necessary. On the phone, she tried to make it sound like fun — like a game — but she felt she had to explain the unfortunate reason behind it, which she did without going into a lot of unnecessary detail. It was only important for them to know that there was a real threat and that their help was urgently needed.

"It's a rather difficult situation," she told them in her calls, "and Myra May and Violet are worried that something may happen to their little girl. We trust that Mr. Moseley is going to handle things on his end and there won't be any serious trouble. But just in case Mr. Hudson shows up here in Darling and tries to locate Cupcake, we'd like to make it tough for him to find her."

"That is totally despicable!" Beulah Trivette cried, when she heard the story. "That awful man had better not show his face in this town!"

"But if he does, he'll never find our Cupcake," Ophelia Snow declared flatly. "We'll make darn sure of that." She added, in a lower voice, "You know, Jed keeps his dad's old revolver under our bed. I won't let him load it, but I like knowing it's handy."

Alice Ann Walker responded differently. "You tell Myra May and Violet that they are not to worry about one single thing," she said in a soothing voice. "That precious sugar will be safe as a baby lamb with her Auntie Alice Ann and her Uncle Arnold. If you'd send her over tomorrow afternoon, that would be perfect. Our little grandson Curly is having his fifth birthday, so we'll have us a big ol' happy birthday party!"

Lizzy hung up, feeling comforted. Surely, with all these wonderful Dahlias linking arms to protect Cupcake, they could keep her safe. And with Aunt Hetty, Bessie, and Verna already on her list, she thought that seven — eight, counting herself — were enough volunteers, at least to start with. On the schedule she had drawn up, Cupcake would stay at one house in the morning, another in the afternoon, and a third overnight. Each of her hosts would take her where she was expected next. And since the little girl knew all the Dahlias and had visited each of them at one time or another, they all seemed like family to her. She would feel perfectly at home wherever she was. And Myra May and Violet would know she was safe.

So on her way to take her bread to The Flour Shop, Lizzy had stopped at the Diner to pick up Cupcake and take her to the first Dahlia on her list — Ophelia Snow. The little girl was dancing up and down and eager to go, adorably dressed in a velvet-trimmed red wool coat and wool bonnet, made for her by her Gramma Ray's friend Pauline, who was an excellent seamstress. With her Little Buttercup doll in one hand and a small cardboard suitcase in the other, she was as cute as cute could be. Myra May and Violet kissed her and said a loving goodbye, telling her to be a good girl and mind her manners.

"I *always* mind my nanners!" she cried, with a stamp of her little foot, and off they went.

After Lizzy left her bag of fresh-baked loaves with Mildred at The Flour Shop, she and Cupcake walked the short distance down Rosemont to Ophelia's house. There, the Snow children, teenagers Sam and Sarah, had just started decorating the Christmas tree, which stood green and lovely — and still quite bare — in a corner of the small parlor. Christmas stockings hung on a nearby shelf, and a row of electric candles shone in the front window.

"Hi there, Cupcake!" Sarah said when she

answered the door. "You're just in time to hang the ornaments on our Christmas tree. Here, honey — let me take your coat."

"Oh, goodie!" Cupcake chortled. "Can I put the angel on the top?"

"Of course," Sarah said. "Sam will lift you up high so you can reach it. Let's do that right now."

While the children were working on the tree, Lizzy and Ophelia sat down in the kitchen over a bowl of hot vegetable soup and an egg salad sandwich. Ophelia's clever stowaway wall-hung ironing board was still down, and her new CCC uniform, freshly ironed, was hanging on the back of the door. She was brimming with excitement about her new job at the Civilian Conservation Corps camp, where she was in charge of reorganizing the commandant's office.

"I love working for Captain Campbell," she said. "He's a little strict but he's nice, and everybody else is so *sweet* to me." With a giggle, she added, "I never thought I would like to wear a uniform, but it's actually fun — makes me feel like one of the boys."

Lizzy ate the last bite of her sandwich. "I'll bet you don't *look* like one of the boys," she said, with an admiring glance at the trim uniform: a light khaki blouse, darker brown skirt, and brown tie. "And it solves the problem of what to wear for work every day," she added. "When we're on a tight budget, clothes are a problem."

Ophelia made a regretful face. "But I really hate leaving Charlie Dickens in the lurch. I'm afraid he won't be able to find anybody to take my place." She tilted her head to one side. "You're only working mornings for Mr. Moseley right now, Lizzy. You have your afternoons free, don't you? Maybe you could —"

"Oh, no," Lizzy broke in. "I already have an afternoon job. I'm *writing,* remember?" It went without saying that she could use the money. Getting by on fifteen dollars a week was no picnic. But while the news-reporting part of Opie's job might be interesting, Lizzy wasn't anxious to operate that balky old Linotype. And she knew she would *not* enjoy selling ads.

"I understand." Ophelia sighed ruefully. "You're doing what you need to do for *you,* and that's right. But I feel awf'lly guilty about leaving Charlie. He gave me a job that kept our family afloat when we were so desperate for cash. I just hope he can find somebody dependable." She pushed her soup bowl away. "Somebody who can actu-ally write a sentence. And who can wrestle that beastly Linotype."

Liz glanced up at the clock over Ophelia's kitchen range and was surprised to see how late it was — nearly twelve-thirty. "Speaking of writing, I'd better head home, Opie. I haven't even started my garden column for next week, and I'd like to make a little progress on my novel." She pushed her chair back and stood up. "Cupcake is scheduled to spend the night at Bessie's. Could you walk her over there after supper?" Magnolia Manor was only a couple of blocks away.

"Sure thing. Jed will want to go with us, I'm sure." Ophelia frowned apprehensively. "You don't think there's any real danger of that fellow — Neil Hudson — showing up here in Darling right away, do you?"

"Nobody knows for sure," Lizzy said, putting on her coat. "He might be sitting back and allowing his lawyer to handle the situation. Or he might take matters into his own hands." She bit her lip. "It's worrisome, Ophelia. I wish I knew."

"Well, she'll be safe and snug as a bug in a rug with us," Ophelia said confidently. "You can count on it."

"Thank you," Lizzy said gratefully. "I know she'll have fun here. The ladies at the Manor will read to her, and tomorrow she goes to Alice Ann, who's having a birthday

341

party for her grandson." She felt that the little game she'd arranged was a good way of dealing with the situation, and was glad for the Dahlias' willing support.

There was something, though, that still troubled her. When she and Verna had gone to the Diner to let Myra May and Violet know what was happening, Myra May had been deeply concerned by the idea that somebody might try to take Cupcake away from her Darling home. Violet, on the other hand, had seemed intrigued by the possibility that Hollywood might recognize Cupcake's talents, especially when she heard how much money Shirley Temple was earning.

"Can you imagine what that much money would mean for Cupcake's future?" She had sounded impressed by the idea. "College and new clothes and a car and . . . and just everything! And think how many people would get to see our little girl in the movies. Why, she would be famous!"

Walking home through the chilly December afternoon, Lizzy wondered. Did Violet *really* want fame and money for the little girl? Did that mean that she would consider a movie career for Cupcake — *if* that were possible?

And what would happen if Mr. Hudson

showed up in Darling tomorrow or the next day and tried to persuade Violet to let him take the child to Hollywood? He might tell her that he had solid connections with the studios — or, more enticing, an offer for an audition. He might even suggest that Violet go along. What would she say to such a seductive invitation? And how would Myra May feel if she left and took Cupcake with her?

The questions themselves made Lizzy deeply uncomfortable. Even worse, she didn't have any answers.

A block away, in the Dickens' apartment over Fannie's hat shop, Mr. and Mrs. Dickens were trading questions and answers in an important conversation.

To start with, Charlie had told Fannie about his meeting at the Cotton Gin the night before and answered her questions about his involvement with the sheriff's investigation at the prison farm.

Fannie shook her head. "That was *dangerous*, Charlie, but I'm glad you did it. It sounds like the information you got has been a big help." She smiled. "Your experience as an investigative reporter came in handy, didn't it?"

"Maybe," he said. "And maybe that will

help excuse what I did." Then he confessed how he had discovered the initials J. C. in Fannie's tidy account books, with the amount of fifty dollars a month. "I apologize for snooping in your private accounts," he said. "But it seemed to me that if we're going to file a joint income tax return in April, the sooner I know where we are, financially speaking, the better."

Fannie sighed. "I can see the logic in that. I know I should have told you. It's been bothering me for months. I'm glad to have it out in the open. But —" She pressed her lips together and her eyes filled with tears. "It's just so . . . so difficult." And then, to Charlie's discomfort, she broke down and sobbed.

Of all things on this earth, Charlie hated to see his pretty wife cry. He gathered her in his arms, smoothed her hair, and whispered "There, there," until she quieted. "Now tell me," he commanded.

Fannie took a deep breath. "Jason is my son," she said. "He's nine — and he has polio. He's been at Warm Springs for a year now. I visit him whenever I take one of my sales trips. The check is for his board and room and rehabilitation. I didn't tell you because Jason was born out of wedlock, and I was ashamed. His father —"

Charlie laid a finger on her lips. "You don't need to tell me that part."

"But I want to. Warren was . . . a terrible mistake. We had been married for three months when I discovered that he was already married."

"Married!" Charlie exclaimed. "A bigamist! That *bastard*!"

Fannie smiled faintly. "He swore he would get a divorce from his first wife, but I sent him away. A week later, I learned that I was pregnant."

If Charlie had been inclined to be judgmental, all that was out the window now. "Oh, Fannie, I'm so sorry," he whispered.

"Life has to go on," Fannie said, in a practical tone. "I moved in with my cousin Amy in Atlanta after Jason was born. I worked in a milliner's shop there, learning the trade. When I came to Darling, I intended to bring him with me, but Amy — she has no children of her own — persuaded me to let him stay in Atlanta with her until I got settled. But he contracted polio and was desperately sick for several months. When he got better, we took him to Warm Springs. He was paralyzed from the waist down, but he's improving all the time. That warm water is a miracle."

"Carpenter," Charlie mused, thinking of

the name on the check. "Is that your cousin's name?"

"Yes. She registered him under both our names: Champaign and Carpenter. He and Amy are very close — he calls both of us mother. Amy is just an hour away from Warm Springs, so she visits him every weekend. I go when I can. And I'm lucky to have enough money to take care of his rehabilitation." Her voice broke. "I should have told you about Jason before we were married, but I . . . I was afraid. I know how you feel about having children, and I didn't want you to feel burdened."

A storm of emotions swept through Charlie. But when he could speak, he said only, "How soon can I meet him?"

Fannie's eyes opened wide. "Meet him?" she whispered. "You want to —"

"Of course I do," he said. "How about tomorrow? It can't be much more than two hundred miles. If we leave by eight, we can be there by noon. Is there a place we can stay overnight? It's Christmas, after all."

"Oh, Charlie," Fannie wept. "This is the best Christmas present I could hope for. Thank you. Thank you!"

CHAPTER TWENTY-TWO:
"THE SKY'S THE LIMIT"

At home, Lizzy changed out of her slacks into a comfortable red sweater and the baggy red-checked flannel pants — her "grubbies" — that she liked to wear around the house. She brewed a cup of coffee and took it upstairs to the small bedroom she used as her writing studio. Daffy, happy to have her all to himself for a few hours, followed her upstairs, where she sat down and rolled a clean sheet of paper into the typewriter.

Over the past several years, Lizzy's weekly Garden Gate column had developed quite a following among readers of the *Dispatch.* Sometimes it was mostly garden club news, because the Dahlias liked to see their names in print, and because they had some interesting (and sometimes amusing) garden adventures. But more often, she wrote about the plants in her garden, or native plants growing wild in the woods and fields and

347

streams around Darling — and always with a personal slant, for she loved plants and liked to imagine that they were her friends. She wanted her readers to share that close-up view, so she let them see the redbird couple busily building a nest in the old-fashioned pink Noisette rose on the fence. Or invited them to enjoy the sharp scent of garden mint along a wet flagstone path, listen to the whisper of the spring wind stirring the willow tree to life, and feel the soft, downy leaves of lamb's ears and woolly mullein.

After a while, she had decided that *Dispatch* readers must be sending clippings to their friends, because she started getting letters from all over the South — not just from Alabama, but from Florida and Georgia and Mississippi — asking gardening questions or telling her what they knew of the plants she had written about. Sometimes they sent her seeds and bulbs, too, which was nice. She would grow them, or try to, and take photographs to send to the donors.

Now, Daffy jumped into her lap, purring comfortably, and she stroked him while she thought about next week's column. This one would be a little different, for she was writing about the poinsettia perched on the corner of her writing table — the one Ryan

Nichols had given her. It was different because of all the gardeners in Darling, only Aunt Hetty Little (who had quite a remarkable green thumb) had ever successfully raised them through several seasons. Also, the plant wasn't native to Alabama. Or to the South, or even to the United States.

In fact, Lizzy knew from her library research that the poinsettia had originally come from Mexico, where the Aztec Indians believed it to be magical. Unlike most of the other plants in their tropical forests, it was at its most beautiful during the shortest, darkest days of the year, when its leaves changed from green to a brilliant, startling red. The gods were said to have sent the poinsettia to remind people that transformation only comes out of darkness and difficulty. How much of this was fact and how much was fancy, she had no idea — but it seemed to her to be a lovely metaphor for their own dark times and the hope for new growth and brighter opportunities.

With that in mind as the subject of her column, Lizzy took out the notes she had made at the library and settled down to work. She became deeply engrossed in what she was writing, and when she pulled the last sheet of paper out of the typewriter and glanced at her wristwatch, she saw to her surprise that it was nearly four o'clock. She stretched happily. The afternoon had flown by and it was almost time to —

The doorbell rang.

"Oh, *drat*," Lizzy muttered crossly. She hoped it wasn't her mother, coming across the street with an invitation to eat with her and Mr. Dunlap. Or Grady, insisting that she have supper with him and Grady Junior. And since she wasn't expecting anybody, she was dressed in her sloppiest, most comfortable at-home clothes. Which wouldn't matter to her mother. And she no longer needed to impress Grady.

Actually, she didn't want to see either of them — and she definitely didn't want to go anywhere to eat. It was Saturday night, and she planned to wash her hair, jump into her flannel pajamas, and snuggle down under a quilt with Agatha Christie's latest mystery, *Murder on the Orient Express* (which Verna had loaned her) while she listened to *Music by Gershwin* on the radio. She would tell whoever was knocking that she was not available.

Irritably, she put Daffy on the floor and started down the stairs. The doorbell pealed again, and she answered under her breath. "Just hold your darn horses, will you? I'm coming as fast as I can." She yanked the door open. "I'm sorry," she said, "but now is *not* a good time —"

It wasn't Grady, and it definitely wasn't her mother.

It was Ryan Nichols. The man from the WPA, who had paid a surprise call back in October. The man who had sent the poinsettia.

"Mr. Nichols!" Lizzy exclaimed, surprised and flustered. "How very . . . nice to see you. Won't you come in?"

He took off his brown fedora. His glance went from her mussed-up hair to her flannel pants. "I'm afraid I'm interrupting," he said contritely. "I'm sorry. I should have telephoned." He half turned away. "I'll try again later."

"Oh, no, please." Lizzy wished she weren't wearing her grubbies. She must look a mess. She could feel her cheeks flushing as red as that poinsettia. "I thought you were my mother or Grady or —"

She stopped herself. Why was she apologizing? The man had come unannounced. He might have caught her in her underwear. Fine, then. Just *fine.* She looked the way she looked. He could take what he got.

"Come in," she said. "It's cold outside. Would you like a cup of coffee?"

Hat in hand, he stepped inside. In a

clipped Yankee accent, he said, "A cup of coffee would be swell. Or tea. Whatever is convenient. If you're *sure* I'm not —"

"Not at all," Lizzy said, and the thought crossed her mind — quite unexpectedly — that she was very glad that Mr. Nichols had dropped in, even without calling. She heard herself say, with more composure than she felt, "By the way, I owe you a big thanks for that lovely poinsettia. It just happens that I had already decided to write my Garden Gate column about the plant this week. Your gift arrived at exactly the right moment." She held out her hand. "May I take your coat?"

"I'm glad you liked it," Mr. Nichols said. He took off his camel-colored overcoat and handed it to her. He was wearing a dark brown wool blazer and red polo shirt with khaki pants. He looked different — more rugged, more down-to-earth — than he had on his previous visit, when he was wearing a business suit.

"I'm always a bit puzzled by poinsettias," he went on. "How they're persuaded to turn red just at Christmas, I mean. There must be a secret to it. Maybe your column will tell us what it is. I'd like to read it."

"It'll be in next Friday's *Dispatch*," she said, as she hung his coat on the rack. "I'll be sure to send you a clipping."

She turned toward the kitchen, disturbingly aware of his physical size. He was something over six feet and broadshouldered, and he moved with a loose, athletic confidence. The blond hair that fell across his forehead was sun-bleached; his eyes, pale blue. His face was darkly tanned. He wasn't handsome; his features — a firm jaw, high cheekbones, pale blue eyes — were too craggy for that. But there was a hint of ironic amusement in his eyes, an interrogative quirk to one eyebrow, and a come-and-go smile that took the edge off his quick Yankee speech. And when he sat down at the table, it was with a comfortable easiness that suggested that he had been there a dozen times before. Even Daffy, curling around his ankles, seemed to think he was a long-lost friend.

"Nice place," he said appreciatively, looking around. "Have you been here long?"

"Just a few years," Lizzy said, checking the coffee pot. "I grew up across the street. That's where my mother lives. This house is small, but when it became available, I knew I wanted it." She laughed a little. "Took a *lot* of fixing up."

"It's almost like a playhouse," he said with a smile. "It fits you."

A *playhouse*? She hadn't thought of her house that way, and it gave her a jolt. What could he have meant? She wanted to ask, but she wasn't sure she wanted to hear his answer. Perhaps it was just a word. Perhaps he meant nothing at all.

She set a cup of coffee in front of him, poured another for herself, and sat down across the table. "What brings you to Darling, Mr. Nichols?"

"Please," he said. "We can't be formal with your cat jumping into my lap." He chuckled. "My name is Ryan."

"Daffy, get down!" she exclaimed, embarrassed. "Oh, dear, I'm so sorry. He's usually more standoffish. Just put him on the floor."

"Put him on the floor, *Ryan,*" he corrected with a twinkle. "But no, Daffy's fine right where he is. Every cat needs a lap." His eyebrow went up. "What do your friends call you when they want to get your attention?"

"Liz, mostly," she said, thinking that he had to be the most *direct* man she had ever met. Was it because he was a Yankee? Were all Yankees like this?

"I prefer Elizabeth," he said decidedly, but with that quick smile. "If you don't mind, that is. Elizabeth."

"I don't mind," she said. She didn't like it

when her mother called her that, but it sounded different when he said it. She repeated her question. "What brings you to Darling? Ryan," she added. His name felt strange in her mouth. It didn't feel like the Southern names she was used to. She rather liked it, but —

"You do."

Her breath caught. "Me?"

He frowned a little. "Why are you surprised?"

"I'm not — I mean . . ." She was irritated with herself. What was *wrong* with her?

"I apologize," he said, but he didn't sound apologetic. There was an odd light in his eyes. "Maybe it would be a little less alarming if I explained that I was accidentally driving from Montgomery to Mobile, happened to remember our conversation of some weeks ago, and said to myself, 'Self, Darling is only a few miles out of the way. Why don't you just pop in and say hello to Elizabeth Lacy?' " His grin was teasing. "There. Is that better?"

She couldn't help laughing.

He picked up his coffee cup, took a drink, set it down again. "That's mostly true." he said lightly. "Sort of. But it wasn't entirely accidental." His voice became serious. "I hope you won't mind if I say that I've been thinking about you."

"That's . . . nice," she said absurdly. To fill the silence — and to sidestep the impossible possibility that his thoughts about her might be personal — she reached for another explanation.

"Then perhaps you've gotten your funding? For the Writers' Project, I mean. The one we talked about when you were here before."

The light in his eyes became amusement. He reached into his shirt pocket and pulled out a pack of Marlboros, tapping it on the table to extract a cigarette. "Yes, that's right. We haven't been officially notified of the funding. Congress always likes to keep people guessing as long as possible. It makes them feel powerful. But the word out of the Budget Office is that it's coming sometime in the first quarter. It's just a matter of time." He took out a gold lighter and lit his cigarette.

She cleared her throat. "So you're beginning to plan the staffing?" Now, why had she said that? He would think she was hinting she wanted to be hired, when in fact it was the last thing on her —

"Right again," he said. And now the amusement reached his mouth. The corners quirked. "We're just about ready to start hiring our state program directors. Why? Are you interested? Available? Or maybe that's too much to hope for. Elizabeth," he added.

Was he making fun of her? He seemed to be ironic, or mocking. Or something. The humor seemed to dance in him, which made him hard to read. And different. From Grady, from Mr. Moseley. From any other man she knew.

"I meant that," he added quickly — and more seriously, as if he had read her thoughts. "Are you interested? Available?"

There was a sunflower-shaped yellow ashtray — *Bank in Darling, The Sun Will Shine on You!* — on the counter. She stood up and got it for him. As she sat down again, she found herself saying, "I suppose I am."

"You suppose?" He sounded surprised. "Really?"

And pleased. But maybe she was imagining that. Because she wanted him to be pleased? Really, she scolded herself. This was all very silly. She had just this morning told Ophelia she didn't *want* another job, which was true. What she wanted was time to work on her book. Why would she let this man believe that she might consider the job he had mentioned to her? But she had boxed herself in, and she had to answer his question honestly.

"I think I told you that my boss might have to cut my hours. Well, that's what happened. I'm working for him just in the mornings, now."

He tapped his cigarette into the ashtray. "You have afternoons free, then? Say, four hours a day, five days a week?" He slanted her a quick look. "And you would be interested in working on the Writers' Project — with me?"

The Federal Writers' Project. As he had described it on his earlier visit (and as she had read about it later, in the *Mobile Press Register*) the funding would support writers, editors, historians, teachers, and librarians — most of them women. Working regionally, they would produce tourist guides, collect local history and folklore, and do social research. Interesting work, yes. But the part of the project that had intrigued her most was the collection of oral histories from people whose stories hadn't yet been told. Older people who remembered what life was like in the old days. Immigrants from other parts of America, and from foreign countries. Colored people, some of whom had slave stories to tell. Yes — *that* would be interesting. Rewarding.

And worth doing.

But it was his "with me" that had made her heart skip like a foolish girl's. Did that mean that *he* interested her more than the job he was offering? That disturbed her, because it meant —

Well, what did it mean, exactly? She had no idea, utterly *no* idea. Which was even more disturbing.

And what about her writing? She had planned to keep her afternoons free for the novel. But she had written the first book on weekends, hadn't she? Couldn't she write the second book that way, too? It wasn't as if she had an editorial deadline looming over her head. There was no guarantee that Mr. Perkins would want to publish it. For all she knew, the publishing business might be so bad that Scribner wouldn't publish *anything.*

She heard herself say "Yes, I'm free in the afternoons. Right now, anyway." The words were very distant, as if they were spoken by someone else. "Yes, I'd like to work on the project." *With you,* she added silently. Whatever that meant.

"Well, *good,*" Ryan said, and his pale eyes lit up. "The job starts at twenty-five dollars a week. Which I know isn't enough to support a living soul. I'm glad to know that you're getting paid for your mornings' work at your other job."

Lizzy caught her lower lip in her teeth. Twenty-five dollars a week for half-time work? Mr. Moseley was paying her fifteen. If she took the job Mr. Nichols — Ryan — was offering, she would be earning forty dollars a week. Forty dollars! Why, that was ten dollars more than Mr. Moseley paid for full-time work! She would be able to afford a car and some new clothes! She would —

He was going on. "There's always the possibility that the hours could increase. In a few months or a year, the job might even become full time. And as I think I told you when we talked back in October, there'll be some travel, overseeing fieldworkers, attending meetings and conferences with other managers across the South — Louisiana, Mississippi, Georgia, Florida. We're setting up a regional office in Montgomery, so I'll be there. Not far away." He leaned forward. "What do you say, Elizabeth? It's a new opportunity for you. It'll take you out of Darling. Give you a glimpse of the wider world. A larger life."

Travel. Meetings and conferences. And the regional office in Montgomery. But could she do it? The work, that is. Did she have the skills? The management ability? As for a new opportunity taking her out of Darling, giving her a glimpse of the wider world — was that what she wanted?

She didn't know. She wasn't sure. But she had never trusted herself when it came to anything new. Change, even the anticipation of change, made her uneasy. She needed time to think, time to plan, to look ahead. To ease into whatever it was. She —

She took a deep breath. "I'd like to try it," she said, and added, "Of course, if it doesn't work out, we can always —"

"Sorry." His mouth became firm and he shook his head. "I can't hire on that basis, Elizabeth. There's training involved, and the expense of setting up an office here in Darling. And you'll be recruiting people who want to work with *you.* I'm going to need a commitment. Six months, at least. More, if I can get it." His eyes on hers were intense, challenging. "If you're wondering whether you're able to do the job, forget it. It'll be easy for you, I promise. Duck soup. And if you run into trouble, I'll be there. I can help."

He would be there. He could help. Breathlessly, she tried to pull her glance away. She felt giddy and fragile, as if she were walking out to the edge of a very steep cliff, and in front of her, there was nothing but empty air. And sky, and space. Wide-open, whirl-ing space.

"All right, then," she managed, finally. Her mouth was dry. "Six months." *Six months?* What had she just agreed to? "Unless —" she began.

"Wonderful!" he said, and slapped his hand on the table. "You're my first hire, and I couldn't be more delighted. I'll get the paperwork started right away. It's the gov-ernment, you know, so there's plenty of it. That's fine, though. It'll give us a head start. You'll be able to go to work the minute the funding is announced."

And now he was laughing, quite openly. "But that isn't why I came, you know."

Was there any end to his surprises? "It isn't?"

"Nope. Hiring you is a bonus for me, and one hundred percent unexpected. I figured that your boss was way too smart to let you go to part time. That was *his* mistake."

"Well, then, why *did* you come?" she asked. It was a real question. What possible reason could he have for —

The phone rang in the hallway. "Excuse me," she said, and went to answer it.

"It's me, Elizabeth," her mother said petulantly. "Are you all right? Who *is* that man? Really, you shouldn't entertain strange men in —"

"I'm fine, Mama," she said, trying to curb her impatience. Living across the street from her mother had its drawbacks, definitely. "Mr. Nichols is a . . . a friend. I'm going to work for him next year. I'll tell you all about it later."

"*Work* for him?" her mother sputtered. "Doing what? What about Mr. Moseley? If it's a matter of money, Mr. Dunlap and I will be glad to let you work at the Five and Dime." She added stiffly, "We offered you twenty-five cents an hour, if you will remember."

"Yes, I remember, and I'm grateful. I promise I'll tell you all about it later. And please don't call back, Mama. I am just *fine*."

"But Elizabeth —" her mother wailed.

"Goodbye, Mama."

Lizzy put down the phone and went back to the kitchen. "Sorry for the interruption," she said breathlessly, sitting down again. "Where were we?"

"I was about to tell you why I came," he said. "Do you still want to know?"

"Yes, of course," Lizzy said.

"I came to ask you if you'd like to go to dinner and a movie tonight. And now we can celebrate your new job." He put out his cigarette in the ashtray. "Clark Gable and Jean Harlow are playing in *Red Dust* at the Palace. It's supposed to be a very good movie. Have you seen it?"

Dinner? A movie? Wordlessly, Lizzy shook her head.

"Good. That makes two of us, then. I have a room at the Old Alabama Hotel, which is supposed to be a swell place to eat. Before I came over, I checked out their menu for tonight. It's Chicken Kiev, which I think is —"

Lizzy found her voice. "Euphoria fries chicken at the Diner on Saturday nights. It's good and quite a bit cheaper than —"

His mouth twitched. "Cheaper. I'll remember that," he said, and she thought again that he was making fun. "But we're celebrating, remember? The sky's the limit. It's Chicken Kiev and a cold bottle of Chablis at the Old Alabama." He glanced down at his wristwatch. "It's nearly five. If we leave for dinner soon, we'll be finished in time for the early show. How does that sound?"

The sky's the limit. Suddenly, it seemed possible. The wider world, a larger life. *The sky's the limit.*

"I have to change," she said, getting up. She would wear the navy mohair dress with

364

the pleated skirt. Put on some makeup. And hope that her hair would behave. "I'll only be a minute."

He looked her up and down, smiling that half-amused smile. "Why change? I've been wearing a suit and tie all week. It's Saturday, and I'm roughing it. I intend to go as I am. You look perfectly beautiful, Elizabeth. Just as you are."

She flushed at his glance. Looking down at herself, she laughed a little. "It's obvious that you don't know the first thing about going out on a Saturday night in Darling, Ryan. A lady *never* wears her grubbies."

"Ah," he said, and smiled gently. "But a lovely lady is lovely in anything she wears."

As Lizzy went up the stairs, she felt she was floating. *The sky's the limit,* she thought again.

The sky's the limit.

CHAPTER TWENTY-THREE:
"GOOD HUNTING,
GENTLEMEN"

"Any questions?" Mr. Moseley looked from one to the other of the five men gathered in the sheriff's office. "Now's the time to ask."

"What about Casey?" Buddy asked.

"He's the kid that drew the map to the still?" Agent Kinnard wanted to know.

"Right," Mr. Moseley said. "Wilber won't be there. He's not going back to Jericho — he's got a new job. But he *will* be a witness at trial." He looked around. "Anything else?"

One hand on his holster, Chester Kinnard glanced at his two deputy federal agents, both armed. They shrugged. Kinnard looked back at Mr. Moseley.

"I take it we don't want any shootin' on this one," he said. Buddy thought he sounded disapproving.

"No shooting," Mr. Moseley replied firmly. "The Board of Prison Administrators knows what we're doing here, and they

366

especially cautioned against any violence. We're after one man, Grover Burford. Go in, find him, take him out to the still, and make sure he watches while you axe it. After that's done, the sheriff —" He nodded at Buddy and Wayne. "The sheriff and his deputy will bring Burford back here. We're charging him on another, more serious matter."

"Got it." Kinnard shook his head. "I've been on some pretty strange raids in my time. Once I raided a sheriff's still — another time, a still that was operated by the town's mayor, out behind his privy. I even busted a still that was run by a widow woman and her four daughters, not a one of 'em over fourteen." He grinned mirthlessly. "But I never expected to break up a still in a goldurn prison."

Buddy respected Chester Kinnard the way he respected a rattlesnake. The agent was tall and stoop-shouldered, with a pitted face and cold, watchful eyes that never missed a trick. He was a brutal man who shot first and asked questions later, especially if he suspected that a moonshiner had a derringer in the pocket of his bibbed overalls. Buddy had been angered and disgusted when Kinnard and his men had carelessly killed Mickey LeDoux's kid brother Rider a while back, while they were axing Mickey's still out on Dead Cow Creek. Darling hadn't forgotten that, and Darling's sheriff hadn't either.

But while Kinnard was cruel, he got the job done. Moonshining had long been a contest between the crafty hunter and the cunning hunted, and while moonshiners were wary and armed for defense, Kinnard was determined, resourceful, and fearless. He went in to do a job and he came out having done it, every time. And since in this case they were aiming to arrest the warden of the Jericho State Prison Farm and golden boy of the Alabama Board of Prison Administrators, Buddy was glad that he and Kinnard were on the same side.

"Just think on it," one of Kinnard's agents muttered. "A damned *prison warden,* goin' into the moonshine business."

"It's a unique situation." Mr. Moseley smiled thinly. "Good hunting, gentlemen."

It was late in the afternoon by the time they got to Jericho — three cars, with the sheriff's black Model T in the lead. The temperature had risen, but the sky was the color of lead, the leafless trees had a wintry look, and the wind had a bite. Not a day to be out, Buddy thought, without a coat and a cap with flaps over your ears.

Buddy got out of the car at the kiosk in front of the compound's main gate. He was glad to see that Leonard was on guard. The two had known one another since Leonard was an acne-scarred, rail-thin senior forward on the Darling high school basketball team and Buddy was the team's water boy. Leonard had gained a hundred pounds, at least. He looked like he would pass out if somebody threw him a ball and told him to dribble down the court. But he always wore a friendly grin when Buddy saw him around town.

"Hey, Sheriff." Leonard came out of the kiosk hitching up his uniform pants. "Good to see you. How ya doin' today?"

"Doin' swell, Leonard. You?"

" 'Bout as good as usual, I reckon." He tipped up the bill of his cap with his thumb. "What can I do you for?"

Buddy gestured to the autos. "The four boys with me are all deputies. We're here to see Warden Burford. You know where I can find him?"

"He's up at the house." Leonard stepped back into the kiosk and took down a clipboard from a nail. "Wonder how come I ain't got you on my weekend Admit page."

Buddy made a face. "Wilber probably

forgot to put it down. We don't want to cause the kid any trouble with the boss, do we? You know how the warden gets when somebody doesn't do his job right."

Leonard rolled his eyes in agreement. "No, siree, I ain't causin' Wilber any trouble. He's a good boy, always real respectful, not like a few others I can name. I'll just put you down." He looked at his watch, noted the time, and penciled a note. "To get to the house, go straight to the rear of the quad, and turn right. You'll see it." He grinned. "Enjoy the party."

Buddy didn't ask "What party?" because he was apparently supposed to know about it. But Leonard had more to say. "Them that has, gets," he went on enviously. "You'll see what I mean when you meet the girls he's got in for this weekend. Real cute — makes a man's mouth water." He looked toward the cars. "But there ain't enough to go around."

Back in the car, Buddy led the caravan along the north edge of the quad to the rear and turned left down a narrow lane. The lane became a circle drive in front of a square two-story house with an imposing white portico that made it look like a plantation house. The men got out of their autos and Buddy and Kinnard led the way to the porch. Inside, Buddy could hear the thump of loud blues with a heavy walking bass, accompanied by a soprano crescendo of girlish giggles. Buddy raised his hand to the doorbell, but paused when he heard a splintery crash.

"Now see what you've done, Grover!" a woman cried. "The whole damn bottle!"

"I'll handle this," Kinnard growled, and Buddy stepped aside to let the agent and his men go forward. Kinnard pounded on the door. "Federal agents! We've got a warrant. Open up! *Now!*"

The door was jerked open by a broad-shouldered man in a neatly pressed khaki guard uniform, a holstered gun on one hip. His black hair was parted down the middle and Brylcreemed flat on both side. "What in the bloody *hell* — How'd you get in here? Who let you into the compound?"

"Shut up," Kinnard barked. His hand darted forward and he yanked the guard's gun out of its holster. "Hands behind your head. Face the wall. Don't move."

The guard's jaw dropped, but he obeyed. Kinnard barreled through the door, followed by his two deputies, guns drawn. Buddy signaled to Wayne and they stepped inside, guns holstered. The two-story foyer was dimly illuminated by a crystal chandelier that hung from the high ceiling. A large parlor opened off to the right, and a flight of carpeted stairs rose into the shadows to the left. Wayne moved to a dark corner and stood with his back to the wall while Buddy went halfway up the stairs and stood, surveying the scene below.

"Federal agents," Kinnard yelled again. "Burford, get your ass out here. *Now!*"

As Buddy watched, a busty red-head in a tight purple dress came to the open door at the end of the hall. She took one look, squealed, "Don't shoot me! Oh, please don't shoot!" and shut the door with a loud bang. Somewhere at the back of the house, a dog began barking, and Buddy remembered that the warden had a big black Rottweiler named Jingo. In the parlor, the blues kept on playing loudly. At the top of the stairs, an abundantly endowed blonde suddenly appeared, naked except for a black garter belt, black stockings, and black high heels.

She spotted Buddy and flung up an arm to cover her breasts. "Oh, my God," she cried, "We're under attack!" She disappeared. It was a good thing, Buddy thought, because his mouth was watering.

"Quiet," Kinnard roared. "Everybody stay where you are but Burford. Grover Burford, out here in the hall. Right now. I want to see your empty hands."

The music stopped with a loud scratch of the needle across a phonograph record. Burford, a heavy man with grizzled hair and a brushy mustache, came out of the front parlor. He was dressed in smart plaid wool trousers and a yellow silk shirt, open to reveal a mat of black hair — a very different man than the one Buddy had seen in uniform. Peeking out from behind him, clutching his arm, was a dark-haired Oriental girl, barefoot, in a pink silk teddy.

His face mottled with rage, Burford shook off the girl's hand. "What is the meaning of this outrage?" he shouted. "What the hell are you doing in my house?"

Kinnard flashed his badge. "Agent Kinnard, Bureau of Internal Revenue," He jerked his head toward a coat tree beside the front door. "Get a coat, Burford. We're going for a ride."

"Bureau of —" The warden puffed himself up, brazening it out. "I am not going anywhere with you." He looked from one to the other of the three agents and then saw Buddy on the stairs. "Ah, Sheriff Norris, there you are. Please tell me what the *hell* is going on here."

Buddy leaned on his forearms against the

banister. "If I were you, Warden," he replied mildly, "I'd do what Agent Kinnard says. He's federal. And he's got kind of a short fuse, so I'd do it quick."

"But a *ride*?" Burford asked, his jaw working. "I demand to know where we are going — and why."

"You don't get to ask questions, Burford," Kinnard snapped. "You can shut up and follow orders. You're in big trouble here."

"Hands up!" The woman at the top of the stairs had reappeared. She was no longer naked, although the silky black shirt she'd put on was unbuttoned and left nothing at all to Buddy's vivid imagination. More important, though, she was holding a double-barreled shotgun.

Gesturing with it, she cried, "Drop your guns on the floor, everybody, and put your hands up!" Her voice went up an octave. "If you don't, I'll shoot. I swear I will!"

Buddy didn't doubt it for a minute. The woman was hysterical. She was shaking so hard that she couldn't hold the shotgun steady. If she pulled the trigger, everybody would get their share of buckshot, at close range. Unfortunately, Buddy himself was the closest, no more than four yards away. And he'd seen what buckshot did to a man. It wasn't pretty.

Kinnard looked up. "Aw, hell," he said. With a clatter, he dropped his gun. His deputies followed suit.

"Thank you, Maisie," the warden said loudly. "That's very good, my dear. You can put that shotgun down now."

"I will *not*!" the woman cried wildly. "They're going to *rape* us!"

The Oriental girl gave a terrified yelp, ran into the parlor, and slammed the door.

"Now, Maisie," the warden said, "you really don't want to —"

"Get their guns, damn it!" Maisie screamed. "You've got to lock them up." She gestured with the shotgun. "Now, while I've got the drop on —"

It all happened at once. The crack of the revolver, the reverberating blast of the shotgun, the crash of the crystal chandelier on the hallway floor, and Maisie's screams as Buddy lunged up the stairs and tried to grab the shotgun out of her grasp. She was stronger than he expected. And since it was the first time he had ever wrestled with an almost-undressed female, he was a little uncertain just where to put his hands and how long to leave them there.

"I'll let you explain the shooting to your county attorney, Sheriff," Kinnard remarked, and picked up his gun. "Come on,

Burford. Get your coat. We've got a job to do."

Later, Buddy decided that Wayne must have shot first, surprising Maisie so that she'd jerked the gun upward and fired into the chandelier. Also later, Wayne claimed to have aimed just over the woman's shoulder, so that Buddy could do what Buddy did. Which Buddy believed, because Wayne was a crack shot. If he'd wanted to shoot that woman, there was plenty of bare flesh to aim at.

But now he left Maisie sobbing on the floor, grabbed her shotgun, went down the stairs. He handed the gun to Wayne. "Thanks. You saved our bacon."

"Maybe, maybe not." With a lazy half-smile, Wayne added, "Mostly, I was keeping Maisie out of trouble. She's too pretty to go to jail for killing a few lousy revenue agents and a no-count sheriff."

"You said a true thing there," Buddy agreed. "As a reward, why don't you get the girls together and have a little talk with them? We'll need their statements. Names, addresses, what they're doing here, how much they're paid, etcetera. I'm going out to the Back Forty with Kinnard. I'll pick you up on the way back."

■ ■ ■ ■

One way or another, Buddy had seen quite a few illegal stills in Cypress County, from the one-family copper "turnip pots" small enough for a man to carry on his shoulder, to Bodeen Pyle's four-hundred-gallon boilers down in Briar Swamp. But the Back Forty operation — which they reached by following Wilber Casey's very accurate map — was the biggest, most industrialized still he had ever seen.

It was operated by about a dozen men, all of them wearing prison garb, working under the watchful eye of an armed guard. Constructed at the foot of a wooded hill, the operation consisted of six "submarine" tanks, wooden-sided blackpot boilers that could hold eight hundred or more gallons of mash. A dense stand of young trees provided the firewood that would keep six concrete-block furnaces going night and day, while a nearby stream provided the running water necessary to cool down the alcohol vapor in the copper worm coils and condense it into high-octane whiskey. A cart track had been graveled to provide an all-weather road for hauling supplies in and white lightning out.

Kinnard put the prisoners to work destroying the boilers, breaking up the furnaces and condensing equipment, and pouring hundreds of gallons of corn whiskey on the ground. Even Burford was given an axe and told to use it. The destruction was complete by the end of the afternoon, and the prisoners and their guard were dispatched back to the compound.

Kinnard and his agents, pleased with their day's work, got in their cars and drove away. Buddy loaded Grover Burford, glowering furiously, into his squad car. On the way back to Darling, he stopped at the warden's house and picked up Wayne.

When Burford asked, all Buddy would say was that the county attorney wanted to discuss the charges that would be filed against him.

"That's good," Burford said, folding his arms. "I'm sure he'll see his way clear to dismissing them — especially after he's had a talk with the Board of Prison Administrators."

"We'll see about that," Buddy said, and there was no more talk.

It was full dark by the time they got back to Darling. The temperature was dropping again, so while Wayne made coffee, Buddy fired up the coal stove in the reception room and turned up the oil heater in his office. Then Mr. Moseley arrived and he and Buddy sat down to discuss a few matters with the warden.

That's when Burford learned that Richards had confessed to shooting Bragg and that Deputy Springer's preliminary test (conducted that morning) indicated that it was Richards' gun that fired the fatal bullet. The sheriff was confident that an examination by ballistics expert Calvin Goddard would confirm it.

Burford pretended shock. "That's damned bad for Richards. But it has nothing to do with me. I took his word for it that Bragg killed himself. I *trusted* him." He shook his head dolefully. "I just cannot fathom what got into the man. Why on earth did he do it?"

Mr. Moseley gave Burford a hard look. "He says you ordered the killing."

"Me?" Burford half-rose from his chair. "He says that? Why that's *crazy!*" He sat back down again. "Why would I do such a terrible thing?"

"Because Bragg had become a nuisance," Mr. Moseley said. "He'd stopped being helpful. He was taking too much on himself. He was getting in your way. Most of all, he knew too much."

"What are you talking about?" There was a tic under Burford's eye. It jerked spasmodically. "Knew too much . . . about what?"

"He knew that you've been treating the prison as a cash cow: overcharging for prison labor and prison-raised crops and products. He knew that the profits were going into your checking accounts in out-of-state banks — and he knew where the banks were. He knew about your clever little foray into the bootleg business, out on the Back Forty." Mr. Moseley's grin was thin, without humor. "He knew about the girls, too. Maybe he wanted to muscle in on the action."

Burford paled. "You don't know — you can't substantiate any of . . ." His voice trailed away.

"The state Board of Prison Administrators has been notified that you've been arrested. There'll be somebody down here from Montgomery, helping with the investigation. They'll have access to all your records at Jericho. And I've made arrangements to share what we know about your extracurricular activities. They are interested in your plans for —"

"I want a lawyer," Bragg said.

"Sure thing," Mr. Moseley said, rising and

smiling pleasantly. "But it's Saturday. You can work on that next week. In the meantime —" He jerked a thumb. "Sheriff, let's lock him up." He stood up and stretched. "When that's done, I want you and Deputy Springer to come on over to the Diner with me. Euphoria is frying chicken tonight."

"Sounds swell," Buddy said. "It's been a long day."

"What about me?" Burford asked plaintively, as Buddy cuffed him for the short walk to the jail. "I only had a light lunch."

"Don't worry." Buddy prodded him toward the door. "I think we can fix you up with a hot dog."

CHAPTER TWENTY-FOUR: "WHATEVER COMES"

Afterward, Lizzy thought she had never had such an exciting evening in her life. The Old Alabama was at its stately best, with candles and fresh snapdragons and asters on the table, a snowy white tablecloth set with crystal and china, and Earlynne Biddle's boy, Benny, dressed up in a white shirt and bowtie and waiting tables.

Ryan proved to be a fascinating conversationalist, captivating her with tales of his travels for Harry Hopkins at the WPA. His stories featured people whose names she recognized from the *Dispatch* and the *Montgomery Advertiser* (Eleanor Roosevelt, Huey P. Long, Frances Perkins, Charles Lindbergh, Lorena Hickok, Amelia Earhart) and she couldn't help being impressed by the people he knew. The Chicken Kiev was good, although perhaps not as good as Euphoria's fried chicken. But the white wine — which they would not have gotten at the Diner — was splendid. Because she wasn't used to it, the two glasses she drank (two!) gave her a pleasant buzz, which lasted through the first fifteen minutes of *Red Dust*. Until Ryan's hand, possessively, found hers.

At which point the buzz from the wine gave way to a giddy buzz from something else. His closeness in the dark theater. The provocatively masculine scent of him. The scratchy warmth of his wool jacket against her bare arm. The disorienting sense that something was going to happen between them, and she had no idea what it was.

Where was this taking her? Where would it end? She had been in the Palace hundreds of times, but this felt like the *first* time, and the place itself felt strange and new and different. It felt unreal, and she felt almost as if *she* were in a movie — only nobody had given her the script, and she wasn't sure which part she was playing.

The feeling of unreality grew even stronger after the film ended and they left their seats. In the lobby, they ran into Verna Tidwell and Al Duffy. Lizzy had to introduce Ryan — "My friend, Mr. Nichols, who is setting up an office in Montgomery, where he'll be managing the new Federal Writers Project" — while she fielded Verna's deeply curious look and raised eyebrows. And then Ryan added, smoothly, "What Elizabeth is neglecting to say is that we'll be working together on the project after the first of the year. She'll be one of our program directors."

Drawing her aside, Verna hissed into her ear. "The man is absolutely gorgeous! Why haven't you told me about him? And a new job, which you haven't even mentioned? What is going on here, *Elizabeth*?"

Lizzy could only shrug and whisper, "I wish I knew."

On the way out the door, they encountered Charlie Dickens and Fannie Champaign, who confessed with a laugh that they were seeing the movie for the second time, because Fannie was delirious about Clark Gable and Charlie wanted to see Jean Harlow take another bath. They had to be introduced, as well, and Ryan had to agree to send material to Charlie about the project, for an article in the *Dispatch* — which would include a formal announcement of Lizzy's new position.

"Swell," Charlie said enthusiastically. "Can we get a photo of the two of you together?"

"I'm sure we can make arrangements for that," Ryan said, and smiled at her. "Can't we, Elizabeth?"

Lizzy nodded weakly. Their photograph in the *Dispatch*? Now everybody would know about her new position, before she had a chance to get used to it herself!

It was still fairly early on Saturday night, and some of the stores were open for late shoppers, their holiday windows a pretty sight. The Christmas tree in front of the courthouse was spectacular, glittering with colored lights and the schoolchildren's cardboard stars. The life-size plywood holiday figures of wise men and angels and reindeer were lighted with a gala effect. Families with children were stopping to admire the display, and children squealed with delight as they found the stars *they* had made, bearing *their* names, hanging on the tree.

Ryan took possession of her arm as they walked along. But they had gone only a dozen yards when they met Mr. Moseley coming down the outside stairs on his way to his car, diagonally parked at the curb in front of the Dispatch office. Lizzy avoided his surprised look and, feeling her checks and throat reddening, muttered the briefest of introductions and silently prayed that Ryan would not tell Mr. Moseley about her new job.

But he did, while Lizzy stood silent beside

him, knowing she should say something but not knowing what she ought to say.

Mr. Moseley seemed taken aback by the news, but he recovered nicely. "Congratulations, Liz," he said with a warm smile. "I'm sure you'll do a swell job. Uncle Sam is lucky to have you working for him, even if it's only part time. When do you start?"

"After the project gets its funding," Lizzy said, feeling relieved. The last thing she wanted was for Mr. Moseley to be disappointed in her. But his comment about her new job being "only part time" — was it meant as a subtle reminder that she was still working for him?

And then he had something else to tell her. "You'll be interested to know, Liz, that Agent Kinnard raided the illegal still at the state prison farm today. And this evening, the sheriff arrested Warden Burford for his part in the murder of Jimmie Bragg. He'll be arraigned on Monday. There'll be other charges coming, so there'll be more work for us on that case."

"That's great," Lizzy said. "I'm glad the murder charge is settled."

"Murder?" Ryan asked in surprise. "In this little town?" He glanced around. "But it looks so *peaceful.*"

"And I just got off the phone with Jake

Gillis," Mr. Moseley went on. "You remember, Liz — the detective you contacted out in Los Angeles? He gave me some interesting information that should help us put an end to Neil Hudson's threat. I'll tell you all about it on Monday."

"Oh, that's good to hear!" Lizzy exclaimed happily. "Myra May and Violet will be *so* relieved. Thank you!" She could always count on Mr. Moseley to make sure that things worked out.

"But we're not out of the woods yet," Mr. Moseley cautioned. "Cupcake is taken care of for the weekend? She's out of danger?"

"Yes, she is," Lizzy said. "Tonight, she's staying with —"

He held up his hand. "Deniability. Remember?" He gave her a quick smile, then shook hands with Ryan. "Nice to meet you, Mr. Nichols," he said. To Lizzy, he added, "Have a pleasant evening, Liz." He got into his car.

"Wow." Ryan was staring at her. "I had *no* idea."

"No idea about what?" Lizzy asked.

"That your work in a law office could be so *exciting*. Murder? And what's this about a detective in Los Angeles?"

"Darling isn't as peaceful as it might seem," Lizzy said. "We may not have much big-city drama, but we have our share of crime."

"Nice-looking fellow, your boss." Ryan's glance followed Mr. Moseley's Chevy as he backed out of the parking space and drove away. "Married?"

That was an odd question. "Divorced," Lizzy replied. They began to walk. "He's dating a socialite in Montgomery."

"Ah. Well, that's all right, then." Lizzy was about to ask him what he meant by that, but he went on. "You've worked for him how long?"

"Oh, years and years," Lizzy replied lightly. "It was my first job." For some reason, she didn't want to discuss Mr. Moseley with Ryan. She was glad when he went on to something less personal.

He chuckled. "Cupcake is 'out of danger' — and Moseley needs 'deniability'? Sounds intriguing."

"It is, a little," Lizzy said. She couldn't see a problem with telling Ryan about Cupcake, her father, and the threat to the little girl.

When she finished telling the story, Ryan was silent for a moment. "I'm sure there must be lots of competition out there in Hollywood," he said finally, "and a movie career is a pretty long shot. But if the little girl has talent, other doors might open for

388

her." He paused thoughtfully. "Of course, it would be better if her mother — Violet, I mean — were involved. Maybe that could be arranged?"

Other doors? Lizzy wondered what possibilities Ryan might be thinking of. But she only said, "Darling would hate to lose our Cupcake, to Hollywood or anywhere else. The same goes for Violet — if she should take Cupcake to Hollywood, I mean. I know that would break Myra May's heart."

"But is she really *your* Cupcake?" he asked. "And is it Darling's decision?"

The questions caught Lizzy by surprise. There were two different answers, weren't there? She thrust her hands deeper into her coat pockets and said, "It's not Darling's decision, no. But she really is *our* Cupcake — in our hearts." She thought of the laughing face, the strawberry blond curls. "If we lost her, we'd all feel the loss, terribly."

"I understand that part of it," Ryan said. "But it's a wide world, and there's so much to see and do and explore." He drew her arm into his. "Darling is a nice place, I grant you that. But it's not the center of the universe."

The night was cold and very quiet — so quiet that Lizzy could hear the crisp crackle of twigs contracting in the cold air, and the

389

faint baying of hounds in the distant hills to the west, toward the river. The air smelled of pine branches and wood smoke. The moon bathed the street with silver-blue light and the stars hung like bits of chipped glass against the blackness of the sky.

Looking up at the moon, Lizzy knew that Ryan was right: Darling wasn't the center of the universe. But it was the center of *her* world. It was home. It was where she *chose* to be. Wasn't it?

And there was another worrisome thought in Lizzy's mind as they turned the corner onto her block. When she and Grady were dating, she had usually invited him to come in for coffee after an evening out. Sometimes they had necked on her sofa until she realized that she had to send him home before things got out of hand. If she invited Ryan in, would he think she expected something . . . well, as intimate as that? She wasn't quite ready for the evening to end, but it might not be as easy to send him away as it had been to send Grady. And she didn't want him to get the wrong idea. What should she do?

She was still wondering as they climbed the porch steps and reached her front door. Still undecided, she turned the knob and hesitantly pushed it open.

He put a hand on her arm. "You didn't lock your door when we left for dinner?"

"No," she said, surprised by the question. "Darling people don't usually lock their doors." She thought of what Mr. Moseley had said and added, "What crime we have usually comes from the outside." It was true, now that she thought about it. There were exceptions, but Darling was an enclave, a little town occupying a place uniquely its own, a safe place.

"From the outside, huh?" Ryan chuckled drily. "Well, maybe that explains the way your boss looked at me tonight. As if he expected me to throw you over my shoulder and make off with you, like a pirate."

Lizzy's eyes widened. "He did no such thing!"

"Of course he did." Ryan grinned. "You didn't notice?"

"Of course I didn't." She pulled herself up straight. "You're making it up."

He pulled his brows together in a mock scowl. "Would I lie about a thing like that?"

"Yes," she said firmly.

"No." His eyebrow arched. "What do you want to bet that he decides he needs you full time again?"

"He doesn't have the money," she said. "I should know. I keep his accounts."

"That, too? Jeez. He's a lucky guy. And dumb, or he wouldn't be letting you go."

Lizzy could only shake her head. She had always just done what needed doing. It was her job.

There was a moment's silence, then Ryan said, "Up north, we Yankees have a tradition. After their first date, the guy kisses the girl goodnight on her front porch." He put a hand on her shoulder. She could feel the weight of it, and the warmth, through her coat. "Do you do it that way here in the South?"

Lizzy felt a quick relief, for he had answered her question. But now, something else was troubling her.

"Yes, but this is . . . well, it's complicated," Lizzy said. "Isn't it?" She was remembering how hard it had been to work with Mr. Moseley in earlier years, when she had thought she was in love with him. "If we're going to be working together, maybe it's not a good idea to . . . you know."

He dropped his hand. "I don't want you to think that I'm in the habit of making a pass at every woman I work with," he said somberly. "Nothing could be farther from the truth. My coming to Darling this weekend had nothing to do with the job. I wanted to see *you,* Elizabeth. Finding out that you're available and interested in working for the project — well, that was a bonus, and I'm glad. But that wasn't why I sent you the poinsettia. It wasn't what I came for." He paused, his voice intense. "I came to Darling for this. For you."

"I don't know what to say," Lizzy said, very low. It was true. She could hear words in her mind, but they were stuck in her throat — or in her heart. She wasn't sure which.

"Then don't say anything," Ryan said, and bent toward her. He was moving slowly, deliberately, giving her time to pull away, if that's what she wanted to do.

She closed her eyes. Don't think, she told herself. For once, don't try to plan or organize or manage how you're feeling. Just . . . whatever. Whatever comes. And then his mouth was on hers, gentle and hesitant at first, then, like the man, assertive, confident, demanding.

Her heart was hammering and she heard herself make a sound. But not a word. She couldn't have spoken if her life depended on it. His hand was in her hair, his body hard against hers. She wanted to respond, but it wasn't exactly a first-date kiss.

After a long moment, he let her go and stepped back. "Sorry," he said gruffly. "That was more than I bargained for. I didn't mean — I hope you don't think —"

And then, as he reached for her again, she saw a light. At her mother's house across the street, the porch light had been turned on. A few seconds later, it went off, then came on again. Laughter bubbled in Lizzy's throat.

"What's so funny?" Ryan asked, sounding a little offended. "Did I —"

"No, no, it's not you," Lizzy said, stepping back, still laughing. "It's my mother."

"Your *mother*?" he asked incredulously.

He turned just as the front door of the house across the street opened and a woman stood in the doorway, wearing a pink nightgown with a blue wrapper over it. She waved a white handkerchief vigorously, then stepped back inside and closed the door with an audible slam. The porch light blinked on and off again.

"Yes, my mother," Lizzy said, and sighed. Whatever the moment had promised, it was gone. But perhaps that was for the best.

"Southern tradition, huh?" Ryan cleared his throat. "I guess that means I'd better be going. I'm headed back to Washington next week. But I'll phone you. Okay?"

"Yes," Lizzy said, and added weakly, "Thank you for the evening. I enjoyed it.

Goodnight."

"Good night." He tipped his hat and went down the steps to his car, parked at the curb. Lizzy went in, shut the door, and leaned against it, closing her eyes.

"Just . . . whatever," she whispered to herself. "Whatever comes."

CHAPTER TWENTY-FIVE: "JIGSAW!"

Sunday, December 23

The puzzle tournament was held on the gym floor at the Darling Academy. Miss Rogers was bustling around, seeing that everything was set up properly and that every team had a sheet of rules (all sixteen of them). The seven competing teams were getting settled at card tables on the gym floor, with the spectators — families, friends, and supporters of the puzzlers — sitting in the bleachers. Almost all of the Dahlias were there, to cheer for their team. Ophelia had brought her two children. Beulah Trivette was there with her beauty associate, Bettina. Earlynne and Mildred had come, with Alice Walker and Lucy Murphy. Beulah was holding up a sign that said "Go, Dahlias Puzzle Divas!"

The Divas themselves — Lizzy, Verna, Bessie, and Aunt Hetty — were seated at their table, trying to contain their nervousness while they waited for Miss Rogers to deliver their puzzle.

"What an exhausting week!" Bessie exclaimed. "So much has been going on!"

"Oh, you bet," Lizzy said. "You've heard that Sheriff Norris has arrested Warden Burford on charges of murder and conspiracy for the killing of Mr. Whitworth — as well as the prison guard who pulled the trigger?" Heads nodded eagerly around the table. "If you don't know all the details," she added, "Charlie Dickens is writing the story. You can read all about it in Friday's *Dispatch*."

"Speaking of the Dickens," Bessie put in, "Have you heard the news about Fannie and Charlie?"

"What news?" Verna asked. "Not bad, I hope."

"Not exactly." Bessie lowered her voice. "You may not know this, but Fannie has a nine-year-old son — Jason, his name is."

Lizzy's eyes widened. "No, I didn't know that!" she exclaimed. "A son? Where *is* he?"

"And why isn't he here in Darling, with his mother?" Verna asked. "Is he with his father?" She narrowed her eyes. "Who *is* his father?"

"Poor Fannie," Aunt Hetty said sadly. "How awful to be separated from your little boy!"

"Jason is at Warm Springs, in Georgia," Bessie said. "You know, where President Roosevelt has his Little White House. The boy had polio, and his legs are paralyzed. Fannie told me about him not long after she came to Darling." She paused and added, "Unfortunately, she didn't tell Charlie."

"Oh, dear," Lizzy said. "Why ever not?"

"Because the boy's father was a *bigamist.*" Bessie's voice quivered on the word. "Fannie sent him packing when she found out he was married to somebody else."

"A bigamist!" Verna exclaimed, wide-eyed. "What a jerk! Now, *that* would really knock the props out from under you, wouldn't it?"

"Poor, poor Fannie," Lizzy mourned. "She must have been terribly hurt."

"Yes, and then she learned that she was pregnant," Bessie said. "She was afraid that if Charlie knew her story, he wouldn't love her."

"But bigamy wasn't *her* fault," Aunt Hetty protested. "And Charlie Dickens is a grown-up man with experience of the world. Bigamy? Surely he wouldn't hold it against her."

"I agree," Bessie said. "But please try to see it from Fannie's point of view, Hetty. Since she discovered the bigamy, she's found it very hard to trust people — especially men. So she put off telling him. And the longer she waited, the harder it got. But last night, she called to tell me that Charlie had somehow managed to track her payments to Warm Springs for Jason's care. She told him the whole story, which was a great relief to her. He wants to get to know Jason. They left this morning for Georgia, to spend Christmas with the little boy."

"How *wonderful*!" Lizzy said eagerly. "Are they bringing him home with them?"

"Fannie plans to talk to the doctors about that," Bessie said. "If they do, though, they'll have to find another place to live. That apartment is handy for the two of them — over Fannie's hat shop and cattycornered from the Dispatch office. But Jason is on crutches. He couldn't manage the stairs."

"The house across the street from me is for sale," Verna said. "It's just one story. And I'd love to have them as neighbors." She put a hand on Aunt Hetty's arm. "Changing the subject — The Flour Shop's grand opening seemed to be a huge success. I heard that they sold all but two of the loaves we donated. How did their first baking lesson go?"

"I was pleasantly surprised," Aunt Hetty admitted. "All Earlynne needed were a few tips and some encouragement. She'll do just fine." She wrinkled her nose. "Mildred — well, she doesn't have the hang of it yet." Her blue eyes twinkled. "She needs more practice, which doesn't suit her style."

"But she's celebrating, she told me," Lizzy said. "Her Christmas window won the Merchants' Association Holiday Window Contest — much to my mother's dismay." In fact, Lizzy's mother had thrown a hissy fit when her window didn't win. She had even threatened to boycott the bakery, claiming that Mildred had used unfair tactics. When Lizzy had asked her exactly what tactics were unfair, though, all she got was a loud *harrumph* — and another warning against allowing strange men into her house.

"Mildred has discovered that she has an artist's hand when it comes to decorating cookies," Bessie remarked. "She says she's going to start decorating Earlynne's cakes, which ought to have a lot of appeal." To Lizzy she said, "Our dear little child is still playing 'Hide the Cupcake'?"

"For the next few days, anyway," Lizzy said, smiling around the table. "Thanks to all of you for helping. Mr. Moseley has been in contact with a private detective in Los Angeles. He says the detective has some

400

information that may put an end to Neil Hudson's threat, at least for the time being. I'll know more about it tomorrow."

"I spoke to Violet after church this morning," Verna said. "She's thinking of taking Cupcake out to Hollywood herself." Her tone was disapproving.

"Taking Cupcake to Hollywood *herself*?" Aunt Hetty repeated incredulously. "But where in the world would Violet get the money? And how would Myra May manage without them? If this happened, she would be devastated!"

"I absolutely agree, Hetty." Bessie was emphatic. "I don't think Violet should do this. I'll tell her so, the next time I see her."

Lizzy frowned. "But Cupcake *is* talented. Perhaps she should have a chance to show what she can do." She hesitated, then added, "That's what Ryan — Mr. Nichols — says. Darling isn't the center of the universe."

"Not the center of the universe?" Aunt Hetty chuckled. "But it *is*!"

"Mr. Nichols," Verna repeated, with a sly glance at Lizzy. "He's your new boss, isn't he?"

"Your new boss?" Bessie asked in surprise. "You're leaving Mr. Moseley? Oh, my goodness!"

Aunt Hetty's eyes widened. "You're not leaving *Darling,* are you?" She put her hand over her heart. "I'm getting too old for this, girls. Too many things are happening. And nothing —" She paused and looked expectantly around the table. She was joined by a chorus. "Nothing ever happens in Darling!"

"No, I'm not leaving Mr. Moseley," Lizzy said. "Or Darling. I promise."

"That's what you say *now,*" Verna muttered. "What happens if Mr. Nichols asks you to relocate?"

Lizzy tossed her head. "I'll just say no," she replied confidently.

"It might not be as easy as that," Verna remarked. She looked up. "Here comes Miss Rogers with the puzzles, girls. Are we ready to beat the pants off the competition?" It was an apt remark, since they were the only all-female team.

"We're ready!" they chorused.

"Here's your puzzle," Miss Rogers said, putting the box on the table. "You may open it and begin when I blow my whistle. You have read all the rules?"

Verna rolled her eyes, but Aunt Hetty replied, "Yes, ma'am."

When Miss Rogers had gone on to the next table, Lizzy held up the box. "Look, Divas!" she chortled. "It's a *poinsettia* puzzle!" And so it was — smaller than the one they had used for practice and with a slightly different background, but otherwise almost the same.

"Looks pretty simple," Aunt Hetty muttered. "I'll take the red pieces."

"Green for me," Verna volunteered.

"I'll do the frame," Lizzy said.

"Which leaves me the background," Bessie said. "This ought to be easy, ladies."

It was. Which is why, exactly fifty-five minutes and thirty seconds after Miss Rogers blew her starting whistle, Aunt Hetty put in the very last piece.

"Jigsaw!" she cried, and waved her cane in the air.

A ripple of applause swept the bleachers. The Dahlias in the audience all stood up and cheered. The Puzzle Divas had won!

CHAPTER TWENTY-SIX:
"I HAVE SOMETHING
TO CONFESS"

Monday, December 24

On the morning of Christmas Eve, Lizzy woke up to an intriguing pearly light, and Rowser's fervent dawn crow seemed oddly muted. When she looked out her bedroom window, she understood why. Her garden was covered in a blanket of glittering white snow. And it was still coming down — large, lazy, lacy flakes that filled the air with magic.

"Oh, how beautiful!" she exclaimed in delight and gave Daffy an extra hug. She dressed in brown wool slacks and a red blouse and red sweater, ready for a chilly day ahead. The snow would be gone soon, but it would be perfect for the children's Christmas party this afternoon. It would be a day they would never forget.

At the office, Mr. Moseley said nothing about Ryan Nichols or Lizzy's new job with the Federal Writers' Project. Instead, he came in, flung his hat on the rack, and said,

404

with gusto, "I'm sure you'll be glad to know that we're done with Neil Hudson, at least for the time being. You can send Cupcake back to her mamas at the Diner."

"Oh, they'll be so glad!" Liz exclaimed. "What did you find out from Mr. Gillis?"

"Coffee first," Mr. Moseley said, taking off his overcoat. "Bring yours, and I'll tell you."

Lizzy put one of the fresh croissants she'd bought at The Flour Shop that morning on a plate. She filled his coffee cup and refilled hers and sat down in front of his desk.

"This is wonderful, Liz," Mr. Moseley said with his mouth full. "Please tell Earlynne she can bake croissants for me any day of the week. I hope the bakery is a great success."

"I'll tell her," Lizzy said. "So what did Mr. Gillis say about Mr. Hudson? I'm dying to know!"

"Jake is a master when it comes to uncovering things that people would like to hide," Mr. Moseley replied. "It turns out that Hudson hasn't had a job for several months and is currently living with his girlfriend — both of which the court would view darkly if he were seeking legal custody of his daughter. But the kicker is that he was arrested late last week. So he won't be coming to Darling, at least not right away."

"Arrested!" Lizzy exclaimed. "What for?"

"For passing hot checks, to the tune of several thousand dollars. He hasn't made bail, so he'll be spending the holidays in jail." He wolfed the rest of his croissant and washed it down with a swig of coffee. "Kidnapping Cupcake won't be high on his priority list for a while." He gave her a serious look. "Which doesn't mean that he won't make another try, when he gets out of jail. Tell Violet and Myra May not to drop their guard."

"I will," Lizzy said. "At least they'll have the holiday free from worry." She thought about what Bessie had said about Violet wanting to take Cupcake to Hollywood and wondered if they had heard the last of that question.

Mr. Moseley was going on. "I'll call Hudson's lawyer today and tell him that we know about the arrest and his client's questionable living arrangements. I'll also let him know that Violet has no intention of surrendering custody of the child and that she is filing for adoption this week. If Hudson wants to contest, he'll have to come here for the hearing. But he won't have a leg to stand on. Jake tells me that last week's arrest wasn't his first, by a long shot. Hot checks, stock fraud, resisting arrest — the man has had several skirmishes with the law."

"Violet is *filing*?" Lizzy asked in surprise. "She hasn't said anything to me about —"

"She doesn't know it yet," Mr. Moseley said comfortably. "When you get a chance, go across the street to Verna's office and get the state adoption forms. Then ask Violet to come to the office and I'll help her fill them out. I'd like to get the paperwork filed before Friday. The sooner we get it taken care of, the better."

Lizzy bit her lip. She was deeply grateful to Mr. Moseley for helping, but there was a problem. "I'm not sure that Violet can afford to do that right now," she said. "There's the filing fee and court costs and your —"

"I'll waive my fee. And the county owes me for the last couple of months as county attorney. I'll take it in trade — Violet's filing fee and court costs in exchange for what Cypress County owes me."

Lizzy was overwhelmed by his generosity. "But do you think . . . I mean, I know what the bank balance looks like. I —"

"And speaking of money," Mr. Moseley went on, "I'm troubled by the thought that you've had to go out and find a half-time job to make ends meet, Liz. I've been thinking about our situation. There are a couple of accounts that I can move here, from the Montgomery office. That should make up the difference in your salary." He grinned at her as if he were very pleased with himself. "You can come back full time whenever you want."

Lizzy was staggered by his offer. She opened her mouth to answer, but the words didn't come. Was he doing this out of guilt, or out of a genuine concern for her welfare? What could she say?

He gave her an interrogatory look. "I hope you haven't signed on with Uncle Sam just yet."

She took a deep breath. "No, but I . . . I —" Her voice faltered. She was genuinely interested in the Writers' Project, and the thought of working with Ryan Nichols was intriguing. But she loved her job here, and she knew that the Writers' Project would inevitably get in the way of her writing. What should she *do*?

"Well, you don't have to tell me now," Mr. Moseley said, to her relief. "We can let it ride until after the holiday. But I do hope you'll say yes." He frowned. "Where is that Santa Claus suit? I suppose I should try it on, in case we need to make a few adjustments before the party this afternoon."

A little later, Mr. Moseley came out of the office, clad in the old red Santa suit, with the white cotton beard hooked over his ears. In a muffled voice, he said, "How do I look?"

"Festive," Lizzy said with a laugh. "Turn around and let me have a look."

He turned, and Lizzy saw that he was holding a sprig of something green behind his back. "What's that?" she asked.

"Oh, this?" He turned to face her, holding it up. "It's just a twig of mistletoe. I thought I'd add it to our office decorations. But first, maybe we ought to give it a try — see whether it works. What do you say?"

"Whether it . . . works?" Lizzy asked hesitantly. Her skin prickled.

He pulled off the white cotton beard. "Don't tell me you've never heard of mistletoe magic." With one hand, he held the mistletoe over their heads. He put the other hand on Lizzy's shoulder and drew her toward him. He bent down and kissed her lightly, almost playfully on the lips, lingering just a little.

But for Lizzy, it wasn't a playful kiss. In a flash, it pulled up all the old romantic feelings, the yearnings she had worked so hard to suppress. It's nothing, she told herself. Just a silly Christmas game. It doesn't mean anything, so don't take it seriously. Don't —

But then his mouth came down hard on hers and the whisper of caution was drowned out by the beating of her heart. Her arms were around his neck and she felt herself responding with a reckless, unruly passion that took her utterly by surprise, sending tremors pulsing through her, weakening her knees.

Finally he dropped his arms, stepped back, and took a deep breath. "Uh, merry Christmas, Liz." He sounded shaken.

Lizzy felt vulnerable and undone, as if the kiss had stripped her — not of her clothing, but of her pretenses, her charades, the calm façade she had built with such effort. She felt bare, exposed.

"Merry Christmas," she managed, trying vainly to control her breathing. She pressed a hand to her heart, feeling its foolish hammering. Shakily, she stammered, "And . . . and a happy New Year, too, Mr. Moseley."

"Mr. Moseley?" He rolled his eyes. "Good grief, girl. We've just shared a kiss that rattled the rafters. Can't you call me Bent?" He looked down at his costume and chuckled. "Or Santa."

Now she could laugh, a little, anyway. "Merry Christmas, Bent."

But her laugh covered a new and wrenching recognition. She had thought she had boxed up her yearnings for Bent Moseley and put them on the highest shelf in the darkest closet of her recollection, out of sight, out of mind. Now, like the genie out of the bottle, they had escaped to devil her. Still feeling the urgency of his mouth on hers, she doubted whether she could put them back. What did that mean? What —

"Liz." He put a hand on her shoulder and gave her a long, searching look, his jaw working, his eyes dark. "I have something to confess."

Here it comes, she thought. He was going to apologize for kissing her, like the Southern gentleman he was. She half turned away, not wanting to hear him say "I'm sorry," or "Let's forget it happened and get back to business as usual." He would be her boss, she would be his secretary. That's all it could ever be.

But he put his fingers on her face and turned back toward him so she could not escape his gaze. "I've been wanting to kiss you for a very long time." His voice was gruff. "I didn't realize just how much I wanted it until I saw you with that good-looking Nichols fellow on Saturday night. I knew he was going to kiss you goodnight. *I* wanted to be the one to do that. And I was hoping like hell that he wouldn't get past your front door."

She stared at him, speechless. And then, to her surprise, felt the laughter bubbling up in her, laughter she couldn't push down. "He didn't," she said, half choking on a giggle. "My mother stopped him."

"Your . . *mother*?"

"She came to her door and turned on the porch light. She waved her hanky at us."

"Her hanky?" His laugh was deep and rich. "Remind me to thank your mother the next time I see her." He held up the mistletoe over their heads. "I'm wondering. How about if we give this a second try, Liz? See if the magic is really real."

Happily, Lizzy was ready to step into his arms, but the telephone rang.

Mr. Moseley dropped his arm and sighed. "If it's Judge McHenry, tell him I'll meet him in chambers, as soon as I get out of this silly suit." He paused, his eyes on hers. "Can I take a rain check on that kiss, Liz? And not on your front porch. I would prefer someplace where your mother can't wave her hanky at us."

Mutely, Lizzy nodded. She stepped to her desk and reached for the phone. She had to clear her throat twice before she could trust herself to speak.

"Law office," she said brightly. "How may I help you?"

###

THE GARDEN GATE BY ELIZABETH LACY

If you're asked what flower you think of when you think of Christmas, you'll probably say, "Why, the poinsettia, of course." And you would be right, for it is the traditional Christmas plant.

The wild poinsettia is native to a mountainous area of southern Mexico, where it flowers during the short, dark days of December and January. The ancient Aztecs prized the plant, using the red "flowers" (they are actually specialized leaves, known as bracts) to make a purple dye and the milky white sap to treat fevers. An early Mexican botanist gave it the botanical name *Euphorbia pulcherrima* — "the most beautiful *Euphorbia.*" Because it flowered around Christmastime, Franciscan priests called it the "Flower of the Holy Night" and used it in their religious celebrations. Now, it is known by many descriptive names: Star flower, Crown of the Andes, Shepherd's rose, and Fire flower — among others.

The plant was brought to North America in the late 1820s by Joel Roberts Poinsett, the first American ambassador to Mexico. Intrigued by the fiery blooms, he sent several to his plantation in South Carolina, where he later propagated them in his greenhouse. He began sharing them with friends and botanical gardens, and they became known as poinsettias.

Here in Darling, Mrs. Hetty Little (Aunt Hetty, to her friends) has been able to grow poinsettias all year long. If you want to keep your Christmas poinsettia alive and thriving until next year, she has some tips for you.

She suggests that you keep your holiday plant in a sunny window as long as its bracts are red, watering it as usual. In March, when the leaves fade, prune it back to about six to eight inches tall and let the soil dry out before you water it. In May, repot the plant in a fast-draining slightly acidic soil. When it starts to put out new leaves, feed it some of your favorite balanced fertilizer. (Or try Aunt Hetty's recipe, below.) Once the new stems have grown out at least four inches, you can begin taking cuttings, if you like. The cuttings should be three to four inches long, with two to three mature leaves.

As the stems grow out, pinch them back

to shape your plant and encourage branching. In October, it's time to begin what Aunt Hetty calls the "dark treatment," to mimic the short days of the plant's native region. Place the poinsettia where it will get about eight to ten hours of sunlight. Then put it in the dark for the rest of the day and night, either covering it with a light-proof cardboard box or moving it into a dark, windowless room or basement. Water and feed it as usual. After about eight weeks (around Thanksgiving), the colored bracts should begin to emerge. Put your plant back in the light and enjoy it through the holidays, patting yourself on the back for helping it survive and thrive throughout the year.

Aunt Hetty says that another tricky thing about poinsettias is the temperature. Poinsettias are tropical plants, and they don't like to be cold. Move them to a warmer spot when the temperature falls to around 50 degrees.

And one other thing Aunt Hetty wants you to know. Don't believe it when people tell you that the poinsettia is poisonous. The milky sap may irritate your skin (it is a *Euphorbia,* after all), and the leaves and bracts don't taste good — they might even make you nauseous. But they won't kill you or your pets, so don't worry. Just enjoy their brilliant red color, so vivid at Christmas time.

Aunt Hetty's Favorite Fertilizer

Aunt Hetty swears by a fertilizer tea she makes in an empty one-gallon jug. Put the following ingredients into the jug and fill it with rainwater. Let it sit for a day or two, then shake, strain, and use at full strength to water the soil around your plants. They'll drink it up!

1 teaspoon baking powder
1 teaspoon ammonia
3 teaspoons blackstrap molasses
3 tablespoons hydrogen peroxide
1/4 cup coffee grounds
1/4 cup crushed bone scraps
2 crushed egg shells
1 dried banana peel

LAGNIAPPE*

If there were no other reason to live in the
     South,
Southern cooking would be enough.
                    Michael Andrew Grissom
                    Southern by the Grace of God

Earlynne and Mildred are still working on a
full list of the pastries and other good things
they plan to sell at The Flour Shop. But in
the meantime, they thought you might like
to try these traditional sweet Southern
goodies for your holiday table.

Pecan Tassies
A longtime Southern favorite, the pecan is
the official state nut of Alabama. There are
over a thousand varieties, many named for
Native American Indian tribes: Cheyenne,
Mohawk, Sioux, Choctaw, and Shawnee.
The word "tassie" — a small cup — has

* Lagniappe: *lan-yap.* A little something extra.

419

been around for centuries, too. Robert Burns, in 1790, used it in one of his poems: "Go fetch to me a pint o' wine, And fill it in a silver tassie." It's easy to see how the word became used to describe little pastries baked in muffin tins. These pecan treats are bite-size finger food, which makes them ideal for a party tray.

1/2 cup butter (room temperature), plus 1 tablespoon butter, melted
3-ounce package cream cheese (room temperature)
1 cup flour
1 large egg
3/4 cup packed light brown sugar
1/2 teaspoon cinnamon
1 teaspoon vanilla extract
Pinch of fine salt
1/2 cup pecans, finely chopped

Preheat the oven to 325 degrees F. Spray a 24-cup mini-muffin pan with cooking spray, or set out 24 silicone mini baking cups.

Beat butter and cream cheese until smooth. Add flour and beat until completely blended. Cover and chill for 1 hour.

Whisk together melted butter, egg, brown sugar, vanilla, and salt until smooth. Set aside.

Divide the chilled dough into 24 pieces, and roll into 1-inch balls. Press the balls into the bottoms and partway up the sides of the baking cups. Drop 1 teaspoon pecans into each cup. Spoon about 1 teaspoon of the egg mixture into each cup.

Bake until the filling is set, about 25 minutes. Cool on a wire rack for 10 minutes. Carefully remove from the baking cups to continue cooling.

Holiday Bread Pudding with Rum Sauce

Frugal Depression-era cooks used every scrap of leftovers — including stale bread — while bootleg rum, made from molasses, was always available. With the addition of raisins, chopped candied fruit, and a heady rum sauce, this bread pudding is a wonderful holiday dessert.

For the Pudding:
7–8 cups torn or cubed stale bread
3/4 cup dark brown sugar
3 cups milk
4 tablespoons butter
1 teaspoon cinnamon
1/2 teaspoon nutmeg
1 teaspoon vanilla
1/3 cup raisins
1/3 cup candied fruit

1/8 cup rum
4 eggs

For the Sauce:
1/2 cup butter
1 cup white sugar
1/3 cup heavy cream
1/8 cup rum

Preheat oven to 350 degrees F. Grease a 9-inch square baking dish.

For the pudding, place the bread in a large bowl. In a medium saucepan, mix brown sugar, milk, butter, cinnamon, nutmeg, vanilla, raisins, candied fruit, and rum. Stir over low heat just until sugar is dissolved. Pour over bread.

In a small bowl, beat 4 eggs. Add to the bread mixture and stir gently, so that the bread is fully saturated with egg and milk. Let stand for 30 minutes.

Scrape bread mixture into baking dish. Bake for 40–50 minutes until the top is browned and the middle is just set.

For the sauce, melt the butter in a medium saucepan over low heat. Add sugar and stir just until dissolved. Mix in the cream and rum. Keep warm (do not boil).

Pour the warm sauce over each scoop of bread pudding before serving.

Forgotten Cookies

The intriguing name for these cookies came from the way they are prepared. They were put into the oven at night and "forgotten" until morning — a good use of the leftover heat of the coal or wood kitchen range. Like other meringues (airy, crisp confections of egg whites and sugar), they are dried in a preheated oven rather than baked. (One early recipe calls for drying them in a "hot closet.") The chocolate chips in this recipe weren't commercially available until 1940, when Nestle began marketing their recently developed "morsels" or "chips." We take our kitchen tools for granted, but as you beat the egg whites, remember how pleased Earlynne was with her 1930s Mixmaster, which saved a lot of muscle power!

2 large egg whites
1/2 teaspoon cream of tartar
3/4 cup sugar
1/2 teaspoon vanilla
3/4 cup chocolate chips (mini chips are
  better for these bite-size cookies)
3/4 cup chopped toasted pecans
1/4 cup dried cherries, finely chopped

Preheat the oven to 350 degrees F. Line a baking sheet with foil or parchment or use a silicon mat.

With an electric mixer at medium speed, beat the egg whites and cream of tartar until soft peaks form (1 to 2 minutes).

Still beating, gradually add the sugar. Beat at high speed until stiff peaks form, about 3 minutes.

Using a spatula, scrape down the sides and bottom of the bowl and fold in the chocolate chips, pecans, and cherries.

Drop 2-inch balls of the meringue mixture onto a large foil-lined baking sheet. (This is easier if you use two teaspoons, one to scoop with, the other to push the meringue onto the sheet.)

Place in preheated oven. After 5 minutes, turn the oven off. Allow the cookies to dry in the oven for at least 8 hours.

Ambrosia

Citrus fruits were a special holiday treat for Southerners, and children loved to find oranges and tangerines in their Christmas stockings. The fruits were in season in the winter, but they were costly — if you could afford them, you would serve them to special guests with pride. During the Depression, a dozen oranges cost about the same as five pounds of flour (which would make five loaves of bread) or a half-gallon of milk. You *had* to have the bread and milk; you didn't need the oranges.

Satsuma oranges, a loose-skinned variety of mandarin oranges, arrived in Florida in 1876 and quickly became a favorite. Christmas was the peak of their season, so the Satsumas were coveted for a fresh fruit dessert called "ambrosia" — the mythical food of the gods. Pineapple (primarily shipped from Cuba) was another prized fruit, added to ambrosia when available.

And there was coconut. Coconuts arrived in Florida accidentally, when the Spanish schooner *Providencia,* bound for Spain with twenty thousand coconuts from Trinidad, ran aground near Palm Beach in 1879. Within a decade, mature coconut palms had grown up to fill the area and the nuts — which traveled well and kept beautifully — were being shipped north.

This ambrosia recipe is complete with helpful suggestions for those who were puzzled about how to get the meat out of their coconut. It is from *Southern Cooking,* by Henrietta Dull, who began selling her homemade food when her husband became ill. Originally published in 1928, Dull's cookbook began as a series of newspaper columns for the *Atlanta Journal,* entitled "Mrs. Dull's Cooking Lessons." It introduced Southern food to a national audience and adapted traditional recipes to gas and electric appliances. A 1989 reprint edition is available from Cherokee Publishing Company.

6 large oranges
1 large coconut
1/2 cup sugar (more or less to suit the taste)

Remove the brown skin and put the coconut through the food chopper or grate. Remove the orange sections from the skin, being careful to remove all of the skin. Mix orange, coconut, and sugar. Put in a cool place for one hour, and it is ready to serve. 1/2 cup sherry may be added. To get the coconut out easily, remove the milk and place in a hot oven until the shell is quite hot to the hand. With a hammer tap over the nut, then give a hard knock to crack the shell, which will break and come apart from the nut meat.

To the requisite coconut and six oranges, a 1913 recipe adds "one pineapple chopped quite fine, one-half box strawberries, six bananas sliced and the slices quartered, and one lemon sliced fine." Another (1904) suggests Malaga grapes, dates, and nuts.

426

A dish fit for the gods, indeed — and perhaps not affordable in Depression-era Darling.

Eggnog

Eggnog was as popular in the South as it was anywhere else, heavily laced with the local rum or brandy. Food historians trace our modern eggnog to early English recipes for posset and syllabub. Here's an American recipe from *The Kentucky Housewife,* by Lettice Bryan. Published in 1839, Bryan's cookbook contained over 1300 recipes, derived from European, American Indian, and African sources and reflects a merging of the three distinct cuisines in Southern cookery. It is available in a reprint edition from Applewood Publishing Company.

Break six eggs, separating the whites from the yolks; beat the whites to a stiff froth, put the yolks in a bowl and beat them light. Stir into it slowly half a pint of rum, or three gills [1 1/2 cups] of common brandy; add a quart of rich sweet milk and half a pound of powdered sugar; then stir in the egg froth, and finish by grating nutmeg on the top.

ABOUT THE AUTHOR

Growing up on a farm on the Illinois prairie, Susan Wittig Albert learned that books could take her anywhere, and reading and writing became passions that have accompanied her throughout her life. She earned an undergraduate degree in English from the University of Illinois at Urbana and a PhD in medieval studies from the University of California at Berkeley, then turned to teaching. After faculty and administrative appointments at the University of Texas, Tulane University, and Texas State University, she left her academic career and began writing full time. Her best-selling fiction includes the Darling Dahlias Depression-era mysteries, the China Bayles Herbal Mysteries, the Cottage Tales of Beatrix Potter, and (under the pseudonym of Robin Paige) a series of Victorian-Edwardian mysteries with her husband, Bill Albert.

Albert's historical fiction includes *The General's Women,* a novel about the World War II romantic triangle of Dwight Eisenhower, his wife Mamie, and his driver and secretary Kay Summersby; *Loving Eleanor,* a fictional account of the friendship of Lorena Hickok and Eleanor Roosevelt; and *A Wilder Rose,* the story of Rose Wilder Lane and the writing of the Little House books. She is also the author of two memoirs: *An Extraordinary Year of Ordinary Days* and *Together, Alone: A Memoir of Marriage and Place.* Other nonfiction titles include *What Wildness Is This: Women Write about the Southwest* (winner of the 2009 Willa Award for Creative Nonfiction); *Writing from Life: Telling the Soul's Story;* and *Work of Her Own: A Woman's Guide to Success off the Career Track.* She is the founder of the Story Circle Network, a nonprofit organization for women writers, and a member of the Texas Institute of Letters. She and her husband Bill live on thirty-one acres in the Texas Hill Country, where she gardens, tends chickens and geese, and indulges her passions for needlework and (of course) reading.

The employees of Thorndike Press hope you have enjoyed this Large Print book. All our Thorndike, Wheeler, and Kennebec Large Print titles are designed for easy reading, and all our books are made to last. Other Thorndike Press Large Print books are available at your library, through selected bookstores, or directly from us.

For information about titles, please call:
(800) 223-1244

or visit our website at:
gale.com/thorndike

To share your comments, please write:

Publisher
Thorndike Press
10 Water St., Suite 310
Waterville, ME 04901